Life is Just Research for Art

Enough! Enough! Shit already e-fucking nuff!

Mornings were the worst. Light, sound, movement; everything overwhelmed. Worst of all the lead like feeling that permeated everything; deeper than sadness, more lonely than death, the relentless obsession that gnawed at his insides. Mornings were the worst because to wake up meant another day in the trenches, sinking into madness and despair. Insanity and obsession intertwined into a driving force not to be denied.

He could lie still for a long while and try to ignore the faint gnawing at his guts and the more persistent feeling of his skin becoming too tight or too clammy or too cold or too hot. He knew his calves and fingers would cramp with spasms if he moved too fast. He had left the fan on while trying to sleep and he knew he would regret that if he started having charlie horses. His bladder ached with pressure and he knew any illusions of returning to the comfort of slumber were the only dreams he would be receiving in the near future.

His eyes remained closed as he struggled mightily to postpone the inevitable. He clung to that brief respite that the loss of consciousness promised. That dreamless coma like state when he passed out. It was the only freedom from his self imposed tortured existence.

The clock by the bed said 9:35. He wasn't sure if that was AM or PM. A half smoked cigarette rested between his fingers with a 2 inch ash dangling languidly over his chest. An ash tray lay on the bed half empty where it had slid off that same chest. He surveyed his surroundings slowly avoiding any sudden movement; more from necessity than caution. Light streaked through a blind hole in a tattered window shade to blossom and grow on the foot of the bed. He thought this bright intruding force of nature had been the source of his irritating return to conscious thought.

Upon further exploration of his surroundings he decided that the sun, although treacherous and deadly, was not the culprit. A garbled cacophony of various electronic devices, all evidently on maximum volume, were blaring from various corners of the room. A large flat screen TV exalted the virtues of an herbal cleanse while a scratched CD repeated the same half chord and click every three seconds.

Up on a debris littered table, beside the bed upon which he reclined, a persistent yet intermittent vibration penetrated through a riotous clamor. A cellphone was tendering its litany of hope and despair; a veritable smorgasbord of possibilities awaited. All he would have to do is pick it up and the cycle would resume.

A phone was a dopefiends lifeline. He couldn't remember what it was like before everyone and everything was instantly accessible. He actually could remember, but it seemed a lifetime ago and the memories were clouded with nostalgia and tinted with a vague, lonely sorrow of a life not lived. Potential wasted in forced hilarity and fear of responsibility.

Thoughts of the past were not to be dwelled upon, no matter how sweet, they always led to the present and the present was a beast to be battled moment to moment with action not reflection.

Like any reasonable person in modern America, he did not answer his phone. He, instead, checked his messages. There were 14 new texts since his last at 3:43 AM. His last pontification upon the world had been a concise directive to a possiblissant fledgling addict named Robert. The post had been brief and to the point. CALL ME EARLY. WILL NEED A RIDE ACROSS THE RIVER. WILL PAY YOU BACK.

Apparently Robert, dope fiend or not, was a man of some integrity and of a reliable nature. He had started blowing up the phone at 6:30 AM and had texted or called every fifteen minutes for the past three hours. Probably a fucking tweeker! Oh God, that's all he needed.

The withdrawal was gnawing at his guts like a fist and he was beginning to feel nauseated.

He would   call the tweeker back but first he needed to piss and hoped he could manage a bowel movement. If had been three days since he had moved anything and he knew from experience it was not going to be pleasant when he did.

Placing the phone back on the pile of empty beer cans and half empty red plastic cups he checked to see if the charger was plugged in. A white cord ran from a wall socket but did not fit the phone's receptacle.

It was then he realized he didn't recognize the phone or the room but that was not a big deal in any way nor in the least alarming.

He could tell by the carpet and furnishings that he was in some seedy motel room probably an extended stay the room was filled with several days worth of trash and it was obvious no maid or cleaning lady had set foot inside the premises. Broken cigarette butts littered the floor their filters torn in half where had used one half to strain a hit of whatever was on the menu from the spoon to the needle.

Bottle caps lay around the perimeter filled with water for the same purpose.

He tried to roll out of bed but got tangled in someone's yoga pants his left foot stuck in the intertwined sheets and pillows. He hopped on his right foot a couple of times and slipped and sank down into a clothes strewn chair. He recognized a worn and tattered pair of Adidas as his own and a pink nike high tops stirred a memory of someone laughing, young, free and alive. It had been a while since he had felt any of those things.

The image made him uneasy so he avoided it. He stood up and scoured through the desolation until he found a lighter. The half smoked cigarette still dangles from his lip its wayward ash sliding down his chest in a mini avalanche of nonchalance and sordid decadence.

He lit the cigarette, took a deep draw and started to cough it was a fucking menthol. Damn what type of degenerate fiends had he been partying with last night fucking barbarians or some // fucking trash from the suburbs brothers didn't even smoke menthols anymore they had all switched to black and milds swishers and those blueberry smelling shits. *Nigga Pleeze!* His first smile of the day.

He took a couple more hits off the nasty choke stick and headed toward a door that stood off to the side of the sink, stove, fridge conglomerate. He assumed this door to be the bathroom and he was correct.

He approached the commode lifted the lid with his big toe on his right foot placed his left hand on the wall leaned forward and removed himself from his blue slightly stained boxers. He coughed up a good sized chunk of phlegm and prepared to spit.

Just as he got a good steady stream going into the toilet bowl. He was startled by a thumping sound off to his right.

Jumping backward his stream followed the sound and splashed against the powder blue and slightly moldy shower curtain.

He quickly stifled his stream placing himself back into his boxers. He tentatively pushed the shower curtain back and held his breath.

Within the light green tub lay a waif like girl with long golden hair.

The thumping sound had been her arm hitting the wall as her body had shifted weight in the tub.

Oh fuck! Fuck! FUCK! His brain screamed no.

He recognized the girl and his heart fell. It was the young girl of the smiling face and the laughing eyes.

He leaned over and put his finger to her neck and looked for signs of life. He felt a pulse and detected a faint breath.

The water was a pale pinkish color and very cold.

He had thought the girl dead from a drug overdose but this was not the case. Beside the tub a small pair of scissors lay; the kind used to trim hair.

The pale waxy figure in the tub had sliced open both wrists in a long vertical gash. She had apparently been serious in her intentions because the slashs were along the veins from wrist to elbow the left one much deeper than the right. This was probably due to her being right handed and cutting the left first.

The ineptness of the cut upon her right arm had probably saved her life.

Beside the scissors lay an empty hypodermic of the variety   sold to diabetics. An empty Mountain Dew code red can sat beside it turned upside down with a brown residue on top. A small pink piece of paper stuck inside an empty cigarette cellophane completed the little altar.

The man acted quickly before he could change his mind. He grabbed the phone from the table dialed 911 stepped outside while the phone was ringing.

He noted the room number and the hotel, gave the information to the operator returned to the bathroom picked up the cellophane emptied the contents of the pink paper onto the mountain dew can. A little brown pebble fell onto the upended can it looked somewhat like a cross between a booger and toe jam. He took the needle drew some water from the sink into the barrel squirted a little onto the pebble. Turned the needle over and used the plunger to break the little pebble and stirred the substance until it was the desired consistency.

He searched until he found another half smoked menthol. Bit the filter in half placed the cigarette end into his mouth lit it. Inhaled, exhaled, set it down. Placed the cotton from the filter on the mountain dew can in the middle of the brownish liquid. Placing the tip of the needle into the filter he drew the entire contents into the hypodermic.

He sat down on the commode and realized he hadn't even finished pissing. He chuckled and grabbed a belt that lay in the jumble of clothes and cosmetics upon the floor.

He wondered briefly how long the girl had been in the bathroom before she decided to kill herself. It looked as though some major soul searching had gone on before that decision had been made. As he stuck the needle in his arm he had the fleeting thought that he would have a few minutes to grab his shit and leave before the paramedics got there. He knew it was a shitty thing to do to just bail on the girl but he really didn't know her and all was going to to happen if he stayed was he would be arrested and charged with who knows what. Plus he was sure they had to be warrants for his arrest floating around.

This line of thinking became most relevant when the contents of the needle had completely emptied into his arm. He tried to stand and the world turned black his body tilted forward and his head hit the wall directly in front of the commode. As he slid down onto the dirty floor his bladder finally emptied itself creating a small   puddle/ upon the floor surrounding the island of his person. Yeah, mornings were the worst.

Chapter 2

Detox

Jail has its own rhythm.

Booking had been a blur. His last memory had been the motel bathroom and a broken angel lying in a lime green bathtub floating on a pale pink cloud of her own tepid blood infused water.

He had lain face down on a concrete floor for seventeen hours after it was determined he was out of danger. The paramedics had come through the door just as his head had hit the bathroom wall.

They had been a block away tending to an elderly lady who had accidentally hit her medic alert button while in the midst of a diabetic mood shift. Her sugar levels had her acting inebriated but the guys on the wagon had fixed her right up.

They were familiar with the motel. They pulled two or three people a week from the place.

It wasn't every day they got a two for one though.

The girl "Sindi" had been taken to the ER and then the psych ward where she would be held for at least three days observation.

Sindi was obviously not her real name and she apparently had no I.D.

The EMT had kept asking him questions about her and he had no idea what to answer.

The shot he had slammed in the bathroom had been pure heaven an instant cure for everything. The world had disappeared and along with it the agony of existence.

His peace was short lived because these EMTs were fully equipped and knew their shit. The larger one held his shoulders while the other blasted him with Narcan in his nose.

That shit truly is evil it simply slayed his high. It was like every iota of peace was just blasted from his body and he just soared into severe withdrawal.

The 911 call had been answered by the police; as well as EMTs, due to the location from which it had been emitted.

The motel was well known for its drug arrests, robberies, prostitution and O.D.'s. It being an otherwise slow day two units had arrived. The four officers in attendance also seemed quite amused at his discomfort.

Only one ambulance was available and a discussion albeit brief was held to determine which person needed the ambulance more. Should they take the unconscious attempted suicide in the bathtub or the semi conscious severely   dope sick possible attempted suicide now sitting up on the bed.

For the EMTs the decision was easy. The O.D. was out of immediate danger, the girl was not. She had lost a lot of blood and was not conscious.

The cops started arguing over whose car he was gonna ride in. Neither set wanted him in their car for fear he would puke or shit inside their cruiser. They flipped a coin and the biggest of the four stepped forward.

In his left hand he held a ripped and very dirty pair of jeans in his right he held a wallet opened to a faded Kentucky driver's license.

"It says here Londale Andrew Hayes. Is that you?"

"Are you Londale Hayes:"

Lonnie. They call me Lonnie or just Hayes. Yes, that's me. I'm Lonnie Hayes.

It occurred to him that he hadn't heard his "real" name in weeks.

Somewhere in his dope fueled madness he had lost his entire identity. He hadn't thought of himself as Lonnie Hayes in a long time.

The officer looked at him closely marking details in his mind. He had a knowing eye and he smirked at Lonnie.

Ain't you a little old for this shit partner? Lonnie had been born in 1985. He was 30 and he knew something the cop didn't.

Dope don't care how old you are and it never let go once it had you.

Lonnie just smiled and nodded his head. "Yeah, I guess I am; shit I was too old for this ten years ago."

"Well Mr. Hayes I need you to get dressed because I'm taking you in."

"Ok, but can you tell me exactly what I'm being charged with?"

"Well possession of narcotics and paraphernalia to start with."

"That girl looked awful young and in bad condition. If she dies, we could be charging you in facilitating in her death and if she's underage we may have a good case for statutory rape charge along with corrupting a juvenile."

The sinking feeling in his gut returned but this time it wasn't just the dope.

Lonnie racked his brain trying to remember the night before and the days previous to that.

Where had he met the mysterious waiflike girl "Sindi" how had they come to be in that motel bathroom together.

His thoughts became muddied. The Narcan was wearing off the dope was taking back over.

Shit must have been cut with fentanyl. The EMTs had left and the cops seemed unaware or didn't care. To them if he died en route to jail it would be no great loss.

It would mean a lot of extra paper work but otherwise he was just another doper and his death was practically a done deal, today, tomorrow, next week, it didn't matter his life had become a brutal loop of waking up, doing whatever it took to score dope, doing dope til it was gone. Scoring more dope. Oblivion. Repeat again and again.

His world had shrunk and drawn in upon itself. His contact with other humans had become out of necessity. His world was only filled with people he could use and/or manipulate for money or drugs.

The last three years had been particularly brutal. His drug of choice had become heroin and heroin did not play.

Lonnie's heroin addiction was due to a peculiar set of circumstances that seemed to be affecting a lot of people.

His story was not unique it had in fact become a very often told tale. The details may vary but the gist of the story remained the same.

Lonnie had started experimenting with alcohol around eleven years old. . He had been a bit of a goody two shoes and subject to ridicule and derision about his reluctance to try alcohol and/or other substances.

He had misgivings for a variety of reasons some he couldn't verbalize. His family had a long history with drinking and partying but they were also hard working people.

His oldest brother and his uncles and cousins had all drank and gotten high but they mostly ignored Lonnie when they did.

It appeared to him that they were having fun and although they seemed silly and acted foolish when they drank; it all seemed harmless and fun.

Lonnie had two brothers, Lloyd and Dale. When Lloyd and Dale drank or got high it was different.

They may be laughing or acting foolish but their hilarity hid something dark and sinister about it. Lonnie was six years younger than Lloyd and seven younger than Dale. The oldest brother Glen, was ten years older and had moved away from home early.

Lonnie having a good strong sense of self preservation noticed early on that when Lloyd and Dale drank that their idea of a good time could be mean spirited. They both liked to be the life of the party and were constantly joking and cutting up for the amusement of their various friends or whatever audience they could gather.

Lonnie had learned the hard way that the majority of their humor would be at someone's expense.

If Lonnie was close at hand he would undoubtedly be a target. Dale loved to give Lonnie hell. Lonnie was a big kid for eleven he already stood around five ft seven and weighted around a hundred and sixty pounds. Dale at seventeen was around five nine and weighed about the same. The difference was Lonnie's one sixty pound preadolescent frame was soft and pliable while Dale's frame was lean and hard. He was one of those people that exuded good health with little or no effort. He was also very good with his fists. Lonnie could bear witness to that for Dale had chosen Lonnie as his personal punching bag and seldom missed an opportunity to improve on his battle prowess at his younger brother's expense.

Lloyd had a mean streak bad as Dale but he also possessed a soft spot for Lonnie.

Lloyd was bigger than Dale but lacked his grace and speed.

They had fought each other many times with no clear winner. Dale had better self esteem due to being the more handsome of the two ;plus Lloyd was about twenty pounds overweight and very self-conscious of the fact.

Lonnie had watched his brothers drink and knew that alcohol changed them.

He thought of it as "The big lie" because it made people into something they weren't. It was a trick and a low and dirty one.

At eleven years old, his resistance faltered and his brother Dale had grabbed him in the kitchen at a neighbor's house. The neighbor an "old" drunk in his forties had a huge house full of dirty dishes and empty beer bottles because his wife had left him. Dale had flattered and bullshitted the old drunk so he would sponsor a huge drunk.

It hadn't taken much, for Roosevelt; the old man was always inclined toward drink.

Dale had gotten Lonnie in a bear hug and squeezed the breath out of him.

Lonnie knew to laugh and pretend it was all in good fun. If he protested or whined about his treatment in any way his brother would become enraged call him a baby and a pussy and leave him covered in bruises.

Dale's dominance was more than the physical abuse he insisted upon humiliation.

Lonnie came to think of it as being fed a shit sandwich and having to smile while you ate it and then asking the host for another and being accused of being ungrateful if you forgot to say thank you.

Dale's heart was in a good place on this day and he felt very kindly toward his little brother.

After releasing him from the bear bug, he turned Lonnie around and said here while handing him a cold Pabst Blue Ribbon in a can.

He looked Lonnie in the eye when he placed the beer in his hand and in his gaze was something Lonnie had never seen. Kindness, goodwill and real affection.

Lonnie didn't hesitate he opened the cold can pulled the tab off and took a long drink. It tasted nothing like he expected while at the same time it tasted exactly right.

He finished that beer and drank another he noticed his brothers were amping up their energy level and knew to make himself scarce.

Lonnie's first time with drugs and alcohol had been a positive one. His brother who he hated and worshipped had treated him as an equal for the first time in his life.

He drank two beers and went home. Never in his life would he ever again drink that responsibly.

Lonnie's drug progression had started when he was eleven his brother had given him his first drink. Beer soon after another family member introduced him to pot.

As he got older he had progressed into hallucinogenic drugs such as acid and muchrooms then later ; speed.

Occasionally someone would have pills and Lonnie would try anything. He had learned to avoid downers because they made him sloppy. He was a big guy and there was always someone waiting to catch him slipping and beat his ass or at least try.

4th Step

Those empty lonely hours of the late night and the predawn have always called to Lonnie.

It wasn't exactly comfort that he felt in those solemn hours. It was familiarity. It was a sense of coming home.

He had always felt alone and the night eliminated pretense.

His mind became unfiltered by the mundane trivialities of daily life. Uncluttered by the inane mutterings of other people. Most of them desperate to be heard with nothing to say.

Chill had told him to stop bullshitting and to get started on his 4th step.

"A searching and Fearless Moral Inventory." He had looked at the book several times and it didn't really, make sense to him.

The "Big Book" of Alcoholics Anonymous had been around a long time and people a lot less intelligent than he had gotten sober and stayed that way by using that information stored within the first 164 pages.

Chill had made it sound so simple. He had spoken as only a true believer could speak. There was no doubt in his voice or hint of insincerity when he spoke of recovery and the "design for living" that the program of Alcoholics Anonymous offered.

That was all well and good for Chill but at 3 a.m. with nothing but a blank page and a pen in his head, Lonnie Hayes felt everything in the world but confident or convinced.

Tormented by so many thoughts and doubts he had no idea where to start. He was determined and scared not to go forward.

The thought of returning to the scared, hunted, haunted, vicious, selfish shameful being that he had been terrified him.

A man in his first or second group meeting at New Hope House had suggested he pray when he felt anxious or unsure.

Lonnie had smirked and told the man   that he wasn't sure he even believed in God.

All his life God had been used as a threat and something to make feel less than.

Much like his family there was little comfort or succor to be found "God" as God had been presented to Lonnie Hayes.

Raised in the Mid South to a family with no serious religious affiliations he had never been forced to attend nor had he been encouraged.

His father seldom mentioned God and when he did the word damn most likely followed. Lonnie's father Brandon Hayes had fathered five children. Lonnie was his youngest. He had never presented or stated a personal belief about the subject of God.

Mary Jo Hayes was a more enlightened soul but she almost never attended church and had left her children to find their own way. She felt it would be wrong to force her views on her children and that something so personal and important should be left up to the individual.

Well that sounds very progressive and enlightened. None of her kids had found any comfort or solace from this point of view.

The men and the meeting had laughed when Lonnie had stated that he didn't think God, if there was one, would listen to a prayer from someone like Lonnie.

The man; an old drunk of about 50 who was in his 12 or 13th rehab had just smiled and said, "Boy, prayer ain't for God, it's for you."

"What?" Lonnie had blurted with incredulity.

Prayer changes you not God. God don't got to exist for prayer to work. Prayer is just a human seeking to focus energy into a positive direction. It's the beginning of hope.

Shit ain't gotta be real to work.

Hell son most the shit we do in our daily are just acts of faith.

How so? Lonnie questioned.

Well you get on the highway and everyone follows the rules of the road. That's an act of faith, an agreement between people and it works.

Money only works because we all agree it has value.

People live, die, kill and work their whole lifes for money and it's just paper. The only value it has is what we   place upon it.

Recovery is a word that we throw around a lot and everyone seems to be pretty sure they know what it is.

But recovery is a personal thing and what recovery is to you may not be the same thing to anyone else.

God is like that at least that's how I think about it.

In the rooms and in that A and A book they keep talking about a higher power of *your* understanding.

Now that sounds simple but what the fuck does that mean?

Well it means a lot of different things but mostly it means an individual has to see it as their very own personal, one of a kind, unique, relationship with some sort of spiritual entity that can provide them with strength and hope!

Bullshit! Who are you? What makes you an authority?

That's just it, boy. There are no authorities. Ha ha!

Lonnie remembered the old man's face and his words but couldn't remember his name. It didn't matter for on this night he decided to follow the old derelict's advice.

He prayed.

He didn't get on his knees and he didn't try to   flatter his higher power with flowery speech and promises.

He simply sat very still, breathed slowly for about two minutes and said very quietly:

Help me.

Help. I do not want to be this person any more.

If there is anything out there help me.

He continued to breathe slowly and his mind quieted a little and he took a pen in hand.

On the paper before he started a list of people that had wronged him.

When Lonnie put pen to paper the "decision" he had made in doing a third step became evidence of his working toward his fourth step.

His personal journey toward spiritual growth was in its early stages.

At some point during this time Lonnie and Chill had a conversation about seeking God's will.

Chill liked to keep things simple when talking to people in early recovery.

He took a cautious stance about inflicting his own views upon newcomers.

The relationship with a higher power should be unique to the individual.

Chill did avoid talking about his personal beliefs.

He tried not to sway others to his beliefs.

Lonnie tended to struggle with the concept of a higher power.

He wanted Chill to tell him how or what to believe.

"It's not some trick Lonnie."

I don't whisper some magic words and do a little dance.

A belief in a higher power is just that a belief.

I believe it and rely on it and even trust in it.

"But you have no proof of it, right?"

Chill laughed. I have proof of it if I wish to acknowledge it as proof.

Right now Lonnie your disease is protecting itself with logic, doubt, justification and whatever else it needs to get you to stop the recovery process.

Lonnie stopped a moment this statement rang true.

Lonnie couldn't figure out Chill's angle.

Why did he care?

What did the big guy gain by talking to Lonnie?

Why was Lonnie's being clean and sober of any concern to Chill?

Why do you even give a fuck? You don't know me.

What do you gain by telling me all this shit?

Chill laughed.

Nothing. Everything.

I'm an alcoholic and a drug fiend. By nature I'm selfish and self-centered.

The best way to trust my disease is to do something unselfish and focus on others.

I sit and listen to another alcoholic and share my experience.

My own concerns seem less important. I stop thinking about my own shit for a few minutes.

I see how sick and anxious and ate with fear that you are and I see that I have made progress.

I get relief.

It's not magic but it is magical.

It doesn't even matter what I say to you if you really want to get sober.

What? Lonnie asked.

Yeah that's right. I can say a thousand things that are brilliant and true and it won't help you any if you are not prepared to listen.

It's only when an individual seeks recovery that he can hear what he needs to hear.

If you truly want to get sober you will find something to later onto and run with that.

People hear what they need to hear. It doesn't matter what is said.

Well ain't that some shit! Lonnie marveled at Chill's words.

We are told that drugs and alcohol are just symptoms of our disease.

Chemicals were how we get relief from being ourselves.

They worked great until they themselves become more of a problem than a relief.

Once we become chemically dependent we now have two issues.

We must trust the disease of addiction and underlying conditions that led to the addiction.

This was new information for Lonnie.

He had just always thought he liked to party.

Like many addicts and alcoholics, he had never considered why he drank or used drugs. It was the drinking and using that caused problems that he contemplated the reasons he used.

Chill broke into the younger man's reverie.

Right now you aren't ready for all that.

That's fourth step work.

Lonnie interjected.

Wait a minute!

You told me once I made a decision to do this shit, the clearest evidence of a completed third step was taking pen in hand and starting a fourth!

True enough! The problem I see is you haven't entirely taken a second step.

Lonnie passed. The second step stated came to believe in a power greater than himself that could solve all his problems.

Chill continued.

The questions you are asking me about God and faith seem to indicate some uncertainty.

Let's do a little review.

Do you think you're powerless over alcohol and/or drugs?

Yes! Lonnie replied.

Okay. Do you think your life is unmanageable as a result of this lack of power?

Fuck yes! The younger man replied with conviction.

Okay, good. Now if you are telling the truth and you believe these things we may have something to work with toward recovery.

Now do you believe you can be helped?

I guess so, I mean I think I can be helped.

Why? Chill asked.

What do you mean why?

Why do you think you can be helped?

Lonnie was confused.

So far, Chill and everyone involved in this recovery crap all been super positive.

This was the first time anyone had even mentioned the possibility that he may not be able to get clean and sober.

Chill continued.

Do you think you deserve to be helped?

Why would God help you?

Lonnie said I don't know. I don't even know what you're asking me?

I know, Chill replied. I know you don't know.

Let me break it down for you.

You are an alcoholic and a drug addict. You have already admitted that much.

Yeah, that is true.

Okay! Now what that means essentially is your life is fucked up and you think is because you drink and use drugs.

Right!

Wrong! Alcohol and drugs were your coping mechanisms. They were what enabled you to function, and at some point their destructive elements to your life outweighed their benefits.

So now you're truly fucked! Your solution—drugs and alcohol—no longer works.

They have in fact become an added burden.

Lonnie looked at Chill and said in a very calm voice.

Dude, this ain't helping. I don't know where you think you're going with this but it really is not making me feel any comfort?

Chill began to laugh a laugh from deep down in his enormous gut. He could already picture himself sharing this story with his sponsor. He would omit Lonnie's name but incident was pure recovery gold.

Chill stopped laughing and looked at Lonnie who seemed to be a lot less amused.

The younger man was looking more than a little pissed.

Chill took a breath and attempted to ameliorate the situation.

I'm not laughing at you! I understand exactly you feel.

I guest need you to realize what you are truly feeling.

I believe you are an alcoholic and an addict very much like myself.

I believe that there is no cure for the disease of alcoholism.

I also believe that this condition is treatable.

The best news of all is the treatment process that I have found most effective for treating my alcoholism also treats the underlying spiritual condition the causes my alcoholism.

In the twelve steps or AA, we admit we are powerless. We than realize we are incapable of fixing ourselves without some power greater than ourselves.

My first power greater than myself that I could relate to was another alcoholic. My sister had drank and drugged much like I drunk and use drugs.

So she had gotten stopped and had become able to live a productive life.

Not only was she surviving on her own, she was no longer taking from or harming the people she loved.

I wanted that more than I had ever wanted anything.

I was truly desperate for a change in my life. I did not care what happened next. I just did not want to go back to living the life I had been living.

Do you think you are at such a point?

Lonnie took a moment: not because he was unsure. He wanted to be honest and certain before he replied.

Yes, sir, I believe I am.

Okay than, back to the second step.

Do you believe there exists a power greater than yourself that can help you?

Lonnie looked at Chill he took a drink of water from a bottle on the table. He spat and then said very quietly: I reckon there's a whole lot of shit I don't know. I reckon there's shit I will never know or even want to know. There's one thing I'm pretty certain of and that is I do not want to keep living this way.

I can't see any reason for you to lie to me hoss.

I really don't even understand why you are even talking to me but I believe "*you*" believe what you are saying.

I also believe that you are batshit crazy and if you tell me you go sober and that I can get sober I'm take you at your word.

You said your sister was the first higher power you used to get sober. Well old son you gonna be mine.

Chill laughed. Okay buddy, if that works for you for now we will let it stand.

It ought to keep you sober today.

That was Chill and Lonnie's first talk about God.

Chill spent a good bit of time reflecting upon that conversation and realized talking another person about belief makes a person examine their own conception of God.

Lonnie had put another question to Chill about Chill's higher power.

How do you know when you're doing God's will, Big Boy?

Chill sighed and gave a low chuckle.

Lonnie you are doing the work. You are asking the questions that show me you are really taking that recovery stuff serious.

Why you say that? Lonnie queried.

Well, you are anxious to do this fourth step but you aren't even sure you believe in God.

Two, you ain't sure there is a God but you want me to tell you how to know if you are doing God's will.

Lonnie chuckled.

You I can see a little inconsistency there.

Well, Chill began. For me it's a little different. I sorta believe little bit of everything and then added to it

Now the "higher power" or "God" that has been presented to me all my life had a lot of very human characteristics.

How do you mean?

Well, the biggest issue I ever had with the accepted traditional version of God was he seemed vindictive.

I'm talking old testament here not Jesus.

The entire concept of hell seems extreme. We are supposed to believe this being is all knowing and all powerful and he created everything.

Man was created in his image and given free will.

Well, God decides to tempt his creation with forbidden things and then judges him on whether he follows directions.

My problem is the normal lifetime for a man is about eighty years. Now if this being doesn't follow directions during those eighty years and just basically resist God created temptations he gets cast into hell for eternity. Wow eternity seems like a very long time in the scope of things.

Why would a supreme being need the affirmation of his own creations?

Is he lonely? Does he have self-esteem issues?

The whole Lucifer as a fallen angel who turns against his father out of jealousy is all very human.

People talk about God answering prayers "in his time."

Why would a supreme being be affected by time?

Wouldn't a being of such proportion be everywhere all the time?

God doesn't wait there is no post, present, or future for such a being. Those are very human limitations.

For myself I believe there exists an underlying force that connects everything in the universe.

Energy never disappears it just changes form.

We can prove their negative energy and positive energy. These forces are in constant flux always changing.

Concepts such as good and bad and morality are all mean made constructs.

The universe is simple.

For every action, there is a reaction. That just breaks down to actions have consequences.

For me to live a life that I deem good I just need to evaluate the possible consequences for my upcoming actions of nonactions.

If I went to flow in harmony with the energy of the universe I choose a path that promises harmony.

If my spirit is in discord and fraught with lots of negative energy this will be what I put out into the universe. The universe will fill that void accordingly.

If you think in those terms moral imperetins(?) such as good, bad, right and wrong are recognized as subjective.

It is never possible to determine with absolute certainty what is absolutely good or bad.

Lonnie interrupted his large friend.

Wait a minute! Are you saying there are no pure good or pure evil acts.

What about the holocaust or any genocide?

What about pedophiles?

Chill paused took a breath and began talking.

Lonnie, genocide is as natural as anything.

Religion is often one of the tools most used to justify genocide. Once a population or grouping of people separate themselves from others they create two groups. They then designate the chosen the group and the unchosen.

If I deem another race of faction of people as unchosen or as less human than myself that free me from feeling guilty about what I do to them.

Traditionally the unchosen are offered the choice to join the chosen group or be killed.

Pedophilia is distasteful but has been recognized as acceptable in certain groups throughout history.

Some countries let take child brides.

Socrates, Plato and Alexander the Great were all practicing pedophiles by today's terms.

The Universe does not contain moral absolutes in my opinion. For every act or force there is an equal act or consequence.

It's not about good or bad; it's about one depends upon the other.

The cycle of life.

Pain makes pleasure more poignant than stress and relief.

Life, death, boredom, excitement all necessary for the other to have meaning.

Pleasure all the time would have no significance it would be meaningless.

Anything as humans that we obtain or attain without struggle or sacrifice we tend to place little value.

The things we struggle for and sacrifice for we tend to place high value.

Lonnie Interjected.

Okay. What about God's grace? I heard somewhere that it's freely given.

Only for those who truly seek it.

What the fuck does that mean?

Chill laughed. God's grace is ongoing. The only people that are aware of God's grace are those willing to see it.

Addiction and alcoholism are distorted perceptions of the world. It's all about perception.

When I got sober the world didn't change.

My view of the world changed.

God or the energy behind the universe is a constant. The way I connect with the force or energy guides my viewpoint on life.

You're saying it's all in my head.

Certainly! As alcoholics, we don't really have a drinking problem in as much as we have a thinking problem.

Dude, you talk in talk in circles. It makes sense when "you" say it but when I get by myself it just sounds like bees in my head.

The problem is Lonnie you want to be "well" all at once. You want recovery to be a task that you can complete and mark off your list.

If you view addiction and alcoholism as a disease and that you were sick from their influence, you can start to see recovery as a process.

We first recognize that there is a problem. We identify the obvious symptoms of that problem. We admit that our lives are unmanageable.

Now if you look closely at the first step of Alcoholic's Anonymous it says: "We admitted we were powerless over alcohol and our lives were unmanageable."

Well it doesn't say alcohol is the reason for that unmanageability. We infer that alcohol is the reason our lives are unmanageable. For many people if you take away alcohol and drugs from their lives their lives remain unmanageable. Some even get sicker.

For myself, alcohol and cocaine were the way I coped with the world. They made existence bearable without these substances I became irritable and nasty, often violent and unreasonable.

Alcohol and cocaine were coping mechanisms. For a long time, they helped make my life manageable.

Once I reached a certain level of tolerance to these substances they were no longer aids to coping. They became further hindrances. Eventually these addictions blossomed into a set of problems that overshadowed everything else in my world.

I had to deal with my alcoholism and addiction issues before I could venture to address other issues.

The great thing about using the twelve principles of recovery outlined in the Big Book of "Alcoholics Anonymous" is these principles address my alcohol issues and if I use them in my daily life they also work on my other issues.

Alcohol was my solution, it led me to my greatest downfalls. Once I surrendered alcoholism led me back to my solution.

Recovery is full of paradot, yin yang, karma whatever you want to call it.

It's like life. For everyone, it has similar features but is also unique to the individual.

You are obsessing over whether or not you are ready to do an honest fourth step? Yes.

Well, I can't tell you that. You want some kind of guarantee and I can't give you one.

I can tell you what I did and what happened to me.

A hundred other people can tell you their experience and you will still have to decide for yourself.

In How it Works, it says "rarely have we seen a person fail who has thoroughly followed our path." That means exactly what it says.

This is the fourth step, buddy.

This is where we separate the punks and crybabies from the true believers.

We do this all the way and it works. Anything but all the way is bullshit and a waste of good getting high time.

If you are ready, can't nothing or no one hold you back.

Recovery is yours for the taking.

Step up and embrace a new way of living.

The thing that holds most people back is fear. They it won't work for them. They fear it will work for them. They fear they will never be happy or have fun again.

Mostly they fear the unknown. As miserable and fucked up as their life is it is still a known entity.

They have survived and coped up till now.

They cannot conceive that their way is wrong.

Plus, why should they believe you or me when we say we know a better way.

A better way for others maybe but I'm not like the others. Every addict or alcoholic at some point encounters these demons of doubt.

For me, it was easy.

I didn't care what was next. I just did not want any more of what had before.

Once I had gotten stopped and had regained a choice I wanted freedom from being owned by my obsessions.

What Now?

Lonnie was bored out of his mind.

Boredom had always been a dangerous thing for Lonnie.

He had called Chill's number had gotten no response.

The guys at the halfway house were all getting ready for a meeting that wasn't going to start for another six hours.

He felt out of place most of the guys were younger and were from the area. This was their hometown.

At thirty, he felt extremely old. Chill laughed when he had told him about feeling.

Shill hadn't gotten sober until he was thirty-four. He talked about wanting to stop for about wanting to stop about three years and hadn't been able to do anything to curtail his disease.

Chill, like Lonnie and a lot of other people, hadn't stopped on his own accord. He had gotten stopped. With the help of law enforcement.

His behavior had gotten so out of control that the police had been called.

A lot of people referred to this as being "rescued" not arrested.

Lonnie and a few of his friends liked to call it a "Commonwealth Intervention" Kentucky being a commonwealth state.

Jails, recovery centers, halfway houses, and other institutions were crammed fall of people that had "decided" to get sober in this manner.

A lot of people felt that forced recovery just didn't work and that a person was just wasting time and energy if in treatment and not ready to quit.

Chill had been ready a long time before he held gotten stopped. Treatment had woven itself around him like a blanket. It hadn't been easy. Not in any way but it had felt right.

He hadn't cared if he went to prison or whatever happened next in his life. He just didn't want to feel "owned" anymore. The dope and whisky had put shackles on his soul that were growing tighter and more restricting every day.

When he had finally gotten arrested he had slept like a baby. Safe and secure in the knowledge he wouldn't have to "go after" anything when he woke up.

Lonnie wasn't anywhere near certain. He teetered on a ledge of not wanting to use and obsessing over getting the next one.

The "Big Book of AA" talks about not being able to imagine a life with or without alcohol. Lonnie and countless others could add numerous other substances.

Lonnie hesitated to call Chill again but he became more and more restless.

A tall skinny boy named Heath noticed his anxiety and approached him.

Yo, L. A. what's eating at you? You more fidgety than whore at a baptism!

"Big Time" (Heath's nickname" I just feel lost and know why. I mean I know a lot of good things are happening in my life. For that I am truly grateful but to be totally honest I'm bored as fuck. Lonnie continued—I mean Is this all there is to it? I mean, okay, I'm sober and all, I'm not in jail, I got a full belly and a warm place to sleep. That's great, but what do I have to look forward to? A shitty job for shitty pay and a bunch of fucking AA meetings to fill my time. Sitting around drinking coffee with a bunch of half dead old fucks retried or on disability. Them sitting around telling me how grateful I should be, while they recite the same old, tired, shitty stories they've told a thousand times.

Maybe I can be one of them smooth old fucks that's constantly trying to fuck all the hot new girls when they walk through the door.

Hold up, Hoss. The lanky youth Heath raised his hand in front of Lonnie's face.

You're getting way ahead of yourself. First thing you said was you were grateful and then everything out of your mouth was anything but grateful.

Dude, you done got too well too fast.

You've lost the sense of desperation they talk about in them meetings.

I know what you're feeling. Hell, I get that way all the time. What I do is just try and remember that it's just my disease fucking with my head.

Have you called your sponsor? I'm sure Ol' Chill could give you some perspective on this issue.

I've tried. He's not answering.

Well, I suggest you keep trying or get out that phone list and call the next person on the list, right now. You is on some dangerous ground.

How long you been clean?

I'm right at ninety days.

Well, have you done a fourth stop and dropped your fifth?

I wrote it out but we ain't went over it.

Hmm well, maybe that would help.

Maybe. Hey, Heath, thanks, man. I do feel a little better. I'm gonna try and call Chill again, soon as I can get to the phone.

Well, you might not have to, because if I'm not mistaken that would be him pulling into the parking lot over behind the horseshoe pit.

Yeah, aint' no mistaking that goliath looking fucker.

Man, your sponsor is one big, mean looking fucker.

I swear he growled at when I went to shake his hand.

Yeah, he does that. It really doesn't mean anything. It's like hello, or fuck you or good morning.

Rising from the crouched position on the curb. Lonnie smacked dust off his trousers and stamped his feet a couple of times to increase circulation.

He extended his hand to the younger man.

Thanks, Heath, you helped more than you know, but I'm gonna try and catch Ol' big Chill and see if he can't shed a little more light on this shit.

Anytime Lonnie, you know new guys gotta stick together.

As Lonnie drew closer to the parking lot he noticed his sponsor was talking to a young man that Lonnie didn't recognize. He briefly wondered who the strange young man was, but he was mainly concerned with why Big Chill hadn't answered his calls.

Nearing the car and the duo standing next to it Lonnie stated to call out his sponsor's name to get his attention.

Big Chill, perhaps sensing his approached, turned in Lonnie's direction and saved him the trouble.

Hey, Mr. Hayes, there you are. Come here, I want you to meet someone.

Lonnie Hayes, this here is Gerald   Phelps.

Chill's companion turned toward Lonnie and extended his right hand in the familiar gesture so prevalent among twelve-steppers.

"People call me Gerry," the young man said in a very quiet but direct voice.

At first glance, the youth was very unimposing.

Standing somewhere between five six and five seven. He probably weighed about a hundred and fifty-five pounds soaking wet.

But there was some width to his shoulders and a calm fierce look in his eyes.

Lonnie's first thought upon seeing these eyes was "banked embers"—a term his granddaddy used to describe hot coals left in the stove covered with ashes.

It only took the slightest of hint of a breeze or even the steady breath of a child and those embers would spark into full blaze.

Lonnie shook the younger man's hand.

The man known as Gerry had one of the faces that gave no hint of his age. It had a boyish charm and not a wrinkle or frown line one.

He could have been sixteen or thirty Lonnie placed him somewhere around twenty-two.

They call me Lonnie or L, or California, or L Haze just about whatever you want.

Well, Lonnie sounds good to me if it suits you.

Lonnie is fine.

Hey, Chill! I been trying to call you all morning. Why haven't you answered?

Well, to tell you the truth, I was busy and you are not the fucking center of the universe.

What the fuck? Lonnie sputtered. You're my sponsor! What if I was about to drink?

Well, that would suck! It would suck a lot more for you than me. But it would suck.

Damn! "It would suck" that's all you got to say. Damn duck I thought we were better than that.

Lonnie looked really hurt so Chill took some mercy upon him.

Lonnie if I died today your solution would not change. Your decision to drink or not to drink would be between you and your higher power. The big book tells us not to place our reliance upon others for people will always let us down. It says we must place our reliance upon a power greater than ourselves.

Now as I recall, you and I got on our knees together in the storeroom at the token star clubhouse and you recited the third step prayer.

Lonnie was confused. Chill had this uncanny knack of turning the tables on him. Lonnie knew that he had a right to be upset. Everyone knew that you were supposed to be able to call your sponsor anytime day or night to save your ass.

That was just like AA rule one. Your sponsor had to help you; that was his job. But no! Not Big Chill, he just turned that shit right around and make Lonnie feel stupid.

The worst part was he did it with so little effort.

Lonnie's accusation and tone had not fazed him even a little he deflected that shit with nary a blink.

Okay, Boy, if I left you hanging I apologize. I was not ignoring you just as you know. I was dealing with a situation the required my full attention.

Gerry is going inside to talk to Harold and Arthur to see if they can help find him a bed.

If you can wait about five minutes I will be able to sit with you and discuss whatever is on you mind.

Oh, by that way, don't you have a fourth step you need to drop so you can please up and begin job searching.

I think today would be an awesome time to go ahead to go ahead and get that out of the way.

So while I'm in here making proper introductions and explaining Gerry's situation. Why don't go put that fourth step.

Lonnie swallowed hard a tight little ball of icy fear formed in his stomach.

Okay, I go get it was all he could manage to mumble.

Great Big Chill said and turned toward the building entrance where the slight but formidable presence of Gerrard "Gerry" Phelps waited patiently.

Lonnie turned and walked toward the other end of the building which housed a screened in porch for smoking and opened onto a patio that had to the back stairway which would take him to his room in which he shared with three other men.

It occurred to him that he wasn't bored anymore.

Get to Stepping

AS Lonnie went to up the steps to his room he reflected back to chill's comment about doing the third step prayer.

It had been a big deal while at the same time it had seemed kinda silly.

Lonnie had a real hard time buying into the whole God thing in this getting sober deal.

It wasn't that he believed or didn't believe.

He had just always tried to avoid thinking about it too much.

He had been raised by his mother and she had been busy.

The whole God and Religion thing had just been avoided.

He can remember asking his father once about God on one of the few occasions that his father was around.

Curtis Hayes had never been much of a father to Lonnie. He had pretty much given up the role by the time Lonnie came into this world.

On this day holding true to form Curtis had responded to Lonnie's inquiry with his usual sardonic candor and cynicism.

Hah! Boy, the shit you do come up with.

Asking me what I think about God.

Hell, boy, that God talk and all that religion shit is just people with shit; telling everybody else how to act and behave so as they can keep their shit.

God ain't never done shit for me, boy, but misery and heartbreak. God ain't no more real than the Tooth Fairy or Santy Claus, boy!

Lonnie had never heard this opinion from anyone.

He asked his father:

Aren't you scared of going to hell?

His father had laughed.

With genuine good humor, he bellowed laughter!

Fuck no! I ain't scared of hell.

Boy, ain't no hell more real than this!

WE IN HELL BOY! Right here, right now.

Ain't a man ever lived known more torment than this.

Curtis Hayes had always been one to glorify his own misery in the world.

He was definitely a glass half empty sort of man.

In later years, Lonnie would often hear his mother bemoan and list his father's numerous shortcomings. The biggest of which was he could never find any joy in life.

Lonnie had spent his summers with father during his teen years.

His mother had finally had enough and had left when Lonnie was ten.

She had said she had stayed as long as she could stand it.

Everyone had been relieved the final years of their living together had been pure hell for everyone involved.

When Curtis would walk into a room Jocelyn would walk into another room.

They never spoke to each other and whenever both were in the same room everyone got quiet.

They had stopped sharing a bed years before and Curtis had taken to sleeping on the couch. She seemed also happy on the couch.

Jos contentment must have irked his wife to some great extent. On a dreary afternoon in the fall of the year, she had Dell and Lonnie drag the couch out into the yard where she set it on fire.

If the loss of the couch had bothered Curtis, he was very careful not to show it.

He never even mentioned it and just took to sleeping on the floor where the couch had been.

The father Lonnie knew from those summers was a very different man from the man that had dueled within Lonnie's childhood.

Curtis Hayes had always been a handsome man dripping with charisma and charm.

He had an easy way with people. Always ready with a sly joke and a kind remark. He was a natural flirt and people were drawn to him.

He could be these things with the world. Strangers always got his best.

It was not an act for someone he just met he could be generous to a fault.

He worked for the park service and his job often entailed mingling with the public.

He carried candy in his pockets to give children and carved intricate little animals. He would sometimes spend hours whittling away on the items and then give them to a stranger as if it was no big thing.

Chill had told Lonnie one time that if you wanted to know the true nature of a man ask the people that lived with him.

If this was indeed the way to measure a man's worth than Curtis Hayes character was in serious question.

Lonnie's fourth step was loaded with writing about his father.

An inventory is meant to be fearless and thorough. The big book of AA goes into great detail on the subject.

It is an attempt to look into the past and find patterns of behavior that need to be eliminated.

It talks "causes and conditions" that led to these negative patterns.

For most alcoholics and addicts, drugs and alcohol start out as coping devices for their lives.

Alcohol and drugs become the relief from intolerable life and unrelenting pain.

The pain of not fitting in not measuring up, not being good enough, the pain of just existing.

Addicts and Alcoholics tend to be self-absorbed and hyper sensitive.

They take everything personal and hung onto insults and injuries from others. These insults can be real or imagined.

Addiction and Alcoholism are discuses of perception. Reality is whatever a person perceives it to be.

One man can see children, a wife, and a home as a blessing. Another man may see the same situation as a burden or a curse.

Happiness and contentment in life is a matter of attitude and gratitude.

Lonnie and Big Chill sat inside Chill's van. It was a windstar. Chill liked it a lot because he could get in and out of it with very little effort.

It was also great for hauling drunks. The van been sold to him for three hundred dollars by a friend in the program.

The man's wife had decided she wanted a new one and the dealership would not give him a fair trade-in so he decided to give it to Chill for what it cost to put tires on his pickup truck. Chill had another friend in the program install the tires at cost and bam he had a van. It had a lot of miles but had been very well maintained.

It had cost Chill another three hundred to license it because the blue book value was so high.

Chill had been sober thirteen years and had come to rely on such events.

He had never had much money but he had never done without necessities.

He would tell guys that he sponsored these stories and they would call them miracles.

Chill would laugh and say:

You know the secret to miracles?

Well, every gift I've ever received in sobriety had a hook to it.

Whether it be a car, a job, or a friend.

Everything I've received required maintenance.

Every gift my higher power gives me he requires me to accept the maintenance of that gift.

The minute I take something or someone for granted in my life, that thing or person is removed.

New guys especially would be impressed by this proclamation. Although, many didn't quite understand what Chill was talking about nor were they sure they believed him.

Chill unfazed by their blunt stares, confusion and sometimes disbelief would continue his philosophy of recovery.

As a result, my life only has people and things I value. I have a worthwhile life.

Do you understand?

I think so the new guy would respond and Chill would hit him with the rest of his theory.

I don't think you do understand. It sounds simple but it is the part of recovery many people miss or forget.

The universe, God, higher power, whatever you call it wastes nothing.

Everything you do, say, or think has power and that power is constantly shifting.

We spent much about freedom of choice without really understanding what the term means. When we accept something into our life whether it be a van, a conversation or even a lover or a child we also accept responsibility.

I'm not saying we are responsible for that item or person or conversation.

We are responsible for our actions toward all these things.

Remember actions always have consequences even if we don't see them right away.

You may spend months or even years building up trust with a person and in one careless remark in a conversation with another person can betray that trust without even knowing you did.

People either hold themselves accountable or the universe will hold them accountable.

Good and bad are not absolutes. My own experience in life has shown me that.

My higher power was everything.

Many of the greatest gifts I received in recovery started out as tragedies.

People have the mistaken idea that once they give up drgs and alcohol that their lives are gonna be easy.

Well, the truth is if you give drugs and alcohol and don't replace them with something more spiritually positive you will probably be more miserable than you have ever been in your life.

Drugs and alcohol have been our solution, our relief. The problem is the relief they once gave has dwindled and the price of that relief has soared.

The big book of AA talks about the fellowship of AA as being a sufficient substitute. Some people find religion or work.

I think a combination of things works best for me.

Now like much of recovery this all sounds great but what does it really mean?

How much does a person go about living a meaningful life?

How do I go from being worthless to having value?

\ Again like so many things it's progress not perfection.

When we begin the journey of recovery it starts with admitting there is a problem.

In AA and other twelve step programs we speak of being powerless over something and as a result our lives have become unmanageable.

That seems pretty straightforward and simple.

A rational individual should be able to sit down with a piece of paper and a pen and in less than five minutes be able to determine if his or her life is manageable and if relieance upon a chemical substance is affecting the management of that life.

Humans are creatures of habit. We become entrenched in our routines.

Change is scary the unknown is always met with suspicion and fear.

Once we determine a problem exists we become faced with the decision to change or not to change.

But even that is not as simple as it sounds.

Because the disease of addiction is progressive change is constant if you are not taking actions to treat your disease it is actively continuing to degrade and compromise every aspect and condition of your life.

The prospect of admitting one is truly powerless and is an addict or alcoholic can be so overwhelming that many individuals cannot do it.

They are incapable of effectively treating their condition beyond brief periods.

The prospect of a never-ending struggle with an unrelenting opponent fills them with despair.

This is why the programs have expressions like "just for today," and "this too shall pass."

The disease of addiction does indeed correct every aspect of the addicts or alcoholics life.

The act of fighting this disease with some form of recovery program makes the most mundane activities more poignant and rich.

Common activities such as paying bills, buying a car, keeping a job, paying child support can all seem like miracles in early recovery.

These acts are miracles but the problem with most people is once the new is worn off these miracles can become drudgery.

Remember Chill's theory of life states every gift has a hook.

The responsibility and maintenance of the gift.

Drugs and alcohol change things immediately but this change is short lived.

Long term effective change takes a prolonged effort.

It often goes unnoticed by the individual involved with the change.

Lonnie was aware of Chill's views about recovery and felt he kinda understood them.

Chill liked to say the greatest gift and the greatest curse in his life was his alcoholism.

Lonnie wasn't sure if he agreed or would ever embrace such a point of view.

He knew that he believed Chill believed and for some reason the big scary fucker made Lonnie more at ease than anyone had in a long time.

He trusted Chill and wasn't exactly sure why.

It seemed odd to Lonnie that a man he had only known in a very short while could instill in him enough confidence to share his innermost darkest shit.

But here he sat with a completed personal inventory in his lap ready to sill it out to this bearded giant of a man who scared him and comforted him at the same time.

Big Chill had a way of talking to you and getting right to the middle of whatever was on your mind.

He loved to cut up and was quick with a joke but very seldom was anything out of the big man's mouth bullshit.

Whenever he dropped Lonnie off from a meeting or ended a phone call he would say "Love you brother you be good" and it didn't feel weird or strange when Big Chill said these things. Lonnie believe the big man meant it when he said it.

Somehow Big Chill was able to love Lonnie just as he was. He could see value and worth within Lonnie even though Lonnie could not.

Chill interrupted Lonnie's thoughts.

Okay, Buddy! Are you ready?

You got your fourth step there?

Lonnie replied yep and started to hand the handful of scrawled pages over to the big man.

Wait up, hoss! We ain't there yet. Chill raised his hand to fend off the proffered pages.

What do you mean Lonnie asked his voice rising. That easy confidence in Big Chill slipping a little. The old familiar animal of fear instantly rising inside him. Was this some trick?

Hold up! Don't get excited we got to go over some shit before we tear into that big ol' fourth step.

What?

Well it is a fourth step so that means we got three steps before it, right?

Well, yeah but we been over all that.

We sure have but it's like I been trying to tell you from day one? This is an ongoing process.

The twelve steps are principles to guide our lives.

The Big Book talks about practicing these principles in all our affairs.

In the twelve and twelve it talks about humility being the underlying principle of all the steps. That's discussed somewhere around the seventh step I believe.

So deep down to your innermost soul do you truly believe you are powerless over drugs and alcohol.

Can you categorically state to yourself and believe with certainty that your life is unmanageable once you place these chemicals inside your body.

Chill you talk like a fucking book sometimes but yes I'm all these things.

Lonnie this isn't a test and there no wrong answers.

These steps work for me and I think they can work for you. I have found success applying these principles in other areas. I have come to rely on them.

Okay, first step down let's keep going.

Do you think you can be helped?

You just said you are powerless over alcohol and as a result your life is unmanageable.

Lonnie thought a second and looked the big men in the eye.

Chill, I know right now at this moment and believe it with all my heart that I am an alcoholic.

I don't always get in trouble when I drink and use but every time I've been in serious trouble I have been drunk or high.

I drink and use when I don't want to and I can never stop once I start. The only way I stop is to lose consciousness or cannot get more. I don't see that getting any better it only seems to be getting worse.

Chill smiled and looked at Lonnie.

Oh man! I believe you. Remember this isn't a test.

The only answers that matter are the truth.

I'm not a judge or your Daddy. I'm just a drunk just like you.

Again I ask you; Do you think can be helped?

\   Chill, big buddy, I don't know.

I go to meetings and while I'm there it seems possible. I sit, I listen, and I can hear in people's voices that they believe what they are saying. Right then, I think yeah I can do this.

I get back to my room and I pick up that big Book and I start reading and it just seems stupid.

People talk about working steps and turning their life and their will our to their higher power and to me it's just talk.

In even heard you talk about AA and recovery being about action.

The only action I ever see is motherfuckers drinking coffee, smoking cigarettes, and fucking their jaws. Oh yeah everybody likes to hit on the new girls.

Big Chill might even tell him to find someone else to work with if he said something bad about AA.

But no here the big fucker sat laughing.

Lonnie thought if he stayed sober a hundred years he would never understand his sponsor. Just when he thought he had him figured out he would go and do the opposite.

What's so funny, Big Time? I'm serious.

Fuckers talk shit into the ground.

One person introduces a topic and the next five step all over their dicks to say the same damn thing.

Occasionally someone will throw in a quote from that fucking book and everybody will kiss his ass.

God forbid a person admit to not understanding or having a doubt during a meeting.

I mean I really try to believe in this shit because I'm scared, Chill.

If this shit don't work I don't know what I'm going to do. I don't want to be the men I was eighty-seven days ago.

Good! That's good you want to be that person.

The big men continued.

It's also good that you have doubts. It's good that you are confused!

You say you aren't sure what constitutes action in recovery.

You just took a whole shitload of action.

Vital, important, necessary action!

You just got honest.

Every meeting we need from the book how it works that's chapter five. The first thing it talks about is the people who fail at the program.

"Those who do not recover are people who cannot or will not completely give themselves to this simply program, usually me and women constitutionally incapable of being honest with themselves."

Can't get honest with themselves. Doesn't say honest with Jesus or Daddy or Big Chill.

A man has to get honest with himself.

I hear you talk and you sound sincere.

But only know if what you are saying is the truth. Let me lay this on you boy!

Chill moved closer and his eyes bore into Lonnie. Lonnie wasn't sure if Chill was trying to intimidate him or if he was just being passionate.

But the big fucker was definitely intense when he got fired up about recovery.

Chill put his right index finger right on Lonnie's chest.

What you believe to be the truth today may not always be the truth!

Facts maybe facts but the way they care perceived by the individual determines *that person's* truth.

You just sat here and told me that you had boudts and was unsure if this could work for you.

I understand those feelings I'm coming up on fourteen years clean and sober and some days I have those same feeling those same doubts.

I've been told that at fourteen years I should be feeling this way or that way and that if I'm having doubts and fears then I must be something wrong.

But the people who say those things don't live inside my head.

Every person comes into this shit with their own set of circumstances and conditions.

We talk about some being sicker than others. Well that's the truth.

It took me five or six years to get any real relief.

Up to that time all I was doing was putting on the brakes and keeping things from getting worse.

I truly didn't believe I had a right to expect anything more than that.

I was very fortunate in a lot of ways when I wanted to get sober.

Part of this process is we share our experience, strength and hope with each other.

We do that for several reasons.

One of the big allies of our disease one of its main weapons is it likes to isolate us.

We share our stories with each other so we don't feel so alone.

You go out in the so called normal world and tell people some of the crazy shit you have done or some of the evil crap you are thinking and they will look at you like you're some kind of freak.

You share that shit with another drunk or addict and they will instantly know what are talking about. They will identify with those feelings and those circumstances. Some of the details may differ but that care will ring true.

That empathy that instant bond is one of the major reasons that twelve step programs are so effective.

It could take months with a counselor or psychiatrist to create that environment of trust that one drunk working with another drunk can establish almost immediately.

Chill's Story 1, 2, 3

Let me tell you about my first three steps. I'm sure I've shared some of this before or that you have heard me share about it in meetings   Remember I told you that facts are facts but the truth is subjective.   Well for me the events of my last drunk is a good example of this.

The facts of that day remain the same but for me the truth of that day has changed a great deal.My perceptions of the day are vastly different then they were and they may continue to change.

One of the things you don't hear much about in meetings is that you never get finished. Remember the steps have principles behind them and that when we talk about working the steps we really are just applying these principles.

According to the Big Book of Alcoholics Anonymous fourth edition the principles are as follows:

Step 1 Honesty   Step 7 Humility

Step 2 Hope   Step 8 Brotherly love

Step 3 Faith   Step 9 Justice

Step 4 Courage   Step 10 Perseverance

Step 5 Integrity   Step 11 Spiritual

Step 6 Willingness   Step 12 Service

Well I'm not sure what all that means or if I'm practicing them correctly. When I read step four I don't see brotherly love and step five confuses me a little with integrity.

I'm not sure if it means just being honest or if the intent of that honesty is imperative. When I share with another person and my higher power ; It does   not   matter the   what   I say it as much as   why   I say it.

If I'm only sharing for selfish reasons such as to save my life am I practicing integrity.

Lonnie looked at Chill.

"Are you asking me?"

The Big man laughed, "No, no, no."

I'm sorry I was put off track.

See what I mean. I been sober almost fourteen years and sometimes I think I know something.

You go what? Eighty-seven days?

You come to me with a fifth step and I start explaining about the principles and realize maybe I don't know as much as I think I do.

We hear all the time that its progress not perfection and that is one of the truest statements of the program.

For years alcoholism and drug addiction has   ran our lives. There are underlying principles at work in living that sort of life.

We practice deceit, arrogance, selfishness, etc. These principles that feed our disease become identified as character traits   and we seek to identify their origin. We call that finding our part. It's the whole point of a fourth step.

A fifth step is several things. It is an act of faith and trust that is obvious.   An individual shares with   his   higher   power   and   another   person   his personal inventory.

 Lonnie what do you think is more important? Writing   the fifth step or sharing a fifth step?

Lonnie furrowed his brow and replied.

"I'm not sure what you're asking, Big Dog."

I guess the information is more important. I don't know. You tell me.

I don't know either, remember it's not a test there are no wrong answers. To me, the information is what it is. It's just a collection of facts.

If I have been truly objective and removed arrogance and self will from the examination of my past, what I will find is patterns of behavior. I will study these patterns and try to determine what motivates me to repeat these behaviors.

For me personally once I set down with another person and examined my shit, we determined the majority of my issues were fear based. I was r able to see when and why I acted out and determined my family was my biggest problem and my biggest strength.

For me the fourth step was easy. I was like you. I was tired of talk, talk, talk. I wanted something solid something I could put my hands on to show I was fighting my disease.

I was determined to get it right. I was in a halfway house in Louisville and about two or three weeks sober. I had a counselor that was   pretty   cool . I told him the book didn't make sense with the whole resentment list bullshit.

He gave me a handout that I think he took from an NA workbook I'm not sure and it doesn't matter.

The handout was titled "A slow thoughtful walk through your life" or some such shit.

It had questions like::

What is your earliest memory?

What is your earliest memory of your mother? Your father?

What type of child are you?

What is your family life like at this age?

It was very thorough and covered your life in every aspect.

Well I wrote eighty-one pages I still have those pages.

I started writing using the questions and it quickly became a narrative.

I only covered events up til age eleven.

That was the age I started using and everything after was just more of the same.

The patterns and the drives were readily identifiable.

I took this "4th step" to my sponsor at the time.

We met in the beer garden of an old pizza joint that shared accommodations with the "Alano" club at that time.

My sponsor was a surly old biker with about nine years sobriety.

I handed him my fourth step and he opened it up and lost it.

Holy shit! Damn boy you may be a little self-indulgent. Fuck I ain't reading this.

You got a fucking Big Book with you!

Well yeah, I stammered.

My sponsor's name was Deacon John and he didn't have time for much bullshit.

Find in the book where the fourth step is done.

He asked me more questions.

1. Do you think you are powerless over alcohol and your life unmanageable as a result?

2. Do you think you can be helped?

3. Are you willing to turn your will and your life over to the care of a power greater than yourself?

Again I answered yes.

Okay then prove it.

How? I answered.

Look, Bobby. That's my real name Robert or Bobby Frieze.

Chill is a nickname my brother gave me.

Bobby I want you to take a blank piece of paper and write down the first ten people you can think of that have harmed you.

We did it just like it's outlined in the big book with the columns and everything. We found the same character defects that I had already identified. We came to the same conclusions.

In forty five minutes with Deacon John I was able to accomplish the same amount of work that had taken me countless hours and much anguish.

He was right. I had been self-indulgent. I wanted my fourth step to be perfect better than everyone's.

It just wasn't.

This program and recovery itself teaches me time and time again I am just another person no better and no worse than anyone else. That use to sort of depress me. But the longer I stay sober the more I realize we are all miracles and truly amazing.

Life use to be a burden a tortured existence and I can remember wanting to die so many times. I can get like that even today but I get that way less and less and feel a certain amount of shame when I do.

Today I try to remind myself that life is a gift a privilege and endeavor to treasure the people and circumstance I find in my life.

I'm not always successful. Some days I'm far from it. These periods of unhappiness and despair tend to happen less frequently and are not as intense when they do happen.

I realize today that much of being happy is a choice. Circumstance and conditions are much less important than my attitude toward them.

Lonnie was intrigued.

I don't understand . Are   you saying since you got sober, you don't have bad days.

No! no! no! not at all! I still have bad days. Everyone does. Sometimes life hands you a bunch of shit.

What I have come to realize that my higher power has jokes.

I don't know your feelings about God and religion and they don't really matter. I can help guide you through the steps anyway. I have a God in my life and it is not one that was handed to me. To me God is a force underlying everything and intertwined within everything.

God isn't about good or bad for me. It's about the universe always levels out. Every action has a reaction, karma, consequences all that stuff.

If I cause harm that will come back to me.

Sometimes I cause harm without intent. That's God using me. My will is not involved so nothing needs to be set right. No correction needed.

In the eleventh step we talk about praying for knowledge of his will and the power to carry it out.If I seek God's will in my thoughts and actions my life goes smooth no matter what happens.

Lonnie said sounds good but I still don't know what you mean.

Chill leaned forward adjusting himself inside the car so he could face Lonnie head on.

Although the windstar was made to accommodate large people Chill still had trouble.

Once he got himself comfortable Chill continued his line of thought.

Lonnie most of the gifts I've received in recovery started out disguised as hardships.

Every   one   including getting sober.

Let me tell you about my last drunk.

I was working as a bartender in some redneck knife and gun club. I was working for twenty dollars a day plus tips. I rented a room in the back. I used this room mainly to sell drugs. I had a girl friend who was fairly young and attractive in a big haired bawdy kind of way.

I think I loved her. I'm not sure. I think the reason I was with her is because she had chosen me and it was just easier to be with her than to leave.

I kept the room in case her and me didn't work out plus she was on section 8 and I wasn't supposed to be living with her.

Well twenty a day and tips was not enough money to pay my bills, especially since I was heavy into cocaine at the time

Somehow without me noticing I had become a drug dealer. I never really thought of myself as one, not at first. ; Eventually I had to admit that cocaine had a big hold of me.

The man   I worked for was an old World War II vet. He had been a marine on Guadalcanal and not one to bullshit.

He was also probably the fairest men I ever met.

He had money but it hadn't changed him. He would give anyone a chance. I seen him feed the nastiest filthiest of drunks. I never seen him deny a drunk a drink if the drunk really needed one.

Don't get me wrong he was no pushover or goody two shoes. He knew something at the time that   I didn't.

He knew we are all the same and that that poor slob down on his luck today could be him or me tomorrow. The place was called Marvel John's and if a guy wanted a drink John would give some job to do to earn a drink.

I asked him once John why fuck with these fuckers.

He laughed and said everyone deserves a chance.

I had said. Maybe but some of these guys are beyond hope.

John seldom got pissed and hardly ever at me.

My comment set him off.

By God! I gave you a fucking chance, didn't I?

You think it was a smart decision to put a big angry guy with a smart ass mouth in charge of my livelihood?I'm still shocked sometimes that you haven't gotten me shut down or yourself shot.

Turns out you're a pretty   damn good   bartender!

At   least   when   you ain't   got   so   much of that   damn   dope   in you that you can't stand still.

I don't know what you all see in that shit.

Well that's how things stood.

I was allowed to drink for free at the bar but I had stopped drinking altogether.

I had never been a little guy and after my first year of drinking all free beer I could stand I had gotten really huge.So I decided to quit drinking beer.

Well whiskey is very dangerous for me. No drug or chemical makes met more pitiful or more violent than just plain whiskey.I often joke that I switched to buying cocaine because it was cheaper than free whiskey because of all the shit that happened when I drank whiskey.Even then I knew I had a problem just had no idea of any way out.So I did lots of cocaine and my world shrank.

My world became three or four rooms the barroom, my room behind the bar, my girlfriend's bedroom, and whichever bathroom that was close.

I filled my life with people that could facilitate my procuring or selling cocaine. All other interactions were kept to a minimum.

I became so paranoid that I ran off most of the bar's alcoholics.

This went on for a long time until God, the universe whatever you call it sent me my greatest gift in the form of probably one of the most painful experiences of my life.

I got sober as an indirect result of my brother's suicide. To tell you the truth, I'm not even sure it was a suicide.

I know on the day it happened I could not accept that fact or I was unwilling to accept it.My woman at the time was a pretty girl named Ellen. She was from somewhere down toward Harlen way.

Her people were country as fuck and not ashamed of it.

Unlike my mother and father, Ellen's family were not what you call hard workers at least not the females.

It seemed to me that the females in her family mainly had one career goal to find a man and work him.

Ellen's people had sent her to the bar to get me. They had scouted me out and decided I was just what she needed.

I didn't know it at first but my oldest brother Hollis Glen was living with Ellen's mother Charlena or Lena. Now Lena had already been married twice.

She had had five kids by Ellen's father who was still alive and well and lived down in some holler in Harlen county.Her second husband had fallen ill and died shortly after marrying Lena.

Now to further illustrate their proclivity to working men, my brother Glen had been scouted out for Lena by her daughter Carol Anne who just so happened to be dating Glen's best friend Clifford.

Now the main requirement for being a suitable mate for these girls was a man had to work and bring home regular money.

It just so happens my family had always been big on work and I'd always kept a job.

At the time of meeting Ellen I think I was working in construction. Either putting in windows or vinyl siding. Iin the mid- nineties there was good money in this type of work and every hillbilly with a truck and a ladder in Northern   Kentucky   would   head across   that   river   every morning to   go gather   up   those   good   buckeye   dollars.

For some reason construction was booming in the Cincinnati area. The housing bubble had not burst and there were jobs aplenty. Cash jobs under the table money. I was working for day wages bringing home about four fifty a week.

I would supplement this income with a little selling of some good bud brought up from Tennessee.   I   grew   up   around Western Kentucky   but   my people   came   from   down around   Eastern   Tennessee,   and   in   the   early   and   mid- nineties we were able to procure the finest smoke available in this region.

I was getting sixty dollars a quarter sack in ninety-one. The only drawback was we were paying premium prices for the shit.   I mainly sold weed so I could smoke for free.

I avoided any hard drugs at this time because I had gotten strung out on crack while in the army. Crack hadn't hit it big in the places I frequented yet and powder coke was mainly around on the weekend.
I preferred psychedelics such as acid and mushrooms and those were sporadic in their availability.

Hardly anyone used needles in the early nineties due to the AIDs scare of the mid-eighties. Those drug users were looked down upon and often avoided.

I've   seen people   asked   to leave parties for shooting up .A bunch of coke fueled drunks yelling at them to get their junkie asses out of their houses.

As far as heroin, it was around but not really in any quantity or quality. An addict would have to rob drug stores   to keep a good habit going.

Well, on the day of my last drink I woke up around noon at Ellen's house, it was an unseasonably warm day in the middle of February. Two days before valentines.

I was taking off work that night and taking Ellen out. Most likely to the bar I worked at and a couple of others within walking distance.

At around noon, Ellen returned from making a phone call.She had went to see when my brother and her mother would be able to pick up her kids for the night.   When she walked into the room, I could see something was wrong.

Chill baby! I just talked to mom.

Hollis shot himself.   Hollis was Chill's oldest brother there was seven years separating the two and Hollis had been more like a father figure than a brother.

Chill can remember a ball of ice running through his body. He knew Ellen was not playing. This was real! this was truth not some sick joke.

Chill's first coherent thought was that it didn't feel right. His brother had the pressures of the world on his shoulders but Chill just couldn't see him   leaving   this kind of hurt   for other   people.

Was Andy there?

Ellen responded . yes Andy found the body.

The body Ha! Rage began to build within Chill.

Hollis Frieze was gone !a vibrant, living, breathing man;who loved and fought and struggled with life, was no more.

He had been reduced to "The body."

Chill's brother had come to him the week before to collect money that Chill had owed him.

Chill had gotten a hundred and thirty dollars from his brother so he could re-up on buying some cocaine.

Chill's habit had gotten out of hand and   between his habit   and   Ellen's he was   barely breaking even.

He could see the future and it was bleak.   He had always   prided   himself on having his dope money on time.   He tried to convince   himself that if he sold dope like a regular job he would be able to maintain. He expected his money to be paid to him on time and so he always tried to pay on time.   He   had   gotten   caught   short and had   asked   Hollis to loan him the money.

Hollis knew Bobby had integrity and didn't even ask what the money was for. He reached in his wallet and handed him the bills.

Hollis looked at his little brother who towered over him by at least four inches and outweighed him by at least eighty pounds.

I'm going to need this back Wednesday. I'm going to the country to see Daddy and I'm going to be short when I get back.

Everyone assumed Hollis had lots of money because he worked all the time and made good money.

The fact was Hollis was struggling. He was having health problems and Lena his new wife, Ellen's mother, was a high maintenance woman.

During their conversation at Chill's house, Hollis had shown Chill a recent acquisition.

Look at this he   had said and handed Chill a short, compact, efficient looking handgun.

Damn boys That's a pretty motherfucker.

Chill poked fun at his big brother what you getting paranoid and taken to packing? He had asked in good fun.

Hollis had reacted strangely to Chill's little joke

His tone deepened and all good humor left his eyes.

"It's not paranoid if they're out to get you."

Chill's blood had begun to race his body tightened.

"Who's fucking with you? Let's get the motherfuckers. Just show me who they are. I got your back."

Hollis had smiled he knew his little brother meant what he said. When it came to family, Chill would fight his heart out. He wouldn't question if it was wrong or right. If a man wouldn't fight for the people he loved he was worthless in Chill's eyes.   This loyalty had gotten him in trouble more than once. He had fought battles for family members and had suffered the consequences of those actions.

Chill sucked it up he knew that if he hadn't helped when he could   help, he wouldn't have been able to live with himself.

Hollis had continued.

"It's Lena and her bunch. Every time we fight she threatens to have her boys bear my ass. You know I ain't afraid to fight but I've gotten old and broke down.   I done told all of them I'm not gonna fight anybody anymore if they come at me. I'm putting 'em down for good."

I've got this nine-millimeter with me all the time.   I bought an AK-47 last week and I got two other pistols.

Chill looked at his   brother.

"Why do you stay? That's fucking crazy you got to live like that in your own home.

"Did she actually threaten you?"

Chill little brother I love her she's the devil but I love her.

"I've lost everyone once and I can't do it again. I'd rather die than go through all the heartbreak again.

If anything happens to me you look into it. These people can be evil."   She's got big Andy staying out there with us and anytime we argue she threatens to sic him on me. I done   told   him   I will   shoot   him   dead   if   he   ever   comes   at   me   and   I   will.

"Damn   Hollis, that   ain't   no   way   to   live."

Hollis had laughed and said something ominous.

"Oh it won't be like this for long. Something will have to give somewhere."

"You just make sure and have my money on Tuesday when I get back in town. Daddy doesn't know we got married so I'm taking Lena down to meet him."

Chill hadn't known either.

"When did tha t happen?"

"Friday before last, little brother! Didn't Ellen tell you?"

"No, I don't think so. If she did, I wasn't paying attention."

Hollis had laughed, "yep you a real hillbilly now. You pre-fucking your sister-in-law's daughter. Ha ha!

I guess that makes Ellen your niece by marriage."

Chill had laughed because it was just twisted enough that he found it funny.

"Well, tell daddy hi for me and that I will probably see him in the spring."

"Alright, will do and brother I want you to know I love you."

Chill did not know how to respond. The people in his family just didn't throw the word love around lightly.

He couldn't remember if his big brother had ever told him he loved him.

Chill hugged Hollis to him and said, "I know buddy I love you too, man."

That had been on Saturday night.

Hollis had shown up on Tuesday for his money and Chill had it ready.

He had had to do some fucked up shit to get the money but he had been determined not to let his brother down. It wasn't just a matter of pride it was also to prove that his word was still good. It would also hide   the extent   that   drugs had taken   over his life. If his big brother knew the truth of Chill's situation he would most likely intervene.   He wouldn't be able to stand idly by and watch his little brother kill himself.

Chill's god did indeed have a fucked up sense of humor.

Chill had met Hollis at the door, money in hand.

"Here you go, brother."

"How was Daddy?"

"Oh, you know; he was Daddy. Lena's in the truck I can't talk. You be good, little brother."

"Thanks for letting me borrow the money, Hollis. It helped me out!"

"Anytime Little brother. I gotta get. I'll holler at you later."

Those were the last words they had spoken to each other.   Those were the last words that they would evr speak to each other.

It hit Chill like a fist. Hollis was Dead! He was dead! Dead! The word really didn't have meaning until someone died.

Everything that person   was   or had been was a finished deal!

Dead meant he wouldn't be there if needed.

Dead meant all those someday plans were now never gonna happen plans.

Chill grabbed his pants and quickly got dressed.

He headed toward the door. Ellen tried to keep up. "Where you going? What are you going to do?"

"The hospital! I'm going to the hospital."

Ellen said to him, "Wait, I will go with you," and Chill had not waited.

He got into the truck without looking back.

He was being overwhelmed with emotion.

His mind raced.

Hollis could not be dead!

Hollis was the success of the family. He had a home, two new trucks, kids, he had bought into the dream.

Hollis had done nothing his whole life but work hard to obtain stuff for the people he loved.

Their father had always worked hard but with a seemingly different motivation. Their father had treated his children as if they were obligations. He had fulfilled his duty to them and was quick to point out his sacrifice.

He had never been one to shower praise or a kind word on his children. These things he saved for the children of strangers.

He took being a father as serious business and was quick to point out his children's shortcomings or areas in which they needed to make improvement.

Chill doubted if his father was even aware that his children felt this way.

Chill's mother had divorced his father when he was ten and he hadn't lived with the man. He spent a couple of weeks each summer with his father and they wrote weekly letters. During his adolescence Every other week a letter would arrive with a check written to Chill.

His sister Anna had long since moved away and Parker his other brother never came around.

These letters had given Chill more of a father than his siblings had known. In his letters Brandon Frieze revealed himself to his youngest son. He had the soul of a poet and dreams. He had only been educated to the eighth grade but his mind was sharp.

He hadn't mistreated his children out of any mean spirit or lack of love. Chill's father for all purposes a very capable man had done his best in the only way he knew.

He was not the self-assured individual he presented to the world. He was a man riddled with self-doubt and nameless fears.

He excelled at everything he did and Chill finally figured out why.His father just didn't do things that   he was   not   already   proficient.

If something appeared in his life that he knew nothing about or looked beyond his scope he would just dismiss it and avoid it altogether. He was not a risk taker and hated to look silly.

After Chill had been sober a few years he realized his father had all the character traits of an alcoholic without the relief of drinking. He also lacked the spiritual solution as a substitute.

He lived his life on self-will and was much better at seeing what he lacked in life rather than being grateful for what gifts he did   possess.

Chill's mother had many of the same fears but she always walked through them. She was determined to at least to make the attempt at her dreams and was not afraid of the opinions of other people.

She was not afraid to try. Her biggest fear was to die without having lived. She still loved Chill's father even though she had left him in the seventies.

He had been a disappointment to her. She was a strong woman and had little time for a weak man.

When Hollis made the comment, "He's Daddy," it was an adequate statement.

For all his shortcomings, Brandon Frieze, Chill's father, was the role model in all his son's lives. All three boys to a various degree had spent a lot of their lives trying to make the old man proud.If they had ever succeeded he had kept it to himself.

Hollis had worked hard like his own father and spent his earnings on his family. He did so with a different heart. He gave to them material things because he had never been taught the value of his heart and time to another.

His family was his biggest gift and if they were a burden he shouldered it with pride.

He never made them feel like they were the reason he didn't have a life. They were the reason he lived.

He seldom spent money on himself unless it was something he could use to make more money.

Any items he did splurge on something   for   himself   he seldom got the time to enjoy. They just sat and collected dust while he worked. When Chill got to the hospital they were bringing Hollis in the ER door.

He   ran   over   to   the gurney on which his brother lay. He would never forget the image seared into his brain.

Hollis's face looked as if made of stone. His body was bloated for some reason. His color was ashen and his beard discolored with blood.

There were no marks on the face but behind the man's right ear slightly tilted was a softball size hole.

Someone had tried to stuff bandages in that cavernous space but it had not been successful.

While Chill observed the groups entrance into the hallway the wadding had fallen from the wound.

A length of bandage trailed loosely back into the hole inside his brother's head.

Small flecks of bone and pink spongey matter were scattered haphazardly throughout his hair.

Some   diabolical   anointing   from a most   foul servant of an indeed   most cruel deity.

Chill's body began to vibrate a rage ran though him like none he had ever experienced.

He felt violated like something had been stolen from him. It wasn't pity or sadness. It had nothing to do with his brother.   This   was personal. It was an irrational fueling but not to be denied.

Don't   they know who he is ? This can't be done to him.

He realized something was gone forever ;something he didn't even know he valued or needed.

His big brother was an untapped resource a nest egg of emotional security.

Chill could not explain or verbalize all the emotions he felt but indignant and full of rage were the two most evident.

The hospital was Catholic and a well-meaning nun approached Chill.She placed a kind hand on his shoulder and said, "Sit, are you okay you are scaring me."

Up to this point they only thing Chill had said was, "Yes that's him, that's my brother Hollis Frieze," when an EMT had asked him to identify "the body."

He had started thinking of the bloated monstrosity as "the body" for it was obvious nothing of his brother remained within that sad place.   Chill could remember grasping one of "the body's" hands and marveling.

They were huge and scarred and cold as stone. Those hands told the entire story of his brother.A lifetime of struggle and sacrifice turned into cold unfeeling uncaring stone. A sadness wrapped around Chill and his heart broke.

He yelled at the nun.

"Why are you scared? You didn't kill him, did you?"

"Of course not," the well-meaning lady replied.

"Well then, you got nothing to worry about then, sister."

Chill remembers grabbing a police officer standing there and asking him, "Sir, can I speak to you?"

"Certainly," the officer replied. "I'm very sorry about your loss." Chill cut him sort.

"Can you do me a favor?"

"I can try. What do you need?"

"There was a man staying at my brother's house. The man is one of his step son's, he's a great big guy named Andy. They call him Big Andy.

My brother told me if anything happened to him that this fucker probably be involved."

The officer said, "My understanding is your brother's injuries were self-inflicted."

"Well, that's why I'm asking you to indulge me. I would like someone to do a gunshot residue test on this Big Andy. He's a felon that just got out of the pen. I'm not even sure he's supposed to be living in my brother's house."

The officer's response to Chill request was, "I'm just an officer. You need to tell the detective ;when he gets here, your misgivings."

Chill could not contain himself any longer he had to get out of the building.

"Fuck it!" Chill had said in the calmest voice he could manage.

"I need a fucking drink," he whispered to no one in particular. He walked out of the ER doorway and encountered his brother Hollis's best friend Clifford Grant.

"Don't go in there you don't want your last memory of him to be that."

He didn't have to explain any further.

Clifford said, "That bad?"

"Yeah, It's that bad."

"Where you going, Chill?"

"To the bar. I got to get a drink"

"Damn! I'll come with you."

"Come on!" Chill had said.

Chill could not remember the ride to the bar. He knew that was when the tears and self-pity started.

Clifford had been like a brother to Hollis and was in many ways closer to him than Chill.

They had lived, worked partied and sold drugs together.

They had had each other's backs for years.

When they got back to Chill's room, the two became very solemn.

Chill had stopped drinking alcohol about a year previous due to the fact that beet was making him enormous and whiskey made him violent.

He had used cocaine daily for the last three years, but he knew there wasn't enough cocaine in the world to numb this hurt.

He had stopped at the bar and grabbed a liter bottle of Jack Daniels old no. 7.

He held the bottle up in front of Clifford and said, "If I make it through this drunk today, I'm never drinking again."

He put the bottle to his lips and pulled hard a good three four ounces of whiskey into his throat. When he brought the bottle back down the neck was empty and a good inch of space shown below the neck.

Chill knew for him that taking that drink was him giving himself permission to act on all the emotion and rage boiling inside him.

He had meant what he had said. If he made it through the day, he planned never to drink again. He didn't figure the odds were real good   he   would   make   it through that day.

After the first drink had been taken, the day became a blur.

Chill, Clifford, his brother Parker had taken over the bar.   Clifford sensing the rising violence within Chill had departed after several hours. A series of friends had come in and out during the day. Only those very close to the fallen Hollis were allowed in.

At one point a good family friend named Kenny Barnes had made a simple drunken statement that enraged Chill.

He had stated:

"If you ask me, he was a coward for shooting himself."

Chill had not said a word. He sat his beer down.

The man had been standing at the bar to Chill's right.

He swung a long roadhouse left that started at his toes and gained power through his hips.

His left fist connected with Kenny's nose and the man flew off his feet and sailed through the air at least six feet with the wall behind him the only thing stopping his flight.

"Nobody asked you, Motherfucker!"

Bobby grabbed the man and pulled him into a headlock with his left arm and was about to beat him until the rage left his body. This was what he needed, he needed to hurt something. He needed to share the pain he felt.

The bartender yelled, "Behind you, Bobby!"

He turned and there was his other brother holding a bar stool high over his head about to hit him in the head.

Chill had smiled and a derisive chuckle escaped his lips.

"You gonna hit me over this piece of shit."

His voice rose but remained icy and calm.

"Our fucking brother ain't even cold yet and this cock sucker is bad mouthing him and you gonna hit me!"

"Not this motherfucker but me they only brother you got left."

"What kind of fucking shit is that!" he yelled.

Chill, I ain't gonna let you kill that man.

He's drunk and he didn't mean no harm.

That man, he's been our friend for years.

Don't let your pain and grief over Hollis make you do some shit you can't take back.

Chill reached up without even thinking and plucked the bar stool   from his brother's hands seemingly with no effort.

It resembled the   plucking of a flower or the brushing of lint from a shirt.

He had hugged Parker to him and sobbed into his chest.

He's dead! He's dead! He's dead and he ain't ever coming back. He ain't never coming back.

Why'd he do that?

Why?

Why did he have to fucking do that?

Why? Why did he do that?

He didn't have to do that. He didn't have to do that! Hollis is dead!

He ain't never gonna be nothing else. He's just gonna be dead.

Parker Frieze was at a loss for words all he could do was hold the grieving giant in his arms.

Whatever had ever happened between the brothers in the past did not matter. Right now, Chill needed someone to help him make some sense of the days tragic turn of events. Chill and Parker had always been the closer of the three brothers.Chill had idolized Parker his entire life and always overlooked his brother's shortcomings. He had fought for his brother whenever asked and never hesitated to have his back when needed.

Parker had always been jealous of Chill's status as youngest in the family.

He had the middle child syndrome in a bad way.He had trouble seeing the good things in his own life but could always see when others had it better.

Chill and he had never fought mainly because for most of his life Chill had feared his brother. Chill no longer feared his brother but he felt no need to fight him.He had thought about it and realized it would always be better for his brother to wonder about the outcome of such a fight.

Chill also knew any fight between the two would be all or nothing. Because he knew if he ever swung on Parker it would be to kill or die. He would not stand the shame of having that foot on his throat another day.

Today all that was history on this day. Parker held his little brother and gave him that little comfort he could.

It was a good thing Parker had been there to comfort and calm the big man. He was probably the only person on the planet that Chill loved enough to let soothe his pain.

The hour grew late the drinking had continued and it seemed like everyone had calmed down.

Parker tried to get Chill to come home with him, but Chill had declined he had decided to spend the night in his rented room behind the bar.

He took another bottle of Jack from behind the bar. The third liter of the day the brothers had also drank a liter of Tequila. For some reason, no one had cocaine on this day and probably a good thing.

Once in his room alone with his thoughts Chill had continued to drink. The pain and the rage had not subsided if anything it had gained power. He could not remember afterward the exact series of the events that followed. Some images were seared into his brain and some were foggy.

Chill had gotten into his truck and driven to Ellen's house. He had given her his key earlier because she had forgotten hers.

His rage returned because she was not home. He was livid with outrage. He needed her and she was not home.

How dare she!

Don't she know who he is?

He had kicked the door in and would later be charged with burglary for this action.

He quickly went through the house looking for what he did not know.

He found a half quarter sack of weed that he had gotten for Ellen.He put it in his pocket out of spite.

The bitch won't be smoking my pot on my brother's death day, By God!

His thoughts were angry and non-sensical. Whiskey often made him indignant and a bully.He hated himself on whiskey and became extremely paranoid and prone to violence.

At some point in his whiskey fueled rage he had latched onto the idea that his brother's wife "Lena" had had him murdered by her son "Big Andy."

To him this was better than his brother committing suicide.It wasn't so much that he was worried about his brother's immortal soul. It was   he   considered his   brother the success of the family.

If   his   brother   Hollis the successful one was so fucking miserable that he killed himself, Tthat meant Chill was in a real world of shit.

He decided "they" had killed him. Hollis and Lena had fought and Hollis had went to sit in his truck and smoke weed and cool off. Lena   had   sent Big Andy to kick   Hollis's Ass.

When he had opened the door. Hollis had pulled a pistol on him.Big Andy knew Hollis was not a killer and that he was in bad health.When Hollis had hesitated to pull the trigger. Big Andy had forced the gun into the man's mouth and pulled the trigger.He had then dragged him out of the truck and laid him in the yard.

The man was not dead so Andy had taken a blanket from inside the truck and tried to smother him. Later he would say he was trying to stop the blood flow.

This was the scenario that played over and over in Chill's brain. It comforted and enraged him.

It comforted in the fact that if it were true his brother had not killed himself.

It enraged him that if it were true his brother had been murdered and no one cared. They killed him and they were going to get away with that murder.

Chill decided that he would drive out to his brother's house and burn all his brother's property so his wife couldn't have it.

Somehow, he never made it to his brother's house but instead wound up at Ellen's older sister's house.

Ellen's sister's house sat upon a hill.He had gotten out of the truck and walked up to the house without knowing. The people inside the house opened the door before he reached it. A young girl of about six years old stood in the doorway she smiled at Chill.

"Mommy and Aunt Ellen are not here. They went to a friend's house. Grandma is here though; do you want to talk to Grandma?"

Something sinister and mean came alive inside Chill.

"Oh yeah! I do want to talk Grandma. Grandma is exactly who I want to talk to."

Chill crossed the living room to the hallway that led to the rear of the house. Lena   Gaskins Frieze stepped out of the back bedroom into the hallway.

She had a cigarette in her left hand an ashtray in her right. Chill began yelling at the woman ..

"You killed him! You fucking bitch! He's fucking dead and it's your fault."

The woman replied.

"I loved Hollis Frieze more than life itself. I will never love another man as much as I loved him."

"You shit! You don't know the meaning of the word love. You fucking whore! He   is   dead and it's your fault!"

While he had been yelling he had been walking toward the frightened woman. She threw   an ashtray at Chill's head. It missed but it was all he had needed to   loose   the rage he had tried to contain all day.

He went to slap the woman with his left hand.

"You bitch! You killed my brother and now you got the fucking nerve to hit me with a fucking ashtray."

He swung that left hand meaning to smack the woman in her face.

What he hadn't realized was he was holding a twelve pack of bottled Budweizer in his left hand when he swung.

The twelve-pack collided with the side of Lena's head and things became a blur for Chill. The woman had run into the bedroom.Chill had turned into an animal.

Like any predator smelling blood and fear he followed.

"Why you running, bitch?" He had screamed.

"If you ain't done nothing wrong, why the fuck you running?"

He couldn't remember swinging again but the two-hundred plus pound Lena flew across the room into the far wall.

The impact knocked the air conditioner out of the wall onto the ground.

When she fell onto the water bed the impact had burst it open.

Chill had grabbed her by her neck with his right hand. Her feet dangled off the floor.

He looked into her eyes and began to squeeze.A click went off inside the big man's head.

It was like that for him on whiskey.

There would be a click and he would black out in a rage and after his anger and adrenaline had burnt the liquor from his body some semblance of sanity would return.

When Chill got the click this time he hadn't been in a blackout. Just the opposite everything was in slow motion.

During the last two or three years Chill had often caught himself wondering how this lifestyle he had chosen would end.

He knew it couldn't go on forever but he also couldn't see any way to stop.

He would ponder daily before leaving the house if that day would be the day.

Would somebody shoot him that day?

Would the cops bust him?

Would he be snitched out by somebody that owed him money? He felt like he was walking a razor blade and any misstep could be the end.

While holding Lena aloft by her throat. It occurred to Chill that this was it.

This was the defining moment.

He had gone too far. This couldn't be taken back. He didn't know what was next but he knew that what had been was a done deal.

He had dabbled at being a drug dealer and a petty thug with the vague idea lurking in the back of his head that someday he would go back to the more   normal life.

He knew with a certainty that he had crossed a line and that his days of being a petty thug and harmless drunkard were done.

All those thoughts ran through Chill's mind in a second while he held Lena aloft. He realized his brother was dead and if he finished choking the life out of Lena his life was as good as over.

"You're not fucking worth it!" He had snarled at the frightened bloody mess.

Saying this he had tossed her aside.

All the fight drained from the big man. He was beaten. It didn't matter if they had killed Hollis or if Hollis had killed himself.

His anger and outrage hadn't been about Hollis. It had been about him. His brother was dead and he hurt so somebody had to pay.

He realized while holding Lena aloft that something truly evil was lose in that house and it occurred to him with surprise that it wasn't them. It was him.

All day he had fed his anger and outrage with alcohol and self-pity. He had nursed and fueled his pain until walking into a houseful of women and children with murder in his heart had seemed like a reasonable course of action.

He had never made the conscious thought to kill anyone but his actions proved he was capable.He had brought evil here and he wanted to be away from it.

He turned to run from the room. The only thing he wanted was to take back the last few moments.

Not because he was ashamed of felt remorse but for fear of what was next.

He knew that actions would have consequences and that his way of life was over the uncertainty of what came next was overwhelming.

Well, a bottle to the head was what came next.

Big   Andy had been at the house to act as a body guard for his mother just in case something like this was to happen.

Chill's action of going to Ellen's house first caused the big man to be drawn to investigate.

Someone had called and reported Chill kicking in the door.The two must have passed each other on the road.

Chill had only beaten the bigger man to the house by less than two minutes. A lot had happened in those two minutes.

A flashing explosion of light burst inside of Chill's head four times.

It was Big Andy breaking all the bottles that hadn't been broken in Chill's initial swing on Chill's head.

The house had been full of people and they swarmed over Chill.Someone had their arms wrapped around his legs. Another had his arms.

Big Andy kept pounding on him but his punches were no longer bringing light and explosions the bigger man was losing wind.

Chill did not cure all the anger and outrage had flown from him. He wanted only one thing. He wanted to get away from the evil that he had brought into the home.

His thoughts were about his eternal soul and justice . The moment was secondary he realized some crucial transcendence was taking place.

The alcohol and adrenaline combined with the days' events had him ensconced firmly within some moral delusion.

God and Satan were at war for his very soul. He had carried evil into this home but he would need God's grace to ever leave.

He would remember thinking these thoughts very clearly while a house full of people tried to subdue him. TheOnslaught finally forced him to one knee.

He heard Big Andy give instruction to his captors.

"Hold him steady! While I get my knife out I'm going to cut this sumbitch's throat! This'll be the last damn fight he ever gonna fight. Hold him dammit!"

Fear flew through Chill's mind. This entire day he had only been concerned with his own loss, his own pain. He had thought only in terms of his own personal tribulations .

For the first time in a long time he thought of someone else's loss. His mother's face flashed through his mind.

She had already lost one son on this day. If he got himself murdered this night she would lose two.

He looked up to the ceiling and did the last thing anyone expected from him.

He begged for his life.

"Please don't kill me! Please don't !"

He was in total panic. Andy looked stunned.! He was shocked.

He hadn't thought Chill to be a coward but here he was sniveling and begging for his life.

What no one in that house knew was Chill was not begging anyone human for anything.

He was begging his God to spare him. The God he had ignored and doubted.

In the moment of impending doom and the thought of his mother's broken heart he had reached out on his knees and asked for his life.

Everyone was stunned by the action. Only moments before   this man had entered this house like a demon straight from hell.

Carrying with him   hate and outrage seeking vengeance for insult and injuries whether real or imagined.

Now here he was meek as a lamb begging for his life.

The meekness did not last sensing his chance he stood up and pushed the people away from him.

He turned and proceeded down the hallway from whence he had first entered the house.

Big Andy pursued but the big men was winded at this point. Chill no longer even recognized Andy as a threat he looked out the living room window. The physical exertions of the last few moments had cleared his mind considerably.

He looked out the window and seen flashing red and blue lights. There were six or seven squad cars outside the house and more coming.

Chill looked at the big man and said:

"You called the cops?"

He could not believe that the cops were there   for him. Not them.

His brother was dead and he was going to jail.

"Yeah, fuck yes, we called the cops, you dumb fuck."

Chill said, "But this is family."

Big Andy looked at Chill like he was from a different planet.

"You is plum fucking crazy."

They had gotten onto the parch and all the police were still at the bottom of the hill.Chill remembered the weed   in his pocket that he had taken from Ellen's house.

Big Andy was talking to him in his heavy accent. "Now look what you done did you got yo'self all likkered up and done came over here and started a bunch of shit. And now you gonna go to jail for I bet a good long time and you ain't helped nothing! Hollis is still dead and alls you done is fuck your own life up."

Andy noticed Chill digging in his coat pocket.

"Hey, what you got there?"

Andy knew Chill sold cocaine and probably thought he had a big rock in his pocket."You got some dope? Quick hand it here and you won't get charged with it."

It was almost funny Chill had been so worried for so long about getting caught with dope that it never occurred to him the several charges he was already facing.

He didn't know if he could trust the big man but he trusted the dope fiend inside the big man.

"Here!" He handed the dope to Big Andy right as the first two police officers came up onto the porch.

The police quickly ascertained who   to arrest and who to congratulate and thank. Big Andy was the hero of the night and Chill was left out in the cold.

Chill didn't know it at the time but the long road back to a sane and sober life had started. His arrest he eventually came to regard as his rescue.

Before taking him to jail he was taken to the Emergency Room for treatment of injuries sustained in the brawl.

He tried to refuse treatment and told the people at the ER that he would not sign anything giving them permission to work on him. He also informed them he would not pay for any treatment since he was being treated against his will.

The arresting officers told the nurse to treat him. He said that the county could pay for it because ;he would not. He never did pay for treatment. The hospital put eighteen staples in his head . He refused any anesthetic for fear he would say something incriminating while sedated.

The police and the hospital staff treated him civilly. After his wounds were treated a dull lethargy settled into Chill's body and mind. The day's rage had been exhausted. All that was left was a deep aching sadness, a quiet resolve. This relatively calm state lasted until arriving at the jail.Upon exiting the police car, Chill was introduced to the detective in charge of his case. Chill started his now familiar self-pitying lament.

"My brother's dead," he started and was interrupted by the detective.

"I know all about it and if you ask me the wrong brother's dead, you piece of shit."

The man's words were like a bucket of ice water in Chill's face.

The cop continued. "It's just a good thing that woman's son arrived in time to stop you, you worthless fuck. I hope you get everything they can throw at you. You fucking crybaby."

Rage ran through Chill. The detective had played Chill completely wrong.

IF he had played into the man's self-pity and coaxed him along; his kind demeanor and a friendly ear would have had the grief stricken man spilling his guts about the day's events. A confession that would have been worth fifteen years at least. The cops attitude instead incensed the man and made him determined not to give the man anything.

Chill did give the cop his opinion of two things. The first was things aren't always as they seem and then he told him to look up Big Andy's prison record to see what kind of hero he had on his hands.

The man's most recent internment had been for first degree assault. A brutal attack in which he had sodomized a grown man with a pool stick in a public pool room during business hours. The man's injuries were so severe that he would have to use a colostomy bag the rest of his life.

Big Andy had done eight years on that charge and that was after he signed a plea agreement.

He also told the man to check and see if Lena hadn't already had one husband die under questionable circumstances. The officer asked him if he wanted to make a statement. Chill had replied, "Fuck you, I ain't tell you shit after the way you talked to me. Don't even pretend that you are here to help me. I ain't making any statement of any kind. Oh yea and   I'd like a lawyer."

The cops face turned to stone and he told the corrections officer on duty to take Chill from the room.

Chill was pulled over by this same officer about a year later for running a red light.

Chill remembered the man and was sure the man remembered him. The cop had him dead to rights. He had ran the light   Something was different. The man was very civil and let Chill off with a warning.

Chill often wondered if the man had indeed checked to see if Chill's remarks regarding Lena and Big Andy's backgrounds were true ? It was the only conclusion that explained the man's change of attitude toward Chill.

Once placed in an eight man cell with ten other people Chill had laid down on the cold concrete floor. He had been   provided   no blankets   nor a mat.

He took his left shoe off and placed it under his head and fell asleep immediately   .Chill woke the next morning with a weird sense of peace. He was facing years in prison and everything he owned was probably lost.

At first he could not explain this sense of well-being then it came to him.

He was alive and it was over. It was over. That impending sense of doom the big book talked was no longer present.

For years, he had dreaded some ominous unknown event that would stop him in this life he had chosen.

He believed in karma and knew he was living wrong. He had been raised with the values of hard work and justice in the world.

He had done the balancing act of addict, drunk and drug dealer for years. The lines of right and wrong had been blurred for him.

He knew eventually his choices would have a price. That ominous unknown thing he had been dreading had happened and he was still here.

It finally hit him that he didn't have to get high that day. Hell it wasn't even an option.A sense of optimism came to life within the man.

He felt free. Freer than he could remember feeling in a long time. He didn't care what happened next as long as he didn't go back to the life he had been living.

He was stopped and determined to stay stopped. The bondage of his addiction was ending. It was time to start the road to his recovery.

Chill was very fortunate in a few ways. Due to the fact that he hadn't drink in a year except for that one day his withdrawal from alcohol was just for a day. Withdrawing from cocaine is not as physically unpleasant as opiates and alcohol .He did itch and obsess and you could smell the dope sweating out of him.

Chill had heard that there was no physical withdrawal from cocaine. He knew in his own case that there was physical withdrawal ..He had cravings and later he noted all through his sobriety he would have using dreams about cocaine.

Another way he was fortunate was he had a sister named Annie who had gotten sober twelve years previous. After four days in jail Chill's brother Parker came to bond him out. It was on a Thursday night. It was almost comical Parker was drunk as fuck and they released Chill into his custody.

Thankfully Parker had a family friend driving. Chill had not gotten to go to Hollis's lay out and they were not sure he would be allowed to the funeral. An emergency protective order had been issued against him. He was not supposed to go within hundred yards of Lena. Lena of course would be sitting up front in the spotlight.

It was her moment to shine. Not only had she lost her beloved husband she had been brutally beaten by his brutish brother.

A special exemption was granted and Chill was allowed to attend with the understanding that if he said anything or same near Lena he would be arrested on the spot.

Hundreds of people were in attendance for Hollis's funeral. It was ironic to say the least. The man had taken his own life. He had felt so alone and alienated that he had shot himself.

There had been no one for him to reach out for help! Yet four hundred people could take the day off work to show up for his funeral.Some people had driven five hours in one direction for Hollis's send off.

So alone he sought refuge in death no one to share his pain.

Four hundred people touched deep enough by his passing to attend his funeral.

Chill could not reconcile these two facts.Before the funeral Chill had called his sister, who lived in Louisville. He knew she would be up later in the day but he had to get something said.

"Annie this Bobbie your brother," he had started the call.

"Hey! Little brother! How you   doing?" This was somewhat of a joke between the two.

Annie stood about four foot ten inches tall and weighed maybe a hundred and five pounds at the time of this call. Her little brother stood around six three and weighed around 350 pounds at the time.

Chill had replied, "I guess I'm alright considering."

"Annie I got something to ask you. It's kind a important."

She said okay.

Chill hesitated then blurted in one long breath.

"Annie I don't want to feel like this anymore. I've been living like an animal and don't know how to stop.

"I know you drank and drugged like I do. I know you did something and got stopped and got your life back.

"I don't know what you did but if it worked for you maybe it'll work for me. I'll do whatever you tell me"

Annie replied, "Well, glory halleluiah I been waiting a long time to hear these words from you."

Chill didn't know it at the time but he did realize later. He had just taken   the first three steps of recovery as outlined in the Big Book.

He had admitted his life was out of control and he was powerless to stop it.

He believed that whatever his sister had done to get clean and sober could probably work for him.

He was willing to turn his will and his life over to her.

To him, his sister was a power greater than himself. Anyone that had managed to stop drinking and drugging had more power than Chill.

This was enough to get him started.

Annie said she would make some calls and see about getting him a bed at a treatment center.

Treatment

Chill's sister Annie was able to get him into a good treatment center. His veteran's benefits were even going to foot the bill.

She knew the people that ran the facility and they pulled some strings and got him a bed without having to wait.   His sister explained some hard facts to him.

"Now you getting this bed   means somebody else has to wait on a bed. If you waste this chance you may be costing someone their life."

Chill had thought at the time she was being overly dramatic.Being in the middle of his addiction he was not yet capable of true empathy. He was self-absorbed and full of self-will.

Fuck the next guy was his feeling on the matter.

If he, Chill, didn't get clean and stay clean he figured he would be dead or at least kill someone. It was life and death but it still didn't matter. One way or another he was determined to get some relief.

He was put into a room with ten   other guys.It reminded him of the military, he had a wall locker and a bunk.

The program was broken   into three phases. Each phase had certain requirements to be met before being able to phase up to the next phase.

The program was designed to be nine months minimum and could take up to two years to complete. Chill had been concerned when informed of this because he had some serious criminal charges facing him.

He was thinking he needed to be making some money and getting a good lawyer.He decided on his sixth day in treatment to trust the process.

He had been in a group and the counselor kept talking about getting rid of old people, places, and things.

The point he was trying to make was if a person wanted to stay in recovery it's a good idea to stay away from people they had used with, places in which he had used and things that were associated with using.

Chill felt himself growing agitated. He was a loyal man by nature and had been raised to stand by family no matter what happened.

He had promised Ellen that his deciding to get sober would not break them apart.

She had stood by him after he had hit her mother. Her family had to be giving her a hard time about this choice.

She came from hard people descended from feud country.

She had three big, strong brothers that were no strangers to violence.

Chill was probably lucky to still be alive.   He really hadn't given it much thought he figured if he had been meant to die it would have happened on the night of his brother's death.

They certainly had opportunity and motive. If Big Andy had cut his throat on that night he would have been a hero.

He wouldn't even have been arrested.

No Chill had made a promise to the girl and he would stand by the promise.

The counselor was a huge bald giant. He had to weigh at least 450 pounds. The clients made a lot of jokes about him. Chill realized that the counselor's, the building, everything were just tools to use.

They had information and experience in recovery but they were just people. This particular counselor only had a little over a year sober.

A tall skinny dark skinned self-confessed freak head kept reminding him that he was also fairly new in recovery.

"Yo Mister Donald, I done had seven years clean and sober before I relapsed! What can you tell me about being clean and sober?"

The big man had smiled and replied. "The key phrase in that sentence is you 'had' seven years."

The minute you took a drink or a drug you removed yourself from the solution.

"Remember we all just have today." Mr. Donald had said something on the first day that had stuck with Chill.

"you can find a thousand reasons to use today but you only need to find one to not use. Look for a reason not to use everyday."

It was simple and sounded kind of dumb but it was exactly right. To stay sober one day at a time all a man had to do was find a reason not to drink or use that day.

When Mr. Donald had brought up the topic of old people places and thing; Chill an he   had clashed.

Chill had stated, "I'm not turning   my back on my people. I got a woman that still drinks and gets high. She's twenty-three years old and I don't have a right to expect her to quit just because I quit."

Mr. Donald had told Chill that, "If you move back into that house with an active drink/drug abuser you will almost certainly use. You will not be able to stay sober under those conditions."

Chill had rose from his seat.

"You don't know what the fuck I can do, big boy!"

Mr. Donald had remained seated. He very calmly asked   Chill to "please be seated."

"Mr. Frieze, why are you getting angry?"

"I'm not angry! You will know when I'm angry! Buddy! Bet on that!"

Nonplussed the big man continued. "Just because you are loud doesn't make you right. You may want to ask yourself what's really going on! Are you perhaps afraid this might actually work? Does your disease feel threatened?"

Chill looked stunned the man's words were like a slap in the face. The big fucking blob could see right through his bullshit.

The truth was his disease did feel threatened and he was defensive.

From that point forward Chill became determined to pay attention to whenever he was getting distressed.

He would figure out what he was being scared of and fight it.

He became very adept at personal inventory .He would try to imagine what he would tell another person if they brought the same issue to him. He began to strive toward being objective with these issues.

By removing the emotional distress from the situation he could often see more than what first appeared.

If he was still unsure of how to proceed he would bring the situation or problem to a friend or someone he respected that he felt applied the twelve principles in their   life.

This was difficult at first because in early recovery Chill just didn't trust many people.He tried not to get too   close to people in the rooms of recovery because he thought most of them were lying.

He had harmed in treatment and from his own experience that alcoholics and addicts were delusional. Some were just more delusional than others.

Just because an individual was passionate and well-spoken during a meeting did not mean that person was being honest or even had a clue about recovery.

He learned to listen close. If someone shared "I've been   around AA a lot of years and I've found" etc. Chill realized the person didn't say they had been sober a lot of years they had said they been around AA a lot of years.

They were implying that they had a lot of recovery and that what they had to share was useful. The truth is they are ego driven not recovery driven.

Chill realized a lot of people were in the rooms of recovery but not near as many people in the rooms were *in* recovery.

He was taught early to watch what people did and see if it lined up with what they said.

The big book talks about placing "principles before personalities" Chill put considerable thought into this slogan. Out of necessity as a child he had learned to read people. In his home as a child you had better be able   to read the mood on everyone's face or risk their wrath. He had   been the youngest and therefore the one most likely to catch everyone's wrath. As a result his bullshit detector was fine tuned.

He did not even have to concentrate to detect inconsistencies in people's shares during meetings. Truth shone through like sunlight through the clouds. He steered clear of people who always seemed to have their shit together.

He knew he wasn't that type of person; his luck did not run to that sort of life. Chill knew the value of pain and understood the necessity of struggle .He did not trust anything that came easy.

It just always felt like a setup. If   life went good for very long he became a little paranoid.It seemed to Chill that gratitude was a key element in a lot of people's program.

The people that seemed the happiest were the ones that seemed grateful. They never hesitated to give rides to newcomers, were glad to give their number out and never seemed too busy to talk about recovery.

One of the things he noticed early on was that the disease of addiction and alcoholism did not play favorites. It struck the smart, the dumb, the rich, the poor, the pious, the greedy, doctors, lawyers, teachers, preachers, whores, thugs, kids and him. The Big Book says the members of AA are people that normally would not mix.

Chill agreed to a point because he knew when he was using he had gotten high with people from all walks of life. He had sold dope to lawyers and used alcohol to sleep with ladies very much above his station.

The disease was the great equalizer. It took everyone to the same place. You could give alcohol everything you owned and cared about and it always wanted more.

Chill had taken the first three steps in a phone call to his sister. In his third week of treatment he wanted to start his fourth step. The fourth step is one in which a lot of people hesitate in their recovery. The fourth step basically is a review of your life.

The book refers to it as an inventory and compares it to a business taking an inventory to determine what goods to keep and what to discard.

When a person reaches the point of admitting powerlessness a lot of bad shit had most likely occurred.

We review out past behavior and look for patterns.

We know what we did and how it affected other people but an inventory can help us identify the factor preceding the acting out. The getting drunk and fucking shit up part is the alcoholic/addict seeking relief from something.

An "honest and thorough" examination as suggested by the Big Book will show these patterns.

Once an individual learns what factors precede his drinking and drugging ; that person should be able to take actions to stop these conditions before they end in using drugs and or alcohol.

Chill was introduced to the disease concept of alcoholism and addiction. The longer he was sober the more he was convinced that it definitely was a disease. He could see people getting sicker.

He was told addiction and alcoholism never went away on their own without treatment or intervention of some sort. The disease was always progressive. If you were doing nothing to fight your disease your disease was gaining ground.

The fourth step is a big deal. People do not want to look at all the fucked up shit they did and admit all the harm they caused.

Chill could not wait to start his fourth step. Everything in recovery to this point had been talk.

People talked about working the steps.

Chill can remember talking to some obnoxious gas bag after a meeting his first week in treatment.

The clients were encouraged to go to outside meetings every day. They were supposed to develop a recovery network to use once they were released from the treatment center.

They were required to attend five outside meetings every week. They could attend narcotics anonymous and alcohol anonymous.

In order to phase up they were required to obtain a sponsor, complete one hundred thirty hours of community service and collect two phone numbers at each meeting they attended.

A lot of sharing of numbers occurred. This was okay because if someone was in the program and practicing the principles of the twelve steps in their lives on a daily basis, they would take the call from any newcomer.

Chill in an attempt to meet his number quota had stopped a burly red faced man of about fifty The man was loud and red faced and very much full of himself. Chill had approached him, explained that he was in a treatment program and asked for the men's number.

The man had made a sarcastic comment about treatment centers and ninety day wonder filling up the rooms. Chill kept his opinion to himself with great restraint. He told the man that he was interviewing for a sponsor.

The man had thought that hilarious. He had inquired to Chill as to just what were his requirements for a sponsor.

Chill had his answer ready. They had role played this entire sequence in group. A sponsor would be someone with long term sobriety who has had a spiritual awakening as a result of working the twelve steps and is willing to walk me through the steps.

The man had replied, "what does that mean?"

Chill a bit perplexed by the question responded, "What do you mean? What does that mean?"

The man got a little nasty to Chill. You just said a whole mouthful of words and they sounded pretty. Now tell me what they meant.

"I don't know what you're asking! What exactly do you not understand?" Chill responded trying to turn it around on the man whom he thought was being a smartass.

"You said a sponsor is a man who has had a spiritual awakening as a result of working the twelve steps. What exactly is a spiritual awakening?"

Chill was stopped cold by the question. Every day since he had come to treatment and started attending meetings he had heard people talk about their higher powers. Spiritual awakening was one of those terms people used all the time in the rooms.

Chill didn't have an answer so he told the truth.

"I don't know. Tell me."

The man smiled and this time it was an honest smile filled with good humor. He was not being snide or mocking.

Young man there may be hope for you.

Chill looked at the man.

"To be honest I don't understand half this shit. "I sit in meetings and hear people talking about working steps. I have no clue what that means. I don't say anything because I don't want to seem stupid."

The man put out his hand. "They call me Big Book Barry."

Chill put out his hand. "My name is Bobby Frieze. Glad to meet you."

"Bobby, don't ever be afraid to ask a question when it involves recovery. Sitting quiet might kill you."

Bobby looked at the man and spoke his mind.

"Okay, in all seriousness, I keep hearing people talk about working the steps and how important it is to get the first step right.

"How do I know I've done the first step right?"

Bobby's new friend put his hand on Bobby's shoulder and said, "You don't take a drink."

Bobby felt tricked.   The man continued.   "I know partner it's frustrating. It'd be great if there was some secret phrase or handshake that I can show you and you become a member insured not to drink.

"The first step is pretty simple. It's just admitting to yourself that you are powerless over alcohol and that your life is unmanageable."

Bobby interrupted the man.

"Those are just words. How do I know?"

"Son, you want this to be something you do   and it's done. "Recovery isn't like that. This is a way of life. The Big Book talks about 'we have a design for living that really works.' The process of recovery is ongoing."

Bobby, more than a little frustrated responded, "Does that mean I will always be powerless?"

"Not   at all. Somewhere around page forty-five in that book. It might be forty-four or forty-six. You got a third edition. I got sober on the second edition?

"Anyway, it says something like 'the main object of the book is to enable you to find a power greater than yourself which will solve your problem.' Now that's not a direct quote.

"Now that paragraph is preceded by one that talks about a lack of power being our dilemma.

"That's important because it doesn't say alcohol is our problem."

Chill very confused at this point explodes.

"Well what the fuck? Isn't this alcoholic anonymous? If alcohol isn't the problem why are we here?"

The man absolutely glowed with good humor at this point.

"Son, I like you!" he exclaimed. "Alcohol was our solution; it made life bearable. Then it stopped working or the consequences of using alcohol became greater than the benefits.

"Get that damn book out, boy. Remember they call me Big Book Barry somewhere in the forward to that second edition it talks about 'To show other alcoholics precisely how we have recovered is the main purpose of this book.' You know what that means?"

"What?" Chill queried.

"You don't got to understand shit! Just do what that fucking book tells you to do that and you will be alright.

"The book uses words like exactly and precisely for a reason. Those words were chosen with care. People may confuse you boy because they don't always know everything they pretend to know.

"Trust the knowledge in that book. People died to gather that knowledge.

"If a man gives you advice on recovery and it isn't somewhere in that book it's probably his opinion."

Chill had asked Barry to be his sponsor and the man had agreed to help guide him through the steps.

The first three steps had been talk, talk, talk, and pray, pray, pray. Chill had talked to the counselor at the treatment center about doing his fourth step.

The counselor had wondered aloud.

"What's the hurry? Recovery ain't a race, you know!"

Chill had pointed out the part at the end of the third step where it says to take pen and hand and start a vigorous course of action and that it could have little permanent effect unless *at once* followed by a strenuous effort to face, and to be rid of the things in ourselves which had been blocking us. This is the part of the Big Book where it talks about liquor being just a symptom and we had to get down to causes and conditions.

The counselor was Mr. Reeves. He was a senior counselor and had fifteen years sober. He was not a very happy man but he did love recovery.

"Alright, Bobby, you are right and I think you're ready. Unfortunately, we cannot take you through a fourth step within the facility."

"We cannot stop you from doing one with your sponsor but state law does not let us take you through a personal inventory. We don't have anyone on stuff with the credentials."

Bobby laughed.

"You guys can't take me through a fourth step because you don't have enough schooling but any drunk in AA can?"

"Exactly! You got it."

Bobby wanted to do a fourth step because it would be something he could look at and physically touch that showed he was fighting his disease. It would be tangible evidence that he was making progress.

He was not fearful he was eager .. He wanted to confront the past and do whatever he had to do to be free.

He wanted to move forward to whatever was next. He had wasted enough of his life he didn't want to waste anymore.

Bobby had sat through numerous meetings in which the fourth step was the topic. This was the step that chased men back out so he was determined to get it right.

The only problem was when he looked at the book it just didn't make sense to him. The little diagram with the columns and resentment list just didn't make sense to Bobby.   Scared that he was going to fuck it up he had went back to Mr. Reeves for advice.

Mr. Reeves provided Bobby with a handout.

The handout was entitled "A Slow Thoughtful Walk Through My Life" and it asked a series of questions that took an individual through their life.

A young man that Bobby would later sponsor would be given the same handout.

Bobby had used the handout and it had helped. But when he had taken it to his sponsor it had been ignored.

Big Book Barry was instrumental in getting Bobby through a major crisis in recovery.

Around June Bobby had been in treatment about four months he received a letter from the prosecuting attorney concerning his upcoming criminal case. In the letter, the prosecutor was offering Bobby a plea bargain deal. If he plead   guilty she would sentence him to eight years suspended and he would have to do eighteen months in prison.

Bobby had   been arged with first degree assault and it had been lowered to first degree burglary. If it went to trial he would be facing fifteen to twenty years with a minimum of doing eight years.

Bobby did not want to go to jail. He was making so much progress in recovery that it just seemed unfair. Big Book Barry told him that this was a great opportunity.

Bobby had wondered how he figured that.

Barry had told him this is an amends. Your higher power is about to show you something. You will never get a better chance to see if this shit works.

Bobby response had been, "Easy for you to say you don't have to do the time."

It really hadn't taken much soul searching for Bobby to make his decision. He understood the basic principle of AA and recovery.

It's all or nothing. He had dank and used the same way.

If his God wanted him in prison he would go.

Bobby refused the deal offered by the state. He was given a trial date in September. It was June and he was broke and didn't even have a lawyer.

He decided to stay in treatment and finish the program. There was nothing he could do about the trial so he gave it to God and he did what was in front of him each day.

He completed treatment three weeks before his trial. He came home and found a job through a temp agency and settled into a routine.

A hearing was scheduled the day before his trial.

He met his lawyer at the same time he met his prosecutor. She was a real estate lawyer hired by his mother and had never done criminal law. It didn't matter.

The prosecutor took Bobby into her office.

She said, "I was very surprised you did not take my offer of eighteen months I thought it was very generous.

"When you declined, I started looking into the background of this case. Specifically,   the background of your victim.

"These are some horrible people. The best suggestion I can give you, Mr. Frieze, is to get far away from these people as fast as you can. Nevertheless, I made some promises.

"One was that you would do some time for this assault.   "If we go to trial and I have to go to the trouble of seating a jury. You will do at least eight years."But I have a new deal for you.

"What do you say to five years suspended sentence with ninety days work release and attendance at AA meeting.   Plus, victim's compensation on hospital bills."

Bobby replied.

"Do you have a pen?"

He considered this as one of the first miracles of his recovery.

One he would share time and time again.

Women!

When Chill finally left Ellen, he found himself reluctant to become involved with anyone romantically.

He still had physical needs but even those he tended to ignore until he just had to seek   relief.

Chill had always had a strong sex drive and was prone to being irritable if deprived for any great length of time.

He had lived with Ellen for eight years. The first four had been with both of them using a lot of drugs and alcohol.   The last four years with Ellen, Chill had been sober and had witnessed Ellen's disease in action.

A person living with someone in active   addiction is affected by that person's using.

Chill as a person in recovery knew he was treading on dangerous ground by staying in the relationship.   He had a whole list of reasons why he stayed.

When he had first gotten sober; even before he had come home from the treatment center, Chill had thought he stayed because he loved Ellen and that he owed her. She had stood by him even after he had almost killed his mother.

Ellen's family was very tight knit in its own way. It had that bonding element of people living through a shared trauma. The trauma in this case being life itself.

Like soldiers on a battlefield being members of Ellen's family all had some form of PTSD. Dysfunctional families tend to lock the world out. They tend to hide their secrets from the outside world.

Ellen's choosing to stay with Chill after he had caused harm to Lena was no little thing. Lena was the glue that held the family together. She was the driving force behind the scenes.

She had been the one to decide that Chill was a good prospect for Ellen. She had done the research to see if he met her requirements as a suitable mate for her daughter.She determined he had a job was unattached had no children or debts.

He was perfect. He could feed and support her baby girl.

Said baby girl had been sleeping on her sister's couch when she had been sent to the bar to snare the unsuspecting Chill with her wily feminine wares and ways. Lena and Chill's brother Hollis were raising Ellen's two kids at the time.

Chill isn't sure but he doesn't think Ellen even mentioned having kids until about their third night together.

Well, they had used together for three years and then Chill had went away to treatment and a couple months in jail.

After coming home, he had moved back in with Ellen but had had to put his mother's house down as his residence for his probation officer.

Chill had never worried about violating his probation because he had known he was doing the next right thing and trusted completely that his higher power would take care of him.At fourteen years sober he can look back at that time and get shivers up his spine.

He had been very naïve. He had been in constant danger while living with Ellen. She still drank and got high every day. Chill often bought her beer and weed.

It just seemed right to him. He was the one that had gotten sober and he didn't feel he had the right to inflict his lifestyle upon anyone.

Whenever they would fight it was usually about how much money it took to feed Ellen's various habits.

Ellen would respond to any complaints with "you never cared how much it cost when you were getting high."

"Yeah well, I paid for the shit I did and yours too. I took the risk, I earned the money.

"You don't hit a lick of work and our biggest expense is you. We spend more money on your cigarettes, beer, and dope than everything else combined," Chill would argue back.

It really didn't matter Chill always gave in.

Ellen had control of the vagina and Chill had always been easy to whip. Ellen may not have had many redeeming qualities but she did have good pussy and as long as Chill kept her supplied in beer, weed, and video games she never denied him. She never tried to hold it hostage that shit didn't work for Chill.

No pussy, no Chill.

Chill was not a man to stick around if the pussy dried up.

It wasn't that he didn't appreciate women as people. He liked women a lot preferred women to anything.

Chill just preferred his own company. He didn't like answering to other people or having to consider others when making decisions.

It was pretty basic for Chill. He would take care of himself except for one thing. He needed women for sex.

This was the truth for Chill or at least he thought it was the truth.

The fact was Chill was careful not   to give his heart to anyone for fear it would be misused.

He associated love with pain for in his life the people who had been responsible for his health and welfare had also been the people that had caused him the most harm.

The two were inextricable the minute he feel in love he would wonder how it would end. The time after leaving Ellen should have been a time of healing.   Somehow Chill managed to stay sober and get meaner.

He attended meeting regularly mostly AA. He kept one regular NA meeting in his routine as a safety measure.

He very seldom started   conversations with people and had gotten into the habit of only speaking to women when they spoke to him.

He had gotten sober at a treatment center in Louisville but had returned to Northern Ky. Treatment had lashed nine months and when he had returned he took great pains to start a recovery program based on the things he had learned.

Old people places and things are often cited as reasons people give for relapse. Chill attended a couple of meetings close to his house. He recognized several faces and a couple guys approached him after the meeting.

Both were surprised to see him at a meeting and neither could believe he was serious about recovery.

Chill at that time wasn't sure his own self. He did know he didn't want to drink or get high that day.   He wasn't convinced on everything that people talked about but he was certain he didn't want to use.

He felt weird and a bit of a hypocrite talking about recovery and spiritual growth around people he had used drugs with and others he had sold drugs.

He started attending meetings at a clubhouse about thirty minutes from his home. It had a more suburban population and no one knew him. He had worked the steps and shared in meetings. He would help people if asked. The place was small and sometimes crowded. He almost always sat alone.

People told him years later that he had growled at them.   He still growled today but hadn't been aware of his earlier tendencies.

The truth was Chill was afraid to be happy. He had made a deal with God and God had fulfilled his end so Chill was determined to uphold his part of the bargain.

He had promised not to drink and drug and that if God would let him live a sober life he would try not to hurt anyone. Chill was scared if he got too close to anyone they would be able to harm him.

He was okay   . He was able to work, pay his bills, meet all his commitments and responsibilities; to ask for anymore would seem greedy.

Chill could have continued this way for years. It was working. He was getting better even if it was slower.

He was practicing what little he knew of the principles in his life on a daily basis.Chill's higher power decided his program needed a little jumpstart.

Chill's spiritual jumpstart began with a sick little girl who just didn't have enough sense to be scared of him.

Kelsey Carter was a beautiful petite nineteen-year-old. She had just recently finished a thirty-day rehab and was having trouble staying sober.   Chill was working third shift at some printing factory through a temp service. He hated the job but showed up every night on time and gave the place a good night's work.

In the mornings after leaving work he had taken to attending an 8 a.m. meeting at his favored clubhouse.

One morning Kelsey started showing up.   She became sort of a regular and he started looking forward to seeing her little face.If she didn't show up his day felt a little smaller, and emptier.

He had hardly ever said anything to her but that didn't seem to bother her.She would sit down beside him and just start talking .She would just say whatever was on her mind.

This type of person would usually aggravate the hell out of Chill. Somehow little Kelsey did not irritate the huge man. She charmed him. She was like a puppy or a kitten. He wanted to pick her up and just keep her safe.

One morning after the meeting Chill was sitting in the coffee room just relaxing before driving home. Kelsey sat down beside him and made a casual remark that she wished, "She had a big old pill that would just make her die." She said it like a joke but it shook something inside the big man.

He didn't know if she was serious or not but he knew she was precious and her life mattered.If it didn't matter to anyone else it mattered to him.

Since his brother's death Chill took talk of suicide serious. He was no crusader but he was determined not to lose anyone else he cared for at least without putting up a fight. He knew the little girl was trying to be funny. He also knew that most humor was used to disguise truth.

He decided that getting home and going to sleep could wait he had to try and help the child woman.

Chill turned to Kelsey and inquired—

"What are you about to do right now?"

"I don't know I need to be a t work at twelve. I guess I will hang out here until the ten o'clock is over then walk to work."

"Where do you work?" Chill asked.

"Oh, I got a job at Pottery Barn. It's pretty easy."

"Okay, why don't you come with me and let me buy you breakfast and talk a little. I will make sure you get to work on time."

Well at the time Chill's vehicle was a 1992 Toyota pickup. It had been wrecked several times. He had been driving it for fourteen years.   The first eight years had been the hardest of his using.

The truck was covered in dents. The bed was bent double and the passenger side window had been broken out and remained missing.

People would ask him why didn't he get it fixed. He had a standard reply.

"Two reasons. One, I didn't break it so I ain't paying to fix it.

"Two, I don't sit over there."

It had never bothered him before to have that window missing but it occurred to him that the morning air may be cold on the girl. It was October and the weather was mild.

Autumn was on its way and it seemed that after five years with no window on the passenger side that Chill was gonna buy one.

Chill was like that he seemed rough and uncaring and indifferent to his own personal discomfort but would spare no expense or hardship to help someone he cared about. Kelsey had the ability to melt the big man's heart seemingly without effort.

It was her lack of guile combined with her beauty that made Chill powerless over the tiny vixen.

The fact that she had no fear of him and trusted him implicitly was a source of wonderment for the giant. Her trust in him was warranted for the man mountain would gladly die before he would harm a hair   on her head.

Once inside the truck Kelsey commented.

"Dude, I like your truck."

Chill told her it was his most treasured possession and that it had never failed him.

He added that she was a very special girl to be able to see the value in "truck."

Kelsey asked, "is that the truck's name? Truck?"

"Yes," Chill replied, "her name is Truck and she's a lady."

Kelsey laughed at Chill and said, "dude, you are fucked up but in a good way." Chill took no offense for some reason the young lady was starting to relax and to smile.

"Okay, little girl, where you want to eat?"

"I don't care. I'm not even really hungry. Let's go through McDonald's and get a sausage and a coffee."

It never occurred to Kelsey that Chill might be hungry. He had just worked all night and then went to the meeting. For him, his day was ending and he was running on empty.

He didn't care. He had been alone so long that the contact with this fascinating creature was working magic upon him.

They went through the drive thru and parked in the parking lot to eat their meager fare.

The old truck was equipped with a stereo. It was an old am/fm cassette player equipped with auto-reverse.

Kelsey reached over without asking turned the radio on.

Immediately loud thrashing metal music filled the truck.

The startled girl quickly turned the volume back down to a more reasonable level.

"What the fuck was that?" she laughed.

Chill said calmly.

"Oh yeah, the cassette player has a cassette stuck inside it.

"it's Pantera's Far Beyond Driven. This is a Pantera truck. All Pantera, all the time."

Kelsey laughed some more. "Okay. If you say so. I am not familiar with 'Pantera' but hey it's your truck you listen to anything you want.

"How long has   that tape been stuck?"

"About five or six years. I'm not mad. I'm just happy it was a good tape that got stuck and not some shit.

"That would have sucked."

Yeah, dude, that would have sucked.

"So, what do I call you I know in the meetings you always say your name is Bobby and you're an alcoholic. But you don't seem like a Bobby."

"I don't know a lot of people call me Chill."

"Chill? Why?"

"Well, my last name is Frieze you know like freeze cold."

"Yeah, I can see that," the girl replied.

Chill continued, "my brother Dale named me that when I got out of the army.

"I had been stationed in California and when I came home I was using a lot of words that I had picked up out west.

"Chill was a word I used a lot so he just started calling me Chill.

"I guess I like it better than Bobby."

"What am I supposed to call you, little fellow?"

"Well, don't call me 'little fellow.'"

"I most definitely am not a fellow. Big Guy."

Chill tried to honor Kelsey's wishes but sometimes he did call her little fellow. It was not out of meanness or to tease her it was pure endearment.

Chill was totally enchanted by the little princess.   He had not a clue how she felt toward him. She seemed oblivious to his obvious infatuation.   To her he was like a big pet.

He didn't mind in the least.

That first day with Kelsey she had spoken about many things. Her family, her dog, her dreams.

She had talked about her job and being lonesome and how she wasn't sure she wanted to be sober.

He had made her promise not to kill herself that day and to call him the next day   and that they would talk about it again.

She had agreed and he took her home to change clothes then drove her to work.

On the way to her work he asked her, "How were you gonna get home to get your work clothes?"

She had laughed, "I don't know I hadn't thought about it." This was going to prove to be standard operating procedure for Kelsey.   She lived on impulse. Her life was a series of reactions to whatever occurred.

This could drive Chill crazy. He was a person that got to work thirty minutes early for a job he hated.

The name Chill was ironic in many ways because he was a definite type A personality.

The two quickly became a familiar sight at various AA meetings. They developed a routine.

Chill would get off work at seven. He would call Kelsey and see if she wanted to go to the 8 a.m. meeting at the clubhouse.

He would pick her up if she wanted to go if she didn't he would go alone.

After the meeting, they would go to breakfast and Chill would hang out until time for Kelsey to go to work.

He would rush home and sleep for about four to six hours and wait for the girl to call.

She would have him pick her up and they would do an evening meeting. Chill had seven years sober when he met Kelsey.

During that seven years he had worked various jobs. All had been second or third shift jobs. As a result he had seldom attended night time meetings. He had heard much about the night meetings.

There was talk about the meeting before the meeting and the meeting after the meeting. Chill had always thought he had been cheated by missing these meetings.

Kelsey had a little book that had listings for every AA meeting in the Northern KY/Greater Cincinnati area.

She liked to pick meetings they had never attended and would convince Chill to drive them.

It never really occurred to Kelsey that Chill may be tired. To her he was immune to such lowly and mundane activities.

Chill followed the little Kelsey around for months. He catered to her every whim. He may have been exhausted but he wasn't lonesome. Chill was obviously in love with the vivacious youngster.

She on the other hand seemed reluctant to let their relationship be more than platonic. Chill was a grown man with needs.

They spent every day together and Chill spent most of his money on Kelsey. He paid for everything they did together and he didn't mind.

There was   nothing   he valued more than her so he never minded spending money on her.

Meetings were over at nine. They would usually go eat and then Chill would either take Kelsey home to her parent's house or leave with friends.   He would then go to work.

Months went by without Chill having any relief of a sexual nature. He didn't want to pressure the girl and risk losing their friendship.

He valued their time together more than anything but he was becoming very frustrated. Chill tried to remain grateful and for the most part his time with Kelsey was one of the happiest of his life.

He knew everything about her. She would chatter on and on and he would listen and contemplate her musings while at work.

He started to notice some inconsistencies within her stories but he tended to overlook them.

Kelsey got her seven-month coin on a Friday night meeting Chill had taken her to dinner afterwards to celebrate.

Some other friends attended and Kelsey left with them leaving Chill the bill.

He was a little peeved that she could just blow him off like that for other people.

He quickly forgave her as he always did.   Later that night while at work Kelsey texted him that her and some friends were attending a midnight meeting.Apparently they were having a blast.

Chill had felt sorry for himself having to work while everybody got to play and with his girl.She might not think of herself as his girl but he most certainly did.

He felt if he just waited patiently she would come to him. Their relationship was not totally platonic at this stage.

Kelsey loved to pose for pictures that Chill loved to take. Chill had studied art in college and was quite talented with acrylics. Kelsey had proven to be an eager and very apt model.

The camera loved her and she became a different girl once she started posing.

Her inhibitions would melt and her clothes would disappear.Chill had hundreds of pictures of his lady love butt-naked but had yet to touch her in the way a man needs to touch a woman.

After posing for an hour or longer she would just turn it off like faucet.   She would put her clothes on and tell the frustrated giant, "That's enough. Let's go eat or a meeting or whatever."

Chill could not help but feeling she was teasing him.

Kelsey was not intentionally teasing the big man. She knew he loved her and she loved the way he looked at her. She was scared.

Guys changed once you had sex with them. Chill was way too important to her to risk losing because of sex.

Once you had sex with a guy they expected it all the time it became the main activity or focus.

This had been her experience.She tried to keep Chill at bay by saying that they were just friends.

Chill was not a bullshitter even in the matters of love. He would tell her that she knew they were more than that and that she needed to step   up   because he would have to find relief somewhere.

Kelsey told him if he needed pussy that bad it was fine with her if he went and found some.

This devastated Chill. He could not comprehend how she could mean everything to him and he mean so little to her.

What he didn't understand was for her if she gave him what he wanted she risked losing everything she valued in their relationship.

She could get anyone to fuck her but Chill loved her, he respected her, hell he practically worshipped her.

She had never told him that they were together but she had never worried about him seeing other girls. It was obvious to everyone that Chill loved her and for him she was everything.

Chill was also able to hold off because he did not want to endanger Kelsey's recovery.   A   lot of people got in relationships early in recove3ry and ended   up using.   They often cited the relationship as a factor in their relapse.

This happened so often that it was referred to as thirteen stepping.

People get sober, work the twelve steps start making a life for themselves get in a relationship and step back out the doors of recovery.

However much Chill may have desired to defile his little princess he did not want to cause her harm.

On the morning after Kelsey's seventh month anniversary everything changed.At about nine a.m. Chill's phone rang. It was Kelsey asking if it was okay to come over to his house.

This was totally out of character for Kelsey didn't drive and Chill almost had to beg her to go to his house because he always got her to dance for him and he would get her naked and he would try to get her to finally give him some of that pussy.

When she got ot his house he could tell right away something was off. She was with a creepy chick and some goofy dude.

Chill could tell something was off.

Kelsey admitted that after the midnight meeting they had smoked some weed in the parking lot. They had then decided what the hell since we relapsed we might as well go all in.

They had went to Cincinnati and gotten crack and smoked all night in the creepy girl's van.

Chill was livid he could not explain his rage. He hid it from Kelsey but the big goofy kid could tell something was wrong.

Kelsey wanted Chill to   help her get more crack or drugs of any kind.

Chill asked her did you fuck this motherfucker?

She told him no! why would you even ask that?

Chill told the creepy girl and the idiot to leave his home. He made it clear that if they didn't leave immediately he would put them out.

Kelsey began crying and Chill lost his composure. He took her relapse personal. He was scared.

His time with Kelsey had been almost magical.   He had been hurting and dying inside without even knowing it.   She had reached out to him for help and had thawed his heart he had followed her around for months and delighted in her recovery. He could not imagine anyone so cavalierly throwing away something so precious.

He had been right not to let people in. He had let this girl in and now it was over. He was wrong. She was a tool that God used to heal him.

She had made him help her and his unselfish love for her was what had made his life open up and become rich.

He would find in the coming months that once his heart had been opened he could not close it.Kelsey went with him to a meeting and then had him drop her off at a friend's house.

She called within a couple of hours for him to come pick her back up.She was shit-faced drunk when he picked her up.

He had to carry her in the house she had a bottle with him. She was crying.

"Big guy, I'm sorry."

I'm sorry please don't hate me. Here, let's do it!

Do what Chill asked the drunken child goddess.

You know let's fuck! She quickly stripped her clothes off.

Please Big Guy just don't be mad.

Chill took the sweet beautiful nineteen-year-old in to his arms and kissed her for the first time.

Tears rolled down his cheeks and inside his head he cursed his God.The only way he could have the woman he loved was if she was drunk out of her mind.

His good guy happy sober self was pushed aside and the deep dark side of Chill came out.He had never had nothing but love for this girl but his love wasn't good enough.

Months and months of sacrifice and frustration and all he had really needed was to hand her a bottle.

He had imagined their first time together in so many ways but he had never imagined it the way it happened.

They made love for the first time with her drunk and crying miserable about the recovery she had thrown away.

He let tears of rage and frustration roll down his cheeks and pumped her tiny body full of his resentment and fear.

Chill's God has jokes.Chill and Kelsey's relationship really didn't change much after they had sex.

Kelsey stayed drunk for a few weeks and gave Chill a lot of pussy.He was overjoyed on the one hand and miserable because he was scared for Kelsey.

His own self loathing grew and grew.Kelsey would disappear for days on end. Sometimes she would call him while he was at work and she would be drunk with party sounds in the background.

Chill knew he wasn't the only person she was fucking.Apparently when drunk or high she became a rather free spirit.

He wanted to hate her but could not.

This was the time when Chill began his real journey in recovery. He learned to love Kelsey in spite of her disease.

He got so full of anger and self-righteous indignation that he almost drank himself.

The term unconditional love means just that.

Love without condition.It's easy to say but very hard to do when the object of that love is an addict or an alcoholic in active addiction.

Kelsey struggled with recovery she would put together thirty days and relapse. She was able to get ninety a couple of times.

The periods she was out started to grow shorter and Chill started to gain some hope.

While Kelsey dabbled with recovery and continued exploring active alcoholism. Chill found it necessary to treat his own disease. He continued the pattern of meetings Kelsey and he had established.

Usually hitting two meetings a day and working at night he kept himself exhausted. He took to sponsoring guys and reaching out to the newcomer.

Kelsey had shown him the magic of working with others and healing yourself through helping another. She had no monopoly on that magic.

Chill kept himself buys and continued to make room for Kelsey whenever she chose to be in his life.

The same old pattern emerged Kelsey refused to commit to a relationship with Chill. She took it for granted he would be there whenever she needed or wanted him. She left her options open and this hurt Chill.

She may not have intended to hurt him but he felt her actions very disrespectful. He would lie awake at night hating himself for putting up with her shit.

He could not understand how he could love someone so much and that person be so indifferent toward him. Chill was forty years old when he had met Kelsey. She had been nineteen when he had first seen her.

Chill had never had a normal relationship with a female. In his youth he had picked up some bad information from some seriously fucked up role models. His brothers found women useful but not equals in a relationship.

His father's attitude toward children had Chill believing all women wanted you to get them pregnant so then could suck the life out of you.

He had often heard his father blame all the woes and misery of the world on the fact that he had a family. He could never remember his father being grateful for his family. There were pictures of his father in the family album when Chill was a kid.

In those pictures his father was smiling that causal charismatic smile. He was a charmer that was easily seen. A tall strong, handsome man.

His father was a hard worker and very competitive. He would die before letting anyone outwork him.   With all his abilities and quick wit, you would think Chill's old man would have been more successful in life.

Chill and the rest of his family could never understand why the old man didn't take the many opportunities that came his way.   Chill finally realized that these opportunities were much like his children for the elder Frieze.

A grateful man armed with faith could see these things as gifts.   A scared man armed only with self will could only see these things as burdens.It wasn't that Chill's father was ignoring chances to better himself.

He just never saw these chances.

Chill over the years of his recovery had started to realize a few things.   When his higher power gave him gifts they often came disguised as obstacles to endear and overcome.

Every "gift" required maintenance whether it be a job, a friend, or a car.   Some work on his part would be required if he wished to keep these things in his life.

If granted a job he would have to be on time and do the work expected. Failure to do so would result in loss of that job.

Friends neglected   or mistreated became memories.

As a result of this manner of living Chill's life had become filled with only things he valued. There were no useless things or people in his life.

Kelsey's youth may have been a big factor in her behavior. She had a lot of things to learn.She had never had to struggle with the same demons as Chill.   Plus Kelsey had her own demons of which she only hinted.

For her love and sex were different things.   Chill would come to find this the case with many of the women in his life.

Not only could they separate love from sex they could break sex down into categories. They could use sex for love, for fun, for profit, for spite, revenge and many other reasons.

Chill was sure that not all women were this way but for some reason he had a knack for finding them.

An old sponsor had told him once that maybe he was the problem. He knew this was probably the case he had done a lot of inventory and realized that he was so scared fo getting hurt in a relationship that he would pick partners incapable of being emotionally responsible or committed to another.

The girls he found himself drawn to were invariably damaged, addicted or immature. He accepted them into his life without rancor or regret. Knowing his tendency toward unhealthy relationship did nothing toward stopping him from getting into one.

He considered himself a coward when it came to love.

Attaching himself to women that he knew would be incapable of sustaining their end of a romantic entanglement was to give himself an out.

When things went bad he could blame it on "them." He knew it was all horseshit and that he was just scared to be alone.

He didn't think he had what a good girl would want. Self-doubt, self-loathing, low self-esteem, and a lack of faith kept him from waiting for a suitable mate.

The funny thing was he was capable of loving these twisted little girls that came in and out of his life.

They got something from him that they didn't get anywhere else. He accepted them as they were and didn't try to change them. He only insisted on one thing.

They couldn't lie to him. Whatever sick and foul shit they were doing he could understand or forgive.

When they lied to him he was no longer a friend the act of deceiving him put him into a category of a trick.

Once dishonesty became involved he was of no use to them if they wished to recover. Kelsey set a pattern for Big Chill.

She was the first of what he considered his girls. Women that came into his life through the rooms of recovery. They would steal his heart fill his world up with energy and life .

To chill nothing was more beautiful than a beautiful young girl finding recovery. Often they would become his world and he would know happiness and contentment.

There was a flip side to the story. Chill was an awesome guy for a sick girl to start a recovery program.

He knew the program and always wanted what was in the girl's best interest even if it conflicted with his own agenda.

He spent countless hours praying fretting about whether he was causing harm.

He constantly examined his motives and often came to realize he was not a great guy. He failed his girls as often as not.

His own ego and self-interest would instigate a compromise of his moral principles. He would give them money or a place to stay when he knew it was not in their best interest. He would rationalize and justify his behavior telling himself they were gonna get high anyway. He came to realize that he would do anything to help a girl stay sober that wanted to recover but if that same girl was intent upon using and had no desire for recovery, well he could accommodate them.

Although he insisted upon honesty from the women in his life he was not naïve. He knew they lied to him regularly but he also knew recovery was about progress not perfection. You could not force the issue.

All he could do was hold up his end of the bargain. He tried never to lie to the women in his life.

He also tried to provide them with a sanctuary of sorts where they could reveal themselves and not have what they shared used against them.He was not always successful and sometimes his ego hurt and his anger would appear. He found himself quicker to forgiveness and slower to anger as time passed.

Liza Beth

After Kelsey had relapsed the first   time she struggled with sobriety.She would come in and out of Chill's life without warning on arrival and even less on departure.

He would drop her off at home or work with plans for later in the day and then not hear from her for weeks. He tried to hold to his policy of not taking another person's disease personally.

She wasn't getting drunk or high to inconvenience him she was an addict/alcoholic and to use was a most natural act for her.

During these absences Chill began to branch out.   Just as he had realized Kelsey was not the only source for his recovery.

She also did not have the only vagina.Chill realized he did have love for the beautiful petite women but he was more in love with the thought of her than the reality.

He hadn't reached the point in his own recovery where he could separate his ego and pride from loving someone. When she ignored him in public or acted like   they were just friends it hurt him.

To know she   slept with other men hurt him more. The sexual aspect of their relationship never ran smoothly.

When the sex was good it was awesome but even then she would be different after.Several times their sex life would get real good and Chill would get his hopes up and she would disappear.

Chill sought comfort in other arms and it was surprising to him that he didn't have to try real hard.

He was starting to learn valuable information about the fairer r sex.One of the first things he learned is women watch and pay attention to people in relationships.

They keep track of how a man acts when he is in a relationship. Is he cheap, ? is he overly jealous,? or controlling? Does he cheat or lie?

Is he useful? Apparently Chill was considered very useful and he could keep his mouth shut.

During his time pursuing the little one; as he liked to refer to Kelsey, he had been very much the gentleman without even trying.

Chill was loyal by nature and steadfast to a fault.It was easy for anyone observing the mismatched couple that the tiny girl held total and absolute power over the ponderous hulk   of a man.

Chill had never worried about how others perceived Kelsey's and his relationship.When they had first started hanging out together the typical rumors were spread.

Old timers spoke in hushed tones about harming the newcomer and thirteenth stepping!

Kelsey was so tiny that she looked like a child and often she would be mistaken for Chill's daughter.

The man would laugh and say no she's not my daughter but she has been known to call me Daddy.

Their relationship was a paradox Kelsey loved crude jokes, porn shops and posing naked. She enjoyed sex immensely but seemed to always feel guilt at some later time.

Chill continued to work nights and attend one or two meetings every day. His home had become a weird sanctuary of sorts for wayward women.

Some stayed a night or two. Some stayed weeks.   At one point he counted up that six girls had keys to his apartment.

They all had their own little drawer and most had left clothes and makeup.He did not have sex with all these girls. He never pressured a girl that was trying to get and stay calm and sober.

If a girl was up to no good and determined to use he had no problem asking them for "rent."

His motto had become "why should the dope boys get all the good pussy."He didn't lie to himself about it or pretend it was right or wrong.   If a girl could fuck a stranger that cared nothing for her in order to get dope she could fuck him for a place to stay and food in their bellies.

He liked to think this was the truth but he cared for all his girls. He loved them all to the best of his ability.

He gave them whatever he had and they gave him their bodies.Some of his best friendships had developed from opening his home and his heart to these girls.

One Friday afternoon he picked the little on up and they headed to the clubhouse for a meeting.

Kelsey had managed to get ninety days clean and sober.   It was the most since her relapse at seven months.

Chill was thinking of all that had happened in just over a year.His life was no longer bleak and although he was still lonely. His life had filled up with people.   He had learned to be a friend and had started sponsoring more men.

He was so lost in his thoughts that he had missed something Kelsey was saying. He asked her to respect herself.

I said there's a hot new girl that just got out of treatment.   "Everyone is all up on her shit like she invented pussy."

"Really?" Chill quipped, "I can't wait to meet her and thank her. I happen to be quite fond of pussy. Maybe she can give me some?"

Kelsey laughed a deep belly laugh so hard she snorted soda out her nose. She wasn't worried about her big guy straying.

It just never occurred to her. They pulled up to the clubhouse and there was a commotion at the door.

A crowd of people were coming out and at the crowds epicenter a very striking, very tall, and very pretty girl was holding court.

"That's her, Kelsey said, "isn't she hot?"   Kelsey liked women especially very pretty ones. It seemed a lot of girls did.

"Yeah, she's pretty fine," Chill replied.Their progress brought them in direct contact with the little gathering. Kelsey grabbed the new girl's arm and dragged her toward Chill.

Here I want you to meet somebody she said to the girl.This is my best friend Bobby but everybody calls him Chill.

Without thinking Chill looked directly into the girl's eyes. He took her hand in his and said

"I want to paint you naked." Her eyes flashed with merriment. Not at all embarrassed or incensed.

"I'd love to see your work,"   she replied and the crowd dragged her away.

Chill turned to Kelsey and said, "Stay away from her. She is up to no good."

When Chill had looked into the new girl's eyes he had seen fiery excitement, she was like a dare.

He had known many women, but none had had a look like that. It seemed as if she had seen right into his soul.

He thought "temptress" an appropriate word for her.He thought her very attractive but sinister.

Something dark and dangerous dwelled   within that angelic face. She was just too good to be real..

She was a genuine bad girl!

What Chill had forgotten, at least for the moment, he was a fool   for just such a girl.

Liza Beth would come into Chill's life and change everything. Through her he would feel his greatest joys and greatest heart breaks.The next day was a beautiful Saturday in mid-September.Chill was supposed to meet Kelsey at the clubhouse for the noon meeting.

He arrived early as was his custom. He parked his truck and entered the clubhouse.He noticed two things. Kelsey was not there but the lovely new girl Liza Beth was in attendance.

He said hey how you doing   today.

She smiled looked him directly in the eyes again and said fine just waiting on my mom to pick me up.

Chill was not accustomed to people looking him directly in the eye. Due to his immense size and general intensity most people tended to glance briefly and glance away.

The little nymph was brazen and again he though she is up to no damn good.

He excused himself and went to the bathroom. When he returned he noted the young beauty was not to be seen.   Oh well she must have left he thought.

He called Kelsey to see if she was on her way and found that she was still in bed.

Well get up and get dressed in on my way.

In typical fashion she had been the one that insisted they attend the meeting and then hadn't even bothered to be ready.

When he walked back outside the long lithesome beauty Liza Beth had stationed herself on the curb.

She was talking to someone on the phone.   He overheard her say in a slightly whiny voice.

Yes, Mother I want to stay for the next meeting, but it won't start for an hour.   If you are not close don't worry about it. I will get something after the meeting.

She ended her conversation and looked up at him.

She had her sunglasses on so those wicked eyes could no work their voodoo on him.

Without thinking Chill blurted out to the wily teen. I'm going to pick up my little friend from yesterday you want to ride with me?

Chill expected a polite no but figured what the hell take a shot.

What was the worst could happen?

The girl jumped up and said hell yeah, I'd love to. I am bored to fucking death. Everybody is nice and all but they just fucking talk and talk.

Chill laughed fucking aye come on then girl

My ruck always looks better with a pretty girl inside.It'll be me and the tall girl going to get the small girl.

Chill couldn't remember that first conversation, but he remembered being at ease.

Years later, he would realize what it reminded him of; being with Liza Beth was like that first drink had felt like.

It felt wrong but nothing had ever felt   more right. Upon arriving at Kelsey's house. Chill waited in the driveway.

His little princess came out through the garage door which was her custom.

In her hand she held a diet coke which looked enormous in her tiny hands.Her other hand contained her ever present Marlboro reds.

The tiny one had her habits and Chill found everything she did endearing.When she reached "truck" she noticed the striking blonde vision in her seat.

The look she gave was one Chill did not recognize on Kelsey.The look only lasted a second and was quickly replaced with her usual quick smile and sparkling good humor.

Well hello? The little princess greeted the vivacious new girl.Hi, Liza Beth returned. I love that top. She said to the tiny lady.

Chill was to notice in the future that Liza Beth often gave compliments to other women upon greeting.

He thought it a very nice gesture. He mentioned it to another girl during one of Liza's absences in his life.

This girl another lovely blonde named Amber was a trusted friend and sometimes lover.

Amber quickly clued Chill in on the facts.

Men are so stupid. She's not complimenting her she's being sarcastic. Girls do that to each other all the time. She was being a complete bitch. Chill was confused and remarked, "I don't think so she seemed really sincere.

Amber knew both girls and knew that Chill, bless his heart, was totally clueless about the ways of women. To Chills' credit Liza Beth was so pretty that she often used compliments to put other women at ease.

She did note that he was one of the few men that she considered teachable.

Chill continued, "Why would she be mean to Kelsey? She barely knew her."

"Chill, baby, sometimes you can be so dense. Some women do not share the spotlight well with anyone."

"What do you mean?" Chill queried.

"Anybody seeing you and Kelsey together can tell in a second that you are crazy about her," She continued. "And any female can tell that Kelsey, don't take this wrong, just doesn't feel the same way."

Chill was stunned Kelsey was still in his life. She may not be his main focus and sometimes months would go but without them being together. But he still had love for her.

"Are you saying Kelsey doesn't love me?"

"No, Chill, I'm not saying that Kelsey loves you just fine. She loves you as a friend.

"Chill, you are my best friend. I know I can trust you with anything. You're an awesome guy you deserve a girl just as awesome.

"I would kill to have a boyfriend as cool as you. You treat women like gold."

Chill looked doubtful.

"Yeah well, if that's true, why am I always the side   guy and not the boyfriend."

"You know too much about us, Chill. All the girls you love need you way too much to become involved with you that way. We can get anybody to fuck us and be our boyfriends, but we can't always get someone to love us."

Chill said he understood but he really wasn't sure.

When Kelsey looked funny at Liza Beth Chill didn't question it. She just said, "Thanks. I love your hair."

There was a pause then they both smiled and there was an awkward silence for a moment.

Chill broke the spell by saying.

"Hey baby! Look what I brought for us to play with."Everyone laughed, and Kelsey said a peculiar thing.

"Lucky me! How many girls you know has their boyfriend bring a hot blonde for them to share."

Liza Beth lit up like Christmas her smile very real this time.

She hugged the small girl tight.

"Oh, thank you so much. You really think I'm hot?"

Kelsey hugged her back and said, "Definitely! Smoking hot!"   Chill laughed and said, "Hell yeah, I don't ride around with no ugly girls."

Chill noticed that Kelsey had referred to him as her boyfriend. She had never done that before. The presence of Liza Beth had shaken Kelsey up a little bit.

Kelsey had always made it clear that they were friends and that Chill had no claim on her.

So far in their dealings with each other this had always worked to Kelsey's advantage.

Chill remained at her beck and call, and she kept her options open for whatever "better deal" she may encounter.

When these better deals didn't pan out she was always able to call up old reliable Chill come get her.

He would answer that call and be so glad to see her that any resentments he had would be forgotten and forgiven.

Kelsey knew Chill loved her and was devoted like a hound dog. She wasn't worried about him straying. She had never even considered anyone even wanting him.It certainly had never occurred to her that a girl as lovely as Liza Beth would show an interest in an old bearded, long haired giant in a beat up old truck.

They spent the day together the three of them and had a wonderful time.

They girls were gracious to each other and seemed like quick friends.

Liza Beth had called her mom after the meeting and told her that she was going to hang out with some new friends.   The girl was a delight to be around. She was pretty and very smart.

She picked up on a lot of jokes that Kelsey missed.

Chill was used to   Kelsey's indifference to his humor.She basically tolerated his sense of humor. This didn't bother Chill because most people just didn't pay enough attention to get his jokes.

It was always a rare and precious treat to find someone that shared a quick wit and   did appreciate his sense of humor.

Liza Beth got his jokes and was quite capable of returning quips of her own.He would make a remark and she would build on it and so on and so forth.

Kelsey smiled through these exchanges and said, "Oh, God! Now I got two of you to put up with! "How could God do this to me?"

The blonde nymph shared her history with her new friends.

She was eighteen had been for two weeks. Chill made her show I.D.

She had just gotten out of rehab and she had a boyfriend named Brandon that most people didn't think was cute but she thought was adorable. She looked right at Chill when she said these things and the simple sentences seemed like a dare.

Chill liked the girl a lot she was beautiful she was every wet dream he had ever had.

He did not trust her at all. He felt she was up to no good and really wasn't trying to hide that fact.

The girl had sized the peculiar couple up in about two minutes. She surmised that the big hillbilly was crazy over the little dwarf creature.

She noted that the little girl had taken the big boy for granted to the point that it would be very easy to upset her little apple cart.

She told her story to the couple and although the words may have been different what she was really saying was.

"Hey Big Boy, right here I am. I'm hot, young, and beautiful."Are you man enough to play with me?

"I am a heroin addict, so you know you can't trust me.

"I have a man but I'm willing to be with you.

"You've been warned! Do you want to play or not?"

Chill had been so careful with Kelsey. He had spent months with her before they ever became romantically involved. He had agonized over her recovery.

With Liza Beth he did not hesitate. It was obvious this little hellion wasn't finished. Hell, she hadn't even gotten started good.

Chill was pretty sure that whatever happened next between the trio would not be boring.

Kelsey had went to great pains to make sure he knew they were not together so she shouldn't be upset if he started seeing another girl.He wasn't sure if the tall blonde with the movie star good looks was serious, but he knew he didn't want to spend the rest of his life regretting not giving it a shot.

On that first day, Kelsey had asked to be dropped off first so she could get ready for Chill to pick her up for the midnight.

Chill asked if Liza Beth needed a ride home. She had said she did but that she lived way out in the country by the airport.

Chill said that was fine he had plenty of gas and plenty of time especially if it meant spending time with a pretty girl.

Liza Beth turned out to be a good listener as well as a good talker. Chill found himself pouring out his story. She seemed to be especially adept at getting him to talk about his and Kelsey's relationship or lack of one.

He thought she was interested in him but not in any serious way. He figured she had some agenda and would use him up quickly but he intended to spend every moment he could with the lovely girl.

She had a way of just taking over his head.

He may have been over twice her age but it was obvious she knew more about relationships than he did.   A cautious man by nature Chill threw caution to the wind.

Liza Beth was an adventure waiting to happen.He had waited his life to meet a girl as dangerous as this one.   He knew at first glance that she was trouble but it seemed she was his kind of trouble.

On that first day when he dropped her off she had taken his number. He figured she had done that to stroke his ego pretty girls loved to play those games.

He hadn't asked her for her number in return because he hadn't wanted to embarrass himself. He knew if he had her phone number he would find a reason to call and that it would probably be creepy.

Hell, he was only a year younger than her father.   He surmised she was just another natural flirt and became determined to put her out of his mind.

He didn't see her for a couple of days and he had pretty much reconciled that she was one of those sweet dreams that just hadn't come true.

That afternoon Kelsey and he went to the clubhouse and there she was. She quickly ran up to the duo. She gave Kelsey a big hug and then hugged Chill in turn. She hugged him very tight and pressed herself against him.

Chill's body responded, and the young girl giggled at the movement in his pants.

She whispered, "Tsk, tsk, naughty boy," in his ear. Chill laughed! This girl was amazing. He had never known anyone like her.

Kelsey's mother was picking her up after the meeting. Liza quickly maneuvered Chill into giving her a ride home. She said she had to work that night but had some time to chill.

After the meeting when they were in Chill's truck Liza Beth asked Chill about his art and if he was serious about painting her.

Chill was quick to respond absolutely!

She said she would need to see his work that she needed to know that the painting would be tasteful and not trashy.

Chill offered to show him his paintings and she agreed. Upon arriving at his house the wily young temptress was impressed.   Everywhere you turned there were paintings.

A lot were older from when Chill was in college.   After he had graduated and gotten heavy into his drinking and using his production had dwindled.

He had probably only completed two paintings in his last year of drinking.After he had gotten sober his art had resumed its importance in his life. He tried to paint on a regular basis.

Paintings were stacked against the walls and hung everywhere.

In his front room he had constructed a stage complete with a stripper pole. Upon seeing the pole and the stage Liza laughed.

"You guys weren't kidding you really do have a strip club in your living room."

"Well, yeah, of course. Why wouldn't I?"

Chill went on to elaborate exactly how the stage had come into existence. The winter before when Kelsey was in a brief sober spree Chill had taken in a stray.

The stray's name was Brittany and she was simply gorgeous. She had a million watt smile and was a genuinely decent human being.He had met her at the clubhouse, just like he had met Kelsey and Liza.   They had become quick friends.

She was as beautiful on the insides as   on the outside.She had been living with a friend and for some reason she had had to move.   She would never tell him exactly why because she was not one to speak ill of others.

She really was that way.She was true blue through and through.   Chill had given her many rides and had joked about the "girls" that came and went in his life.

At the time of meeting Brittany three girls had keys to his house. One was Kelsey of course another was the beautiful Amber and a third was a peculiar little hustler name Netta.

He hadn't seen Amber or Netta in weeks but it was not strange for him to come home in the morning and find one of them asleep in his bed.

His home was a refuge of sorts. These girls felt safe with Chill.

Well, Brittany called him one day and asked if she could stay with him. Chill never hesitated an instant. "Yes! Of course, anytime."

Brittany came back with, "Can you come get me? I have a little money for gas! I just really need to get out of here." She never gave the particulars, but Chill was able to piece together that a handsome young men had befriended Brittany and offered her a place to stay when the place she was at had gotten to be dangerous to her recovery.

Once she had moved in some type of relationship had developed or was assumed by the man.

Chill had surmised that the young man had pressured Brittany for sex and had used the threat of putting her out as leverage.   Brittany had a lot of heart and pride and had made arrangements immediately to be gone.

She had called Chill and within thirty minutes he was loading her meager belongings into his truck.

The young man was an okay chap   as far as Chill was concerned but if he wanted to get aggressive or be an asshole about letting the girl leave, Chill had no problem with beating his ass.

The man was indeed making some feeble attempt to mend fences with the young beauty.

Brittany had flashing cat-like eyes and was truly a beautiful girl.

Old boy knew he had done fucked up a good thing and if Chill had been a little smaller and a little less intense of a person he might have pushed the issue.

Chill did hear him tell the girl in the relative privacy of the kitchen.

"What are you gonna do if that big fucker tries to crawl into bed with you?"

Brittany had laughed and said, "Cuddle, I guess. Don't worry about it. I'm not your problem anymore."

She was truly a classy girl in every way.

"I want to thank you for letting me stay here and I appreciate everything you have done for me I wish you only good things."

The young man had considerable class his own self and replied with"

"I wish you the same and you could tell he meant it."

He shook Chill's hand looked him square in the eye and said, "Please take care of her. She's a pretty awesome girl."

Chill looked back into the man's eyes and shook his hand and told the young man.

"Don't worry that girl wears God like a coat ain't nobody gonna hurt her," and he meant it.The lovely Brittany had moved into Chill's home and filled it with her peculiar brand of magic.

Every day was an adventure, and Brittany was a fearless explorer embracing recovery and the new life it was offering.

Well, the stripper pole had come about one day while riding Kelsey and Brittany around in the truck.

For some reason, Kelsey had started sleeping over at Chill's house.

In the two years, he had known her she had only stayed at his house a handful of times and most of those had been while she was using or drunk.

Chill was kinda amused and kinda pissed.   It had long been his dream to have the little girl live with him but it seemed she was only using him to try and get with another girl.

He wasn't good enough to stay with by himself but she couldn't get enough of his house now that Brittany had arrived.

The lovely Amber actually laughed at him when he shared this with her. She took great pains and effort to explain to him the situation as she saw it.

Dumbass, she wasn't chasing Brittany she was making sure Brittany didn't steal you.

What? Chill was flabbergasted.

Yeah, the little little bitch was cockblocking you.

She might not let you think she wants you but she don't want anyone else to have you.

"Well, that's bullshit. That's fucking wrong." Chill was astounded. He considered himself pretty astute. How could he have missed that?

Amber filled him in because men are stupid?! She had laughed.

Back to the stripper pole and how it came into existence.

Chill loved women and he loved painting them. He now had two very beautiful young ladies staying at his house.

They constantly walked around half dressed or naked.He took dozens of pictures of them. It was all innocent and harmless.

He had videos of them in the shower together and he treasured this time with these girls.

One day while riding in "truck" Brittany had opened a conversation with a question.

Chill you know what you need?

No Baby doll what do I need? I think I got everything a man could want right here in this truck.

Occasionally Old Chill could get off a good one.

The girls smiled   and Brittany continued.

You need a stripper pole for all your little girls to play upon.

It hit Chill like a fist! Of course how had he overlooked it. How had he lived forty one years and not installed a stripper pole   in his home.

Kelsey confirmed Bittany's proclamation.   Yes you got to get one.

He did indeed get a stripper pole and it was one of the best decisions of his life. The lovely Brittany moved out before the stage had gotten installed.

She had worked as a stripper when using and Chill wanted very much to see her dance. In one of his higher power's cruder jokes Brittany never danced on his stage.

She had met a young man at a meeting while living with Chill and had moved in with him.

Chill and her had never been lovers. Chill had never even tried he was pretty sure she would have let him one night if he had wanted but he had truly valued her friendship too much to risk it plus he didn't want to hurt Kelsey.

He knew if he slept with Brittany he would want more and it would be a kindness on her part.

He considered his and Brittany's friendship   one of the most special in his life. Over the years, their lives had drifted apart but he knew he had a life long friend if he needed her.

Brittany had embraced recovery and used Chill as a resource for her recovery. She had not taken advantage of him.

Chill learned some valuable lessons from Brittany. He got to be selfless and found immense reward.

One day she had called him and asked for a ride to go get her license. He had just gotten off work and was tired.

He had been taught to help when asked plus she was beautiful and if he went home he would just lie awake and wonder why he hadn't helped the girl.

First she had to get a social security card. He took her to do that and she told him how she had lost her license in the first place.

She had gotten a DUI in Louisville several years before.

She said it had been a second DUI.

Chill had sked her if she had paid a fine   or taken any classes.

She had told him no but it was okay because she was getting her license in Ohio.

She had a letter that said she needed to do was pay a $40 reinstatement fee.

Chill had a few years sober at this time and he got a sinking feeling. He recognized an amends when he saw one.

He didn't bother to argue the point because the girl had such a good energy he didn't want to shoot it down.

She had moved in with her sponsor in Ohio. The drive was forty minutes each way.

Chill had already spent one day with her getting her social security card straightened out. He had gotten off work at 7 am after working all night and drove straight to pick Brittany up.   He was exhausted until she got in the car. She radiated energy.

Any resentment or regret Chill had been nursing vanished in front of her onslaught of vitality and sparkling beauty.

Brittany is one of those girls that wears recovery like a crown yet somehow remaining humble.

She knew she was hot but she was not vain. She has a generous nature and a kind soul.   Her positivity nurtured Chill, who could be a morose bastard.

If you've never experienced a true amends pay attention.   Brittany had a goal: To get her license back.

She did some research she had called the Ohio DMV to find out the requirements. They had told her she needed a social security a card and $40 reinstatement fee.

Sounds pretty simple and straight forward.

She did not have transportation so she called a friend and asked for help. Remember most gifts in recovery come disguised as hardships.

Chill agrees to help Brittany.

The first thing they do is get her a social security card.   The following week Chill gets off work at seven drives the 40-minute trip to Brittany's house. They go to breakfast and he takes her to the Ohio DMV.

She is armed with her social security card a valid ID and the $40 that she has been told is required.

Chill is skeptical but does not want to burst her bubble.

He has been around recovery a while and encountered several people that have gotten a second DUI.

He doubts that she can get a license until she clears up the old DUI.   Chill waits in the truck and tries to doze .

The lovely Brittany returns to the truck in tears.She is very disappointed and frustrated.

The people in the DMV have told her she can get her license but she needs a reinstatement letter and the $40.

Brittany's Amends

Brittany keeps her composure and asks the lady to tell her exactly what she needs to do to get her license.

The lady tells her all she needs is the $40, a valid ID, her social security card and a reinstatement letter from the state of Kentucky's DMV.

Brittany was devastated she felt she had been lied to and misled.

She was crying and distraught.Chill tried to soothe her but she was angry clean through.

He had never seen her negative.He hadn't realized how hard the little girl was trying.

She was doing everything she could to the best of her ability and now it seemed despite her best efforts she was stopped cold.

Chill knew she had come too far to quit.

Okay girl you are not the first person to have to get their license back.Other people have done this so that means it can be done.

But how? That fucking bitch said I have to go to driving school in Kentucky.How the fuck am I supposed to get there every fucking week.   It's fucking hopeless. I'm never gonna get my license back. I fucking give up.

I might as well fucking drink.

Stop it Chill told his friend let's do this right.

What do you mean. I've done everything right so far. You know I have. The distraught girl would not be assuaged.

Okay Brittany I know you are doing everything you can but this is pretty straight forward.

If you want your license you have to go to driving school.

Did she give you a number to call to enroll in driving school?

She did but I have to go to driving school in Kentucky because I got the DUI in Kentucky.

Okay so did you get a number for driving school in Kentucky.

Yes! But how the fuck am I gonna get there it's every week for six months. I don't have a fucking car.

Chill placed his hand on her arm.

Calm down. First things first.

Call the number and find out when the classes start.Enroll in the classes.

Chill you're not listening I don't have a way to get to Kentucky every week.

Brittany I will take you until you find a way. If you step forward with willingness your higher power   will make it possible.

It's just like getting sober. We do it one day at a time, right?

Yeah the pretty girl replied a glimmer of hope coming to light in her eyes.

Chill went on—"You enroll find out when the classes are and we will figure out which one you can take."

Brittany made the call there was a class starting the next Tuesday. The groups ran from 9am until 11:30am.

Inwardly Chill moaned but he kept nodding to keep the girl talking.

She had brightened considerably and he could tell she was already tackling this next obstacle in recovery.

Can we go enroll today? Please!

Chill cringed it meant driving 40 minutes to Newport, Kentucky. Then driving Brittany back home another 40 minutes.

Then finally driving himself another 40 minutes to get home.

Of the final 40 minutes was goona be during rush hour so that 40 minute drive was going to be more like an hour.

Sure baby doll anything to put a smile back on that face.   Chill had been up since six the night before. He wouldn't get home until around six that night. He had to be back at work by eleven.

It was all good. He was finally useful to someone.

Tuesday became the highlight of Chill's week.

He would get off work at 8 drive the forty minutes to get Brittany and make it back to just in time for her DUI class to start.

He would usually sit in "truck" and try to doze for the ninety minutes the class lasted.They developed a routine after her class they would go back to Chill's house to workout with free weights and Brittany would run on the treadmill while Chill got cleaned up. They were very comfortable around each other.

Chill often brought up one of his favorite memories from when Brittany had stayed with him.

One night while Kelsey had stayed over the girls had decided to use the treadmill.

They were dressed in their sports bras panties and running shoes.

Chill got out his camera and took video because while they ran they were smoking Marlboro Reds.

They joked that they could sell a lot of cigarettes with that footage.

After their workout they would go eat lunch then Chill would drive the girl home in time for her to go to work. He would then return to his house to sleep the day away with his mind totally at ease.Brittany decided to make a Saturday evening meeting her home group.

It was in Kentucky so Chill would make the drive on Saturdays. They would attend their meeting. Brittany would meet her boyfriend at the meeting or afterwards and ride home with him.

It was not as strange as it sounds.

At this period in Chill's life Brittany was a stabilizing element.   Chill's life was full of discord and chaos as a result of his relationship with the lovely Liza Beth.

You remember Liza Beth. Chill was showing her his stripper pole and she had asked him how he had come to possess a stripper pole.

Well the short answer is a pretty girl told him he needed one.

Liza did dance for Chill on that first night but she didn't get naked.

Chill called it nekkid and she like that.

She took her top and bra off and let him take some pictures.Chill did not try to take advantage fo the girl. He didn't want to scare her away.He was grateful for whatever she wanted to show him.

He still thought she was up to no good but did not care.He was determined to enjoy his time with her and to treasure every moment.He was quite certain she would be in his life only a short time.

He was not going to waste that time.

After she danced and let him take pictures they talked more.She was enrolled at a local college and sked him if he wanted to see her dorm room.

He was quite comfortable where they were and was trying to figure out how to get her to again remove her clothes.   He said sure because he knew that was what she wanted to hear and he really couldn't think of any reason not to go look at her room.

When they got to her room something peculiar happened. The sultry sex pot disappeared.

The girl that had always been so sassy   and bawdy became almost demure.

She shared poetry she had written with Chill.She let herself become vulnerable and her youth emerged.

She shared her dream,s she talked of lost loves, she entrusted him with herself.

Chill could tell that for all her bluster and image. She was at her center so very lonely.

Her life   was a series of performances.She gave people what they wanted her to be meanwhile keeping her true essence from everyone.

That night she shared a brief glimpse of what really mattered in her heart. It was nothing earth shattering or soul searching but it was profound.

Her youth and her beauty were precious items.Treasures that she took for granted and bestowed upon the unworthy as only the young can.

They know not the value of what they   squander.

Chill knew, Chill had the soul of an artist and he could see in the woman child something magical.

That night she shared more she may place little value upon her beauty and youth but her heart she did not take for granted.

Chill's heart melted he began to develop real feelings for Liza Beth.He had thought her jaded and up to no good.

Those things may be true but that wasn't all she was. That night her soul connected with Chill's.

The simple act of sharing her real feelings and dreams had ripped away any pretense of Chill's resistance to her charms.

He would remember the magic of that night. She weaved her girl/woman magic around his heart with innocence and trust.

Chill forgot that his higher power had jokes.

The following morning Liza Beth called Chill early "hey let's go pantie shopping."Chill said hell yes!

He was more than willing because the night before the lovely girl had refused to take her pants off for pictures because she didn't wear panties.   They went to the mall and went panty shopping.That was the day Chill had fallen in love with the nymph named Liza Beth.

Her spirit was soaring that day and she shined like new money.She was flirtatious and funny and made him feel like the only man on the planet.

She had charmed him the night before with her poetry her letters and her outpourings of her heart.

On this day, she sealed the deal with her beauty her zest for life and her clever wit.She was too good to be true but Chill was forgetting that more and more.She bought ten pair of panties just go he could watch her take them off.

That night he kissed her for the first time as she danced for him.

Wearing only a black sheer pair of glittery panties.

She had tilted her beautiful blonde mane of hair to one side and raised her head slightly and he had kissed her sweet lips.

He kissed her once and then pushed him away.We should stop! Kelsey is my friend.

Chill was like what the fuck?Kelsey has no hold on me and that's of her choosing.

Let's don't argue it's been a great day and I just want you to take me home.

Chill as always did as the lady asked. Liza Beth and Chill quickly grew closer.

The threesome of Kelsey, Chill and Liza Beth thrived for a little while but Kelsey was soon edged out.

Within a month of meeting Chill, the sultry young vixen; Liza Beth decided to move in. It had came sort of sudden but Chill seemed the only one surprised.

He had met the lovely girl the second Saturday in September.

She had moved in by the first of October.

She became his world and he had never been happier. He felt like a king whenever he walked into a meeting with the stunning girl on his arm.

She was a true bombshell and never failed to turn heads wherever she went. He was aware that many people were laughing at him during this time. They were waiting for it to go bad.

They could not believe the young girl loved him.

It was viewed as classic 13th stepping.

Wily old man stalking   innocent sweet newcomer. People started taking bets on when he would drink.

Because they believed there was no way a predator like him could stay sober after taking advantage of such a sweet young thing.   He was a huge man with a history of violence and quick to anger.

There was a lot of whispers and rumors, but no one said anything to his face. Older wiser people with long term recovery were not so quick to judge.

Chill had been around the program for about seven years at this time. He had been rough in his talk and mannerisms. But his actions had been consistent with the principles of recovery. Those who knew what to look for could see spiritual growth within the men.

His   sponsors sponsor saw him with the young girl and told him if he survived and didn't drink he would find out a whole lot about himself.

Sometime about the time Liza Beth moved in Kelsey announced she was pregnant and that Chill was the father.

Now Chill's world was   rocked off the beaten track.t Liza Beth   was living with him and having an intimate relationship was not upset at the news.

Chill was overjoyed Kelsey had been hesitant to tell him but he had been nothing but happy about the news.

He wasn't sure it was his and really didn't care. If Kelsey wanted him to be the father he would be the father.   One Tuesday after Brittany had gone home, Chill was relaxing and trying to sleep before work.

He hadn't heard from Kelsey in a couple of days.

Liza Beth had taken her to a doctor's appointment on the previous Friday and both girls were acting strange. Kelsey was staying with the couple and they saw less and less of her.

He tried to call her and she texted him she was at the hospital.

Chill quickly got dressed and went to the hospital and she wasn't there.

He finally texted her back and she seemed very angry.

Chill could not figure out what was going on and finally Kelsey sent him a text that made his whole world crumble.

She texted him that the baby she was carrying was not his. She had lost his baby and gotten pregnant the same week by someone else.

Furthermore to add insult to injury she didn't want him texting or calling her anymore.   He told her he didn't believe her and she told him to ask his girlfriend she was there when the doctor told her the news.

Chill felt doubly betrayed he could not remember anything hurting like this.His brother's suicide and the subsequent rage that came after had been as painful but in a different way.

He went to his mother's house and got his brother's pistol. It was a super Blackhawk 44 magnum with an 8-inch barrel.

He sat at his mother's kitchen table loading and unloading the weapon.   He wanted to kill something. He wanted to die.

He wanted not to feel this incredible hurt!

In the seven years, he had been sober he had learned a few things. One was to call somebody to share that pain.

He was unable to get a hold of his sponsor or his sponsor's sponsor.

He kept dialing number.s   His sponsor's grand sponsor answered his call.

He explained what was going on and the bastard chuckled.

Chill almost lost his mind. The man, he name was John M., told him to calm down.

He said well big boy sounds like God done handed you a whole bucket of shit and you're in a world of pain. He went on to ask Chill some questions.

What does the book say to do?

I don't know that's why I'm calling you.

Bullshit, you know. You got the tools use them.

Find your part!

Chill exploded, "find my part!" You got to be kidding. This little cold hearted bitch tells me my baby is dead and she no longer wants me in her life.The worst part is she can't even face me or give me the fucking courtesy of a phone call.

She fucking text me this shit.

Okay, write it down then call me. We will meet and go over it.

Chill was struck dumb.

What? Was all he could manage.

Use the steps! Write it down bring it to me and we will go over it.

Chill in spite of his pain and anger knew recovery worked.

He had seen miracles in his own life.He considered Kelsey and Liza Beth blessings in his life.He did the only thing he knew to do.   He put his dead brother's pistol back into his sweet mother's closet sat down at her kitchen table took pen and hand and wrote it down.   He poured out everything he was feeling onto about six sheets of paper

His hand moved furiously across the pages trying to keep pace with his racing mind.

Once he had written it out he called John.

Oh I got it written down.

John laughed Damn! Boy you must be hurting. Usually when you tell a person to write about something you don't see them for a few weeks and when you do they're drunk.   Meet me at the clubhouse and we will thrash it out.

Chill made the twenty minute drive in less than ten.John was already there sitting in what was known as the half measures room.

This was the room outside the meeting room. The Big Book had a line it that stated, "half measures avail us nothing."

To sit in the half measures room while a meeting was going on was tantamount to doing nothing for your recovery.

A lot of people hang around the rooms of recovery without ever fully committing to the program as it is outlined by the first one hundred and sixty-four pages.   They rarely succeed at recovery.

John looked over at Chill and quipped "There he is all huffing and puffing. Stand back he could blow at any time."

John had been sober thirty plus years and had a very fucked up sense of humor.

He wasn't scared or ashamed of anything as far as Chill could tell. He would stand in front of a room full of drunks and tell them they were all doing it wrong and fuck 'em if they didn't believe him.

He believed in working a spiritual program and his higher power was not a finicky one. He may have seemed like he was enjoying Chill's discomfort, but he was not having fun at the big man's expense.

Let's see what you got.

Chill handed the man the crumpled sheets of notebook paper. His hands were shaking and there were tears streaming down his cheeks.

Calms down big feels it's gonna be okay.

John read what the giant had written and pondered a moment.

Chill good buddy when I read this all I see is a man wanting to be loved and appreciated.

Chill snorted—"How could she do this to me?"

Hold on buddy ain't nobody done anything to you.

Let me ask you something. This Kelsey, is she the little half pint girl you been following around for the last year or so?

Yeah, you know she is.

Well, how old is she? About twenty-five years old.

No, She's twenty, Chill replied.

Okay, now look here put yourself in her situation.

You a little girl about four foot ten inches tall. You weigh about ninety pounds soaking wet. You got some bad news to tell someone that you know is going to just simply devastate that person.

You got to tell this person that loves you that what he wants more than anything is not going to happen.

Do you think that was easy for her?

Chill was taken aback.

What the fuck? No, I know it wasn't easy. Chill's voice started to rise with self-righteous anger but she could have at least told me face to face she didn't have to text it to me.

Wrong, John shot back. She didn't have to tell you anything. You sit here all hurt and put out. Did you ask her if she was okay? Did you inquire to her health or the health of the child she is carrying? You aren't the only one that lost something here.

That little girl lost that baby too. It probably cost her a lot more anguish than you feeling. It was a living part of her.   At twenty years old the last thing she needs is your big sad ass piling on more shit.

You are wanting something from her she is not emotionally mature enough to give. That's not her fault. There are two people hurting here and you have been so hung up in your own selfish shit so hard that not once today have you considered that little girls pain and heart break.

She not only lost her baby she's lost you and from what I've seen that little girl sets a pretty high store in you.

Just like that the anger inside Chill evaporated to be   replaced by shame.

He said to the elder man, "How do I make this right?"

John laughed. Son you don't make it right God makes it right God and time.

The incident was a crucial turning point in Chill's recovery.

He had thought himself a very objective person.   He was big on inventorying his actions and quick to make amends when he felt he had wronged someone.

Somehow he had completely missed the obvious fact that Kelsey had also suffered the loss of their child .

Hell he wasn't even sure it was his child.He was pretty certain he was sterile.He was in his forties and hadn't been careful at all about birth control.

In his twenties in college he had had some scares.A couple of girls had come to him with that awkward conversation about how they might be pregnant.

At that time he had been a complete and selfish prick and the last thing he had wanted was a child.As the years passed, his attitude had changed.He sorta daydreamed about being a father.

Kelsey's miscarriage was not about the loss of a child for Chill. It was the death of a dream.

Dreams were Chill's stock and trade he depended upon them to give him a reason to get up in the morning.

Chill realized he needed someone to help to analyze his behavior.His self-examination as thorough as he could make it was sorely lacking at times.He began to review his behavior closely and began asking his higher power for some relief on this issue.

Chill had his concept of a higher power. It had developed from necessity more than choice.

The traditional representations of an ultimate power just did not work for him.Religions seemed to always stack the odds in their favor.

They used God as a way of dividing the world between the chosen and the unchosen.Throughout the history of the world men had used these systems as a justification for many injustices and atrocities.

Their actions may have originated with some divine force and a genuine interest in helping others.At some point, the selfish nature inherent to man would surface and religion and the dogma produced would be used to push less divine agendas.

Recovery had shown Chill that there was no clear line between what is right and what is wrong.Often fate and circumstance could place an individual into a course of action that seemed totally at odds with that person's core beliefs.

He had seen in his own life where situations had occurred in which he had committed acts and made moral compromises that he felt he would never make.In the midst of his disease, he had lied to friends and family to facilitate further use.

He had stolen money from his employer .He had always replaced the money before the end of the night but he knew it had been a slippery slope.

The program of AA often talked about doing the next right thing. Well determining what the next right thing is could prove to be a tricky thing. He   had found himself in situations in which the kindest thing he could do for his fellow men was to buy him a drink.

He had had girls live with him that he loved with all his heart and wanted only good things for them.He had seen these girls dope sick and pitiful driven by their obsession and need.He had given them money knowing they would use it to get high.

He hadn't known what else to do.

He knew that to stand in the way of an addict in the midst of their disease was to rick being trampled. If someone's higher power was determined for that person to experience some consequences for their actions; to interfere in that process would only endanger your own health and serenity.

God seemed to get his way.

The word God was a tricky thing for Chill. He used it a lot but didn't want it misunderstood.

To him God was a title used by people as a convenient way to talk about the infinite energy that connected everything in the universe.

Chill felt that anytime a person attempted to explain their conception of a higher power to another that person doing the explaining would somehow fall short. Self interest and self-will would almost certainly taint the experience.

He understood the need for religion and valued it. He had learned from his own experience that people could use religious books and values to justify and rationalize almost anything.

Facts are facts, but truth can be subjective.

In the big book it talks about seeking God's will.

That seems simple but if every person has his or her own conception of a higher power wouldn't that mean a lack of agreement on what constitutes God's will.

Chill realized early on that his mind under the influence of alcoholism and addictive thinking could make him over think everything. This over thinking would keep him sick.

He decided to just "do" things. He asked people that were sober and seemed somewhat content what they felt would be "good" or appropriate things to do to stay sober.

When people suggested actions for him to take he did them without question.

He didn't care why these actions worked he just wanted to stay sober for that day.

As time went by and his mind cleared from the alcohol and drugs, he started to notice some consistencies in these actions.

These actions that afforded the most relief from alcoholic thinking were invariably actions in which he was being useful to other people.

The Big Book of AA talks about selfish and self-seeking behavior being the root of the alcoholics' problem. Chill found that for him this was true.

Once Chill realized that being unselfish was the key to "his" God's will it became a lot easier for him to seek direction in his life. Anytime a situation arose that made Chill uncertain about how to proceed in life, he would ask himself a few questions.

He would ask himself who benefits from this course of action and does anyone get harmed by this course of action?

A third question would always appear.

Am I willing to suffer the consequences of my actions?

Chill discovered over the years that he was unwilling to let go of some of his old thinking and actions. He had made programs in these areas but his own self-will and lack of faith kept him ensconced in certain actions.

His fear of loneliness and low self-esteem led him to seek relationships with women he knew were emotionally unwilling or unable to treat him in a decent and loving manner.

He found himself in one sick relationship after another and had to admit he was the common denominator. He went to his sponsor and sought counsel.

His sponsor was of little help because when it came to relationships with the fairer sex, his sponsor was sicker than Chill.

His sponsor was twenty plus years sober but had been divorced four times. Three of his sponsor's divorces had occurred since he had gotten sober. His sponsor was in his mid-fifties and lived with his parents and little brother.

He had a bad heart and grumbled constantly. He did however insist that he was happy.

Chill needed someone in his life that could manufacture delusion of this magnitude at regular intervals.

Chill's sponsor was happy for all his sad sack demeanor. He was a man who every day strove to help "his" higher power's children on a daily basis. He did AA a lot better than he spoke AA.

He applied the principles in his daily affairs by consistently putting his hand out to help other people.

He was blessed with the ability to work on mechanical things and to repair them.He often was asked to work on people's cars and usually had to pull money out of his own pockets to do the work.

A lot of times these people were less than grateful.

He tried not to care and liked to say:

"We do it for free and for fun." He tried to mean this when said it but that wasn't always easy.

Chill's sponsor was not the place he sought counsel for relationship advice.

He had a special person for this.A beautiful young lady with the face and the heart of an angel.

Pixie Skye was the unlikely moniker of the loyal addict/alcoholic that had entered into Chill's life and had become his best friend and sounding board for his recovery.Chill had met Liza Be3th in September she had moved into his home by October.

On Halloween she relapsed on heroin.Chill had thought when he met her that she was up to "no good."

Her beauty and personality had made him ignore his own good instincts.He had made a conscious decision to get involved with the lovely but sinister wench.

She had a delightful devilish streak that made life interesting to say the least.She had been involved with a young man when he had met her.

Chill was a firm believer in the old adage that "what a lover will do with you they will do to you."

If she was willing to cheat on her boyfriend with Chill at some point Chill figured she would cheat on him.

She was so hot that he didn't care he had to have him some of that.He never figured her to be in his life for long so he set out to get as much of that sweet ass as he could while he could.

Chill may have been convinced that he would be able to shield his heart from the girls' wily ways but he was sorely mistaken.

She stole his heart and took it whole.He had never loved anyone to such a degree.

She was like a drug for the big hillbilly.His good sense flew out the window.By the time she relapsed he was smitten, head over heels in love.

He was never certain if Liza Beth loved him or if she found him convenient.He had given her the use of his other pick up truck which looked better than "truck."

The truck was a ranger in good condition and ran fine .Chill continued to drive "truck" because truck had served him faithfully. He had some weird sense of loyalty to the beat-up jalopy. Every dent and spot of rust was for Chill like a wrinkle or mole on a lover's face. It didn't make truck ugly to Chill it represented the truck's sacrifice and service to their relationship.

He often joked that "truck" and his relationship was the most successful one in which he had been involved.If he thought about it much he had to admit it wasn't a joke.

Liza Beth continued to stay with Chill until February of the following year.During that time her drug use increased.

Since Chill worked third shift she mostly stayed at her parent's house or wherever her disease took her.She gave up any pretense of going to school and lost her job.

She attended meetings with Chill but often as not she would nod out during the meeting. Chill did not know what to do.He had taken a job as a drug counselor in a treatment center for men.He constantly reviewed his actions and inventoried his motivations toward the girl.

He had no doubt that he loved her he just wasn't sure that he was beneficial to her.She decided to enter into a methadone program and moved backed into her parent's house.

Chill had had to take the truck back from her because she was using it to maintain her disease. If she pushed him hard enough or used her female cunning she could get it from him for the day. The truck was started with a screwdriver and Liza Beth stole it more than once.

Within a couple of weeks of starting the methadone program Liza Beth moved in with a boy close to her own age. The boy lived with his parents. The whole family was addicted to heroin.

Liza Beth had met them at the methadone clinic. Liza Beth never bothered to tell Chill she had found a new boyfriend nor that she was living with him. She continued to stay with Chill on the weekends and talk to him on the phone.

He knew something was up because her whole demeanor and behavior had changed. She never texted him anymore and if he called her phone was always off.

During this time "Pixie Skye" entered his life. She had flashing eyes and a smile as pretty as anyones She reminded him of Brittany with her beauty and good energy. That's what you noticed most about "Pixie" She was good.

Not in a boy scout, holier than thou kind of way. She was good in that she just didn't waste her energy on being mean. She was a nice person and had a kind heart.

She was genuine and for Chill had the thing he looked for most in a newcomer. She was uncertain. She had just finished treatment at a care unit. She had had the mandatory treatment center romance.

Chill had tried to see if he could fuck her but she wasn't down for that.

She had been extremely nice with her refusal and they had become very good friends and confidants.

She had wound up homeless for a very brief period and used Chill's home for showers. She had something that none of the other girls had had that had entered in Chill's life.

She had the ability to see Chill as more valuable as a recovery resource than as a man to be manipulated. They entered into a friendship built on trust, honesty and mutual respect.

Chill often used "Pixie's" way of handling people as a blueprint in his own life. He fell way short of being as kind and fair as she but her involvement in his life did cause vast improvement in his dealings with other people.

Pixie got to experience Chill work through the greatest struggle in his recovery. He was unable and unwilling to eliminate Liza Beth from his life.

As a result of continuing this relationship Chill had to find a way to keep her in his life while staying sober. Many late nights had Chill on the phone talking to "Pixie."

She would listen as he walked himself through extensive and exhaustive inventories about the subject.

When he had first confronted Liza Beth about her infidelity she had denied it. He had told her that what was really important was she needed to be honest. He could handle it if she was with someone else.

It would suck but it wasn't the end of the world. She was eighteen years old and shit happened.

The reason he insisted on her being honest was because in order to get sober a person had to be honest. When Liza Beth put a lie between her and Chill, he could no longer be a factor in her recovery.

It also meant that all the time they spent together after the lie would be tainted. Dishonesty put them on adversarial plane.

True friendship cannot exist if a person does not reveal their true self. If all you give to a relationship is a presentation of self instead of your true self, the other person does not get the opportunity to love you.

Time spent with that person afterwards becomes a performance. Your friend becomes a job. Each time you see them you have to become the person you presented to them.

Eventually a person would become exhausted.

If in every interaction with others you present a person that you feel that person wants every relationship becomes a performance.

If you do this long enough you become at risk of losing your own identity.Chill wanted whatever happened between them to be real no matter how unpleasant.

Liza Beth heard the words but could not take them at face value.

Deception and manipulation of others had become so routine to her that Chill's sincerity was lost.

Chill surmised that the girl may have feelings for him but that her disease was calling the shots.

He told her if she wanted to keep her other relationship that the other guy would be her boyfriend.

Chill preferred to be the man she cheated with not   the man upon whom she cheated.

It did suck for Chill to know the girl he loved more than anything could lie in another's arms.He told himself all the lies he needed to hear to keep her in his life.

He started seeing other women and thought that would make him feel better.He enjoyed the sex and if helped keep him sane but in the middle of the night his heart ached so deeply he would pray to die for relief.

He didn't drink and he didn't use.He went to work and tried his best to carry the message of recovery.

He strove to be objective and to believe the message of recovery as pure as possible.He would tell the men in his treatment groups that he wanted them to have the message as honest as possible just in case he drank someday and needed them to give it back to him.

He would pour his heart out to "Pixie" about his feelings for Liza Beth.He realized that Liza Beth was not his problem.

She was a young girl in the midst of her disease and incapable of being honest or treating anyone with love and respect.

Her disease was calling the shots and it didn't matter if she loved someone or not. He learned that in order to keep her in his life he had to learn to not take her disease personally.

It was almost impossible to believe that she could do the things she did and not realize how much they affected him.

Pixie had to remind him in her own sweet way that "she's not doing anything to you, she's just doing what it takes to get the next one.""That next one" could be anything from heroin, crack, or a lover!

Over the next four years Liza Beth would let the disease of addiction take over her life. She ran through a series of men and a few women. She had a baby that was not Chill's and she started getting arrested.

Only two things stayed consistent within her life. Her disease and Chill. Chill realized that she was too sick to love him. She was too sick to love anyone.

Her lies had gotten very unimaginative and it was almost funny that she even tried to deceive him.

Chill had long ago reconciled that she was incapable of being faithful. Pixie sometimes wondered out loud how he could stand being treated the way Liza Beth treated him.

He explained after you forgive the same behavior twice and it continues. It's obvious to everyone involved that it's acceptable behavior.

Chill guessed there was nothing that Liza Beth could do that he couldn't forgive. Over the years of their relationship he had learned what the word unconditional love really meant.

He loved her! His love wasn't dependent upon her behavior.

His love was not dependent upon her loving him return. His love was absent of ego and pride.In the early days, he had loved to have her on his arm when he walked in a room.Over time he had learned to loathe encountering her in public.

It was the pretense that bothered him.If she was not living with him, he had to pretend they were "just friends."

Sometimes she would be involved with other people and he would have to pretend it didn't bother him.

He was good at it and these encounters excited her For Chill it just cemented for him the falseness of her life. All her relationships had become   performance art.

He began to doubt that she would be able to get sober when she finally decided she was done.

The Big Book of AA talks about how the people who fail at getting sober are the one s"incapable" of being honest.It declares that such people do exist and states that they are unfortunate.

Chill had taken classes in grad school that had dealt with addiction.He could recall a study that had been conducted that compared the pet scans of convicted serial killers with those of long term opiate addiction.

The scans showed that the frontal lobe of the brain had been compromised in almost exactly the same areas.

The frontal lobe is the region of the brain associated with impulse control and decision making.

People with this region impaired have trouble with simple human emotions such as empathy and tend to objectify others.

In essence long term narcotic use gave a person many traits of a sociopath.

Chill was not sure of the science but on more than one occasion he had wondered if Liza Beth was indeed a sociopath.

Chill had also realized over the years that people are seldom only one thing. To classify Liza Beth a sociopath would be convenient for Chill's ego but it didn't feel true.

Chill was no angel and had found himself in an odd situation. In one of her periods of relative lucidity, Liza Beth had gotten Chill to agree to be monogamous. Chill had laughed when she made the suggestion.

She was staying with him at the time. She was working and attending meetings. It was a relative calm before the storm period.

This was no the first time Liza Beth had come home to Chill. He seemed to be her fallback plan whenever everything turned to shit. He often thought of himself as weak for keeping her in his life. The truth was really very simple if not noble. Chill kept Liza Beth in his life because there was no real reason to keep her out.

She was beautiful and the physical relationship between the two was strong. No one else had the same impact on Chill as Liza Beth. He had other women in his life but she was his most dependable source of physical satisfaction. He was a coward when it came to commitment. The relationship met his physical requirements and required very little from him.

It was a relationship of convenience.

Bullshit!

He could sit down and list all this shit on paper or tell it to Pixie on the phone but the truth was Chill loved the girl! With all her wicked ways   lies, deceit, infidelity it didn't matter his heart stayed true.

After agreeing to be monogamous, Liza Beth had soon after gotten involved with someone. She even got engaged but she never quit seeing Chill.

She would show up once or twice a week and he would live for these visits.

Chill knew she was mostly after money and he didn't care. He couldn't think of anything he'd rather spend his money on than her. He knew the value of her beauty and youth even if she didn't.

In his mid-forties, Chill knew that her volatility and looks were fragile thing to be treasured.

With the cockiness of youth the girl was squandering her priceless girlhood on idiots and filth.

Trading youth's   vibrant energy for a few numbed hours of nothingness.

In his own youth, he had never had the nerve or felt himself worthy enough to approach such a beauty.

Chill began seeing two or three other girls. One almost everyday. Her name was Amber and they were real friends.

She would lie in his arms and confide in him her deepest secrets and fears. She would share her hopes and dreams.

She was also an addict and knew Liza Beth.She would lie in Chill's arms and talk about her boyfriend.

She would talk about how much she loved him and how it hurt her that he didn't trust her.

Chill would suppress a laugh and point out that the man may have a point.

Amber would say, "he doesn't know I'm doing anything and without proof it's just wrong to always be accusing me of shit."The funny thing was Chill understood Amber and girls like her.

Amber did love her boyfriend with all her heart.When she fucked other men, it was for money or to feed   her disease.

It wasn't cheating because she formed no emotional attachment.She told Chill these things best to help him out.

She could call him up and say she really needed twenty to get right and he would give it without question.

Chill started feelings guilty that he hadn't told.Liza Beth about seeing other women after agreeing to be monogamous.

He told "Pixie" that he felt he owed Liza Beth amends for these indiscretions.

Pixie had laughed and   laughed but in a kind way.

"After all the shit she's pulled with other men you are going to tell her you've been seeing other girls?"

Yes Chill replied. He went on to say—"I know she's living with someone now and that it seems stupid for me to 'confess' my sins but I've learned over the years that this shit kills people. People drink over shit like this.

I'm responsible for my behavior and I have no control over hers. just because she routinely lies and cheats does not afford me the sane luxury.

I have to be honest with her even if it means losing her.

Pixie laughed, "You're not gonna lose her you're gonna confuse her."

Chill laughed in return you're probably right. I know it's stupid but I also know the longer I live in a lie the worse damage it will do.If I ever want to be of use to her in recovery I have to model the behavior that is recovery. I realize the absurdity but I also see the necessity for making this amends.

Upon Liza Beth's next visit he sat her down and told her.

"I got something to tell you and I'm knd of nervous about it."

Liza Beth could sense that he was serious. "Okay, just say it. That's the easiest way."

Chill told her that he had been having sex with other girls.

She remained calm and asked if he had been using protection and if these girls were clean.

Her response had been very practical but very anti-climatic.

Chill was a little disappointed with her reaction. She wasn't angry or jealous.

At times like this Chill realized that at twenty-four years old Liza Beth knew more about relationships than he did.The physical set of love just didn't carry all that significance for her.

He asked her if she was mad at him or hurt?She told him that in truth she was just disappointed that she loved him.

That that hadn't changed but hat like he had told her on mor than one occasion.

"It sucks but I can't do anything about it. I'm a little hurt but just mostly disappointed."

Chill realized that he child woman had a valid point.He also realized that whatever actions she had ever done with other people he doubted if any were about him.

She had taken lovers out of boredom or to get drugs or because they interested her.

He had taken lovers because he couldn't have her.   To her, he was not crucial to him she was crucial.

She had went to others because he no longer was enough to stimulate her mind or heart or feed her disease.

He had sought others to fill the void until she returned.   In many ways, Liza Beth was Chill's drug of choice.

He made compromises and told himself whatever he needed to hear to keep her in his life.During this period of Chill's life, he had started going to a lot more AA meetings.   He was working as a counselor for a while but had lost that job through arrogance and pride.

He had went back to school and gotten his Master's degree to find work as a counselor.He started working as a janitor cleaning hospital clinics at night.

It was lonely work he had the places to himself. The buildings were outpatient clinics and he found his brain working overtime.

He had started picking up carloads of men from treatment centers and taking   them to AA meetings.It helped him work his own recovery program while he helped others.

The Big Book of AA talks about nothing insuring continued sobriety as much as intensive work with another alcoholic.

His relationship with the woman in his life continued to be chaotic and confusing. He found younger men coming to him and seeking his counsel. The gentlemen that approached him all seemed to have much in common.

They used and drank much like Chill had used and drank. These men also seemed to have many of the same issues Chill had with women.

The Big Book of AA also talks about the past being our biggest asset. Chill Found his experiences being very beneficial in working with newcomers.

When he spoke to a new guy often the things he would tell that men were the things he needed to hear himself.

The solution never changes we just sometimes stray   from the solution.

Chill was able to appease some of his spiritual demons with this intensive period of active recovery. The act of forgiveness gave him strength. He knew he had expected behavior from people that they were incapable of doing. These expectations had ceased resentments and kept him spiritually sick.

Liza Beth continued to weave in and out of Chill's life during this period. She was deteriorating fast her need for drugs had become a constant driving force. This obsession had made her reckless in her decision making. Each time she would show up at Chill's home she would look haunted.

She was losing weight and not taking care of herself. Somehow her appeal to him increased—he found her beauty ethereal.

It was her at her core   No makeup unwashed uncaring about her looks. One Friday night she showed up and stayed the night and it was like old times. They had gotten a movie and she became that young girl again.

They talked and laughed and held each other. She went to sleep in his arms and he held her for hours.

She left the next day to go get well as she called it but she called within a couple of hours and had Chill pick her up in Cincinnati.

Chill did not like to have dope in his car. He had finally gotten a nice car and he didn't want to see it impounded because he was using it for bad things.He believed the car a gift from his higher power.

It had come with a payment and he knew if he didn't take care of it it would be removed from his life.

He believed he would be spitting in his higher power's fare by using a gift like a new car to help another person stay sick.He believed proper use of the vehicle was to give rides to people early in recovery needing to get to meetings.

It may seem a little superstitious to some people but Chill believed in these things to the bottom of his soul.

Actions had consequences they may not be immediate consequences but they could not be put off forever.

Against his better judgement he crossed the river into Ohio and picked Liza Beth up from a not good part of town.

He tried to ascertain how she had some to be stranded in such a place but she was not forthcoming with any answers.

Chill decided no tot push it. If he kept asking she would just start lying.

Although she had only been gone about four hours it was easy to see she had found plenty of "medicine" she was feeling very "well."

He could tell she had gotten some "hard" (crack) as well as "dog"—heroin.

He hated when she smoked crack. It made her twitch and she just seemed distracted.He endured it because the sex was often good when she was cracked up.

He knew he was taking advantage of her at these times but he would rationalize it to himself. If he didn't take her home she would just call someone else.He was just happy it was his turn again.

He intended to make the most of the opportunity.It could be weeks before he could see her again.He had a theory that she called him out of some sense of nostalgia.

Whenever whoever she was living with or partying   with that day got on her nerves or started to bore her she would start reminiscing and call him.He refused to waste his time with her arguing over why she hadn't been around or called him.

He realized about the third month he knew her that every time he saw her could be the last and he didn't want his last memory of their time together to be a bad memory.When they returned to his house they quickly fell into their routine.

When she was high on crack she liked to spend an inordinate amount of time in the bathroom picking at imaginary bumps.

They would make love and she would get   high. This cycle would continue until she ran out of dope or passed out of consciousness.

This day the cycle was interrupted by her phone ringing.Chill could tell by her end of the conversation that the call was about dope.He also surmised that the person on the other end of the phone was probably the same one that had left Liza Beth stranded in Cincinnati.

Chill was unable to hear the entire call for Liza Beth went into the bathroom.He could hear her voice rising in anger and he could tell by her tone she was scolding a man.He was familiar with that time and he got a sinking feeling that his lady love would soon be departing.

She came back into the room and Chill couldn't resist taking a sarcastic jab at her."Well how long we got?" he asked.

What do you mean? The nubile young beauty replied.

How long till you leave with whoever that was on the phone?

She smiled unfazed.

"Don't worry I'm gonna take care of you right now but we gotta hurry and I need you to do me two favors."

Chill started to protest but Liza Beth knew him. She rewound the only article of clothing she was wearing. A tattered pair of pajama bottoms.

Chill said, "Fuck it" and reached for the girl.

Whoever the fucker was she was leaving with he was definitely not getting first shot at this ass today.

Chill made it quick because he wanted to get her on her way before things turned ugly. He knew nothing he could say would deter her from her course of action.

The only way she would stay was if he was willing to take her to get more dope then whoever she was having with had promised.

Even then when that was gone she would just call the guy then.

He went to a meeting.

Sunday morning came and no word from Liza Beth. She had agreed to come over around noon.

He started texting around eleven no reply. He started calling at noon and started getting pissed off around two.

He felt so stupid, betrayed and played.

He kept picturing her fine little body entwined around some faceless man.

Then it became a series of men.

He tried to paint so he wouldn't be thinking of her. He kept thinking that she knew she wasn't coming over today that she had never had any intention of coming over.

He felt like a complete fool.

Around five the phone rang. It was her she sounded extremely agitated.

She was very fucked up, he could hardly understand her when she spoke.

Chill baby please come get me please I don't want to be here.

Someone grabbed the phone from her and he could hear a man's deep gruff voice.

"Ain't nobody coming to get you! Give me that damn phone!"

Chill was screaming into the phone. Where are you? I will come get you just tell me where you are.

The man's voice came on the phone. "Don't worry buddy she's fine right where she's at." The line went dead.

Chill spent the next few hours trying to get her to answer the phone. It was turned off.

He had no idea where she was at or who she was with. She could be dead or raped or tortured Thousands of sick, twisted scenarios went through his mind none of them good.

He did what he had been taught by eleven years of recovery. He prayed. He got on his knees and cleared his head of every thought.

Chill did not try to manipulate his higher power with prayer The eleventh step of AA talks about seeking knowledge of his will and the power to carry it out. Chill sought to find God's will in the day's events.

He gained little peace and the phone continued to not ring. He spent a restless night fearful for his friend. He did drift off to sleep and was awakened around seven am by his phone.

It was Liza Beth! His heart soared she was alive! His prayers had been answered.

She said to him:

"Can you come get me? I need to stay with you for a while. Is that cool?"

Yeah. Sure where are you? Are you okay.

I'm in Ohio at the house where you usually pick me up. Ginnie's house.

Liza Beth had been staying at a friend's house for over a year.Chill had figured out a long time ago that Ginnie was a guy name Kris.It didn't matter the lies were more for her than him.

He sometimes found it insulting that she thought him so naïve or stupid to believe that she wasn't involved with someone.

It was also pretty disappointing for him to consider the fact that he was so whipped that he allowed the lie to continue.

Every good stripper, whore, tramp etc. knows that the trick will tell himself what he needs to hear.

Chill knew he was more than a trick to Liza Beth but not by much.He made the drive quickly and she texted him to meet her at a bar about a mile from where he usually picked her up.

By the time Chill arrived at the bar parking lot it was close to nine o'clock and he had had time to think.

The more he thought the more pissed off he was getting the little selfish bitch had absolutely no regard for anyone but herself.

She met him in the parking lot and told him to wait one moment she had to call her friend.She made a call and within ten minutes a beat up old green Camry pulled into the parking lot.It was a typical doper car. It was piled to the roof with trash and clothes.

The owner probably had everything she owned inside that car.Waiting for the inevitable police intervention that would end this "run."The girl got out of the car and she and Liza Beth hugged.

She opened her trunk and Liza Beth removed her things.Two hefty garbage bags and a couple of school backpacks.

Over the years Chill had accumulated several little girls worldly goods. They all seemed to have the same type of "luggage" when they arrived within his home.Once she had put her stuff into his trunk she got into the passenger seat.

She was shaking, and Chill figured she was all tweaked out. She had probably been smoking crack all night.

He could tell that it was going to be a long day.Before she could open her mouth and start to run game on him Chill decided to get some boundaries.

"Liza Beth I love you and you are welcome in my home but I will not help you to get dope. If you show up high that's on you. I'm not gonna kick you out but I'm not going to take you to get dope or let you use my car."

Liza Beth instantly flew into a rage. Well, I wish you had fucking told me that before I let her leave.

Chill's heart sank. He had thought the girl on the verge of being done or at least ready for a break from her disease. his was not the case. Her disease was   running strong.

It   would not be denied.

She quickly dialed her phone and spoke into it.

"Hey can you come back and get me?"

Yeah he's being a dick too. Ha! She laughed sardonically with no humor.

"It seems like everybody's turning on me today. I can't catch a break. The one time I really need these assholes they all turn their back on me."

Please come back I got to get well. Girl, I'm about to really lose it. She started to cry and the rears were real. They were not some attempt at manipulation.

Chill stood firm. He had to he   knew if he got caught up in taking her to get dope that eventually he would get high.

He had taken her a handful of times and been consumed with guilt.His self-loathing and shame were overwhelming .She seemed not to notice how much it bothered him.

The truth was when he took her to get dope he knew it wasn't anything about love or recovery anymore .It was about control and manipulation. He was not with someone he loved. He was turning that person into an object and using that object for his own gratification.

Chill had come to believe the message contained within the Big Book of AA and trusted that message.

In the Big Book, it says if a person continues to knowingly harm others without regret or trying to change that man will drink.

He knew that taking Liza Beth to get dope was causing   harm. He could not rationalize or justify this action. He had to stand by his guns on this point. Even if it meant she went away for good. In the midst of her disease, she could not see why it was a big deal.

The girl in the pale green Camry returned.

Liza started to get out of the car.

She paused, "Can I still stay with you? I need to get well   right now I really need you."

Of course Chill replied you know you can.

Liza I love you. I mean I really love you. I don't know if that means anything to you but it's the truth.

The girl took the big man's hand. There were tears rolling down her face.

"Baby, right now that means everything. I will call you in a little while, okay?"

Yeah, sure.

Chill figured he would hear from her in a couple of weeks. Then he remembered her stuff was in his car.

That didn't mean a whole lot. Liza Beth had a habit of starting over from scratch. She thrived on recreating herself with new people.

He decided to go home and try to sleep. Once he had gotten home and had settled in the phone page. It was Liza Beth.

Hey she said in that lazy drawl she used when the dope was just starting to take hold.

"Can you pick me up. I'm at the shell station right off the Interstate on the Kentucky side."

Chill was confused.

Sure, I'll be there in like ten minutes.

Hell, she had practically followed him home.

He got to the shell and she got in the car.

Damn, girl that was quick.

"I tried to tell you I just needed to get well but you were being a dick. Forget it I don't want to argue can we just go home. I want to lay down and maybe you can hold me. Just hold me, okay?"

Sure, yeah! Whatever, Chill loved holding her but she was not the typical girl that liked to cuddle.

She liked to nod out in his arms but usually the drugs in her system had her bouncing out of character.

When they got to his house or "home" as it were. She put on some old sweat pants and a t-shirt. She even put on panties which was definitely odd. She rarely ever wore panties. Said she quit wearing them when she was sixteen.

It added to her sex pot nymph mystique. Chill loved her naked but he had to admit panties were nice to pull off a girl. Sometimes the right underwear made a lovely young ass even lovelier.

He wasn't going to push the issue. If she didn't like to wear panties that was her business. She obviously had a lot of confidence in her hygiene.

She certainly had nothing to hide there was no part of her that wasn't beautiful. Chill had seen his share of pretty girls but Liza Beth was something special. She was long of limb and had clean strong lines. He often thought of her as a thoroughbred. He had never told her this for fear she would take it the wrong way.

She was a sensual animal and like an animal she didn't apologize for her sexuality it was just a part of her.

As the day progressed, Chill noted a definite anxiety rising within Liza Beth. He could tell something was disturbing her and that she wanted to tell him but something was holding her back.

Chill broached the subject a couple of times with little success.

Baby is something on your mind? He had asked and then later. Liza girl I can tell something is wrong do you want to talk about it?

She took a long moment before responding.

I can't talk about it.

You will hate me.

Chill's gut went cold. He   hesitated.

I doubt that baby girl.

I've always told you you can tell me anything.

Your wellbeing means more to me than anything. I know we are lovers but I was your friend first. I am still your friend. It looks to me that right now you need me to be a friend.

Oh baby I do Ireally do.

Chill hugged the girl to him and she began to sob.

He had never seen Liza Beth this distraught. She quivered and whimpered and squeezed him with all her might.

They held each other for a long time neither speaking.

They were both hesitant to speak, to go further into the next thing. They knew that what happened next would be a defining moment for them. The girl needing the man to be understanding and supportive.

The man hoping he can give the girl what she needs.

Tentatively they moved apart both hesitant to break the spell and comfort of that embrace.

The girl again took the big man's hand in hers.

Baby, I don't know how to start. I got to tell somebody or I'm going to bust.

The man looked her in the eye and said:

"Just say it."

The girl started speaking and everything changed.

Liza Beth began her tale. As she progressed Chill's blood began to rise. He was torn between anger and compassion.

Their relationship was far from a traditional situation. Chill at this time had nine years sober. He was forty-five years old. Liza Beth had just turned twenty. In some ways, the girl was more experienced.

Chill had only been involved in a handful of long term relationships. He had had a lot of one night stands. He was for the most part monogamous. This monogamy was due to when he was with someone   he made them his world. For Chill there was nothing more important than taking care of the people he loved?

Liza Beth was well versed in "relationships." She had had a boyfriend of some   sort   since she was twelve years old. She often found herself involved with several people at the same time. Her pattern was to meet someone become infatuated make them feel like they were her world. They would fall in love with the person she presented to them. Once the new began to wear off or the whole thing became tiresome she would start looking for the next one.

Chill knew   she was living with someone or had been until this morning.

As she spoke it became clear she had been involved with at least one other person besides the one with whom she had been living.

Chill really didn't care about all that he knew she was in the middle of her disease and that her obsession .was making the decisions.

Alcoholism and addition made an individual consumed with self

He knew he loved her and it was not a love based on her treatment of him. He loved her unconditionally he had never understood what that meant before he met Liza Beth.

Without   condition.

Her actions toward him   were often deceitful disrespectful and worst all oblivious. When he awoke, he would think of her. All through the day his mind would wander to thoughts of her throughout the day. She stayed on his mind.

Most nights he fell asleep wondering if she was safe. But another part of him not so loving would be more inclined toward thoughts of a less forgiving nature.

Yeah, she was safe. Safe in another   man's arms. She was safe and could care less about Chill or his love for her.

He realized over the three years he had known her that she had gotten sicker. At times he had gotten sicker with her.

The chaos and destruction in her life had overflowed into his. For Liza Beth, Chill had become a convenience and a fall back plan. Whenever her plans and relationships fell apart she would come back to Chill.

Chill's friend Pixie Skye had watched it happen time and time again. She had asked Chill why he put up with it. She had told him he was a great guy and that he deserved a girl that would treat him good.

Chill had laughed sadly.

Liza Beth was Chill's heroin. He knew she was unhealthy for him but a   part of him was obsessed with her.

There were other girls in his life. Liza Beth sometimes stayed away for two and three weeks.

Chill never knew when she would make an appearance. He maintained relationships with two and sometimes three other girls. They all were involved in other relationships.

Pixie told him he was a professional "side guy."

He had agreed with her. He was real good friends with all the girls in his life.

They shared their deepest secrets with him.

They told him about their relationship problems and he was able to give kind caring advice from an objective point of view. They all knew Chill cared for them but they all also knew that he loved Liza Beth.

They listened to his tales of woe and seen how in their own lives they were guilty of treating some men the way Liza Beth treated Chill.

This time Liza Beth had gotten herself in a situation where she could have been killed. It was hard to get her started. Chill could sense she wanted to tell him what had happened.

She was shaking and scared and it was imperative that she tell somebody.

Chill knew that something bad had happened. She had tried to numb herself with dope but it wasn't working.

Chill figured the problem was she wanted to tell Chill what happened but was determined to hold something back.

Chill coaxed her.

Is this about when you called yesterday?

You asked me to come and get you but you never told me where you were.

Some man took the phone from you and cut you off.

He had said "She don't need no fucking ride. She's right where she needs to be. Ain't that right, bitch?"

Then the phone cut off.

It was from a private number and I had no way to track you down.

She asked Chill. "What time was that?"

Around five you were supposed to have been here by one yesterday. I was already mad.

Why were *you* mad?

Liza Beth had trouble seeing any point of view but her own.

That's great. You were sitting here pissed at me while some maniac was about to kill me.

No! Chill started to get angry. "If you had came here like you said you was going to do you would not have been there to get hurt."

If you hadn't lied and ran off with another man that man would have been able to hurt you.

Fuck you, Bobby!

I don't need this from you right now. Can't you see I'm hurting? Can't you for just once think about somebody but yourself?

You're just all upset because I didn't come over here yesterday and give you some fucking pussy! You don't even care that I almost got beat to death by some maniac!

Chill stepped back as if struck!

How in the fuck am I the selfish one here?

I need you, Chill, right now and I don't need you mad at me. You are always telling me how much you love me. Well that's what I need right now. I don't need to be told, "I told you so." I don't need to be judged. I need you to listen to me and I need a friend.

Chill's heart melted. She may be a world class bitch and a treacherous whore but she was also the woman he loved.

Right now she was his friend and she hurt.

She was right in this instance. However, she had wound up hurt or in harms' way was not relevant.

She was in pain and did not need him to harm her more.

It was not his place to punish her. If he couldn't accept her, he always had the opportunity to exclude her from his life.

Chill softened.

You're right, baby! I apologize. This is not the time for my shit.

You know I love you. You know that.

Tell me what happened.

This man picked me up and we want to get dope.

Who is this man? Where do you know him from?

He was a friend of Anna's. You remember my friend Anna.

Yeah, so why were you with him?

Anna and Robert said he was alright. We all went to High School together.

Chill knew something wasn't right with this explanation. He also knew she wasn't going to tell him the whole truth.

The man was probably someone she had been seeing and did not want to admit to Chill.

He had told her hundreds of times that she didn't have to lie to him. He would rather have the truth no matter how bad. When she lied to him about anything it placed an obstacle between them.

The disease of addiction thrives on dishonesty. Once she puts a lie between them the nature of their relationship changes. He can not be a resource of true comfort or recovery. It becomes adversarial in that she has deceived him and must now continue that deceit.

He becomes a job.

The lie takes the relationship from friend lover and changes it into something along the lines of trick, sugar daddy, or side dude.

If she ever decided to get sober, the dishonesty placed between them would exclude him from being a resource in her recovery. She would not be able to share her complete truth with him without causing harm.

What was the guy's name?

She told him some name like Peter Jacobs or some shit. He didn't say anything but he remembered her using this name in a lie the previous year. He had noticed this pattern about six months after they had met. She had certain names and scenarios that she used again and again. Whenever she used them he knew she was lying.

One was to be dropped off somewhere and that her mom was picking her up. That always meant she was meeting someone to go get drugs. Another one was she would have him pick her up at a gas station or store.

This meant she didn't want him to see with whom she had been. It meant most likely a man.

He could tell by the way she was telling her story that she knew the man that had attacked her. He also knew she was not going to tell him the man's name.

Liza Beth continued her tale.

She said that Anna and Robert had left her with the man. The man was supposed to give her a ride home. He had instead said that he had more money and asked if she wanted to get more dope.

Liza Beth had no idea how her cavalier attitude of just getting into the car with some "stranger" to go get dope was twisting Chill's guts into a knot.

He struggled to remain quiet to let the girl continue.

They had gotten dope and gotten high. He had bought heroin and crack. Once they were out she had insisted he take her home.

This was when he had turned on her. He got real angry and started screaming at her. He told her she owed him some pussy. She tried to get out of the car and he had smacked her. He drove her out to the country where he lived.

Chill figured the attack had occurred at the man's place. He had calmed her down by saying he had more dope at his house.

He told her he had pain pills and Xanax all she could ever want. The drug fiend part agreed to go to his house for the dope.

The man's house was way down in the country about eighty miles from where Liza Beth lived.

Chill had asked her if she could find the place.

She had replied no because she had been really high.

Once inside his house the man had tried to get her to undress.

She had insisted on seeing the drugs he had promised. He had gotten angry again. He started yelling that she had done did three hundred dollars worth of his drugs and by God it was time she gave him some of that ass. He threw her on the bed and tried to get his hand down her pants. His weight was on top of her. She started to swing and kick.

The man grew more and more violent. He reached his hand across the bed toward a night table. He fumbled in a drawer and pulled out a large pistol.

He placed the pistol to her forehead and screamed into her face."Shut the fuck up Bitch! Quit your fucking bawling. You knew all along what this was about!"

While he held the gun to her head he resumed his exploration with his other hand. He had reached into her pants and forced his middle finger inside.

She had been dry and the pain had been tremendous. She had screamed and pushed at his face. He smacked her ear with the pistol. He was very careful not to bruise her face. He kept hitting and smacking her on the back of the head and the stomach.

He resumed the assault with his fingers This time he forced two inside her. He fumbled at his belt and pulled his own pants down to his knees.

His penis was not completely hard and he continued the assault with his fingers.

Liza Beth felt something being ripped from inside her.

The man had pulled her birth control device out of her body.

The device had been placed inside by a doctor. It was not meant to be removed. The pain had been so overwhelming that she had folded up into the fetal position. Her attacker had become unseated and struggled to retain his spot on top of her.

He had placed his hand over her mouth and waited until she calmed down.

He put the gun to her head and told her that if she didn't do everything he told her to do he would beat her face until no one would ever look at her again. He told her he would go to her mother's house and kill her whole family.

He had even threatened to kill her nine-month-old son.

Told   her that he had "never shot a retard before but he was sure he could do it."

Chill remained silent but inside his head was a whirlwind of mixed emotions. He could tell by her story that the attack was real. A man had put a gun to her head and forced himself inside her.

Furthermore, the details about threatening her family told Chill that the man was no stranger to Liza Beth.

She had told this man about herself. She had shared about her child and her mother. He knew how to hurt her because she had entrusted him with this knowledge. Chill can remember similar conversations with Liza Beth.

These   conversations occurred usually after lovemaking. Pillow talk. She would lie in his arms her head upon his chest a cigarette dangling from her left hand. Her legs would be crossed at the ankles and with her right hand she would idly rub and stroke Chill's body.

These were some of Chill's most pleasant memories. It was when she let her guard down and all her pretense would fall.

It was when the true Liza Beth would come out. The Liza Beth that Chill loved and held dear. Tears started rolling slowly down the man's cheeks. The tears were not for Liza's pain and her ordeal.

These tears stemmed from Chill's certainty that at some point his precious Liza Beth had shared with this man that part of herself that Chill had thought his alone.

He was able to live with the thought that she gave her body to other men. Somehow the physical act of sex was far less intimate.

She had shared her fears, her dreams, her hopes.

She had given to another what Chill had thought his.

What's more this interloper had used it against her.

He had not seen the beautiful treasure that a young girl's heart held.

Liza was a beautiful girl but she had no sense of her true worth.   Youth and exuberance abounded within her long supple form.

Oh the insolence of youth. Thinking itself invincible and its glories inexhaustible it squanders God's most precious gifts on fools and fiends.

The artist's soul inside Chill had seen and recognized Liza Beth's truest and greatest prize.

That same artist soul now sorrowfully contemplated the loss at least in part of that youthful naivet' .

He also felt betrayed to the depths of his soul. Apparently in no way was he special to Liza Beth.

No part of herself had she thought of as his and his alone. All these thoughts flashed through Chill's head in a moment.

He endured and strove to show no hint of his realization. Whatever her actions she needed him now.

He was only responsible for his actions. He was determined not to cause her further harm on this night.

The man's threats had caused the opposite effect of the one   he had desired.

Instead of becoming compliant and letting the man   continue his rape with more than a couple of fingers; Liza Beth became galvanized into action.

She started screaming from anger and wailing and tearing at his face.

She kicked and thrashed and   again the man was unseated.

This time when he fell to the side she pushed at him and dove to the other side of the bed toward the floor and the bedroom doorway. He slid headfirst into the same end table that had held the pistol.

He hit his head on the way down and began cursing. Liza Beth seeing an opportunity for escape ran for the doorway.

She struggled to button her jeans as she ran. She felt something hot and slick and realized she was bleeding.

The motherfucker had torn something inside her. She could hear him struggling behind her.

She ran through hallway into the kitchen toward the backdoor. The house was old and used a wood stove in the winter for heat. The kitchen door opened onto a mudroom. In the corner of the mudroom was an ash bucket.

Inside the bucket were nestled a poker a small axe and a little shovel for shoveling embers. Liza grabbed for the poker and flung it at the running figure. It glanced off the door frame and split his cheek.

It didn't stop him. She grabbed the little metal shovel in a two-handed grip. She sung it like a baseball bat.

It missed the man's nose by half an inch.

Meanwhile, his right foot landed on the abandoned poker and it rolled when he jerked his head back from the girl's swing.

The   impetuous   of the man's movement combined with the rolling of the poker made the man came crashing down.

All his weight landed squarely upon his right elbow which landed on a concrete step that led from the kitchen door into the combination porch mudroom. The man screamed.

Oh fuck! You've broke my fucking arm, you stupid cunt!

I'm gonna kill you for this!   Come back here, you bitch!

The girl grabbed the axe as she ran out the door.

It was of little use for she tripped over a five gallon bucket full of crushed beer cans in the dark. She dropped the axe and didn't stop to look for it.

She quickly headed into the dark tree line behind the house.

She knew if she got over the hill there were houses   on the other side and beyond that lay the highway.

Somehow her phone was still in her jeans. She tried to get a signal but to no avail. She could only get one bar and the low batt light was blinking.

She lay behind a tree for a long time and kept to the tree line.

Chill stopped her.

What happened to dude?

I don't know. He just sat waiting and shivering until I couldn't stand it anymore. I started walking down the highway.

Some old man picked me up and drove me to a little store.

Why didn't you have him drive you to the police.

The man that attacked me said he knew all the cops in that town.

He said he had grown up with them and that   he still got high and drank beer with most of them. I was afraid they would take me back to his house turn me over to him.

Shit Chill had said. You are lucky to be alive. You really are.

Chill began to realize how close he had come to losing her.

She may be a treacherous, lying dope fiend slut, but he loved her more than anything. She was the light of his life. He couldn't imagine not having her   in his life.

Those infrequent phone calls that preceded her taking over his life were his biggest motivation in life.

The quiet periods in between the chaos of her visits he spent painting. He knew loneliness and heartbreak, but he lived on hope.

If Liza Beth were to disappear from his life completely he doubted he could maintain even the slim thread of hope. He had no children and his family was not close.

Sometimes the phone didn't ring for weeks.

If he disappeared tomorrow no   one's life would be greatly disturbed. As fucked up as she was, Liza Beth provided Chill a purpose. She needed him. She showed up consistently and she told him she loved him.

He doubted if it was true but at least she made the effort. He could count on the fingers of one hand the women outside of family that had told him they loved him.

He hadn't believed most of them. Liza Beth's love was not much to nourish a man's soul, but Chill was like a cactus in the desert. He could thrive on what would kill most people.

After Liza Beth told her tale, Chill kept talking with her.

The more she thought about it the more angry she got.

Chill convinced her to go to the hospital and get everything checked out.

He stressed that this man had probably done this shit before and if he wasn't stopped would probably continue to harm other girls.

Chill wanted to kill the man himself. Right now he needed to attend to his woman.He took her to the same hospital in which he had identified his brother's body.

Where he had watched his brother become an object. He was no longer the living, breathing, loving man Glenn Frieze. Just the body remained.

He had accompanied Liza Beth into the E.R.

They had explained why they were there.

A couple of nurses' quickly filled out some initial paperwork and asked Liza Beth some questions .She worried about being able to pay. She was assured that it wouldn't cost her anything as long as a police report was filed.

Two police officers arrived and Liza Beth asked Chill to wait outside while she made her report.

Chill didn't argue. He knew she wanted him to leave so she could tell the police the entire facts of the night.

He knew her attacker was no casual acquaintance from high school. He was not a fool there had been many holes in the girl's story. He had heard so many lies from her that he   had little trouble spotting them.

He just knew better than to press the issue. He seldom got to see her and he didn't want to waste what little time they had together fighting over something that wasn't going to change.

He hated fighting with her if she left his house with them angry at each other his life became pure hell.

He knew she was a heroin addict and that on any given day she could die. He did not want his last moments with her to be unpleasant and fueled by anger.

It was obvious she knew who attacked her. It was a testament to her anger about the incident that she was filing a police report.

Chill grew antsy in the waiting room. He needed to talk to someone. He started to call his sponsor but hesitated.

Chill loved Frankie with all his heart and trusted him implicitly with his own issues and problems.

He did not feel comfortable telling Frankie about Liza Beth's being attacked. Frankie had been Chill's sponsor for about five years. He had chosen him because he seemed happy and he was always helping people.

Frankie had   been married four or five times. Three since being sober.

When it came to issues with females Chill had found Frankie could be less than compassionate.

He loved women but he had been badly used by women. Chill didn't need a lecture he just needed a friend.

Someone to listen and not judge him   or Liza Beth.

He called his best friend Pixie Skye.He had known Pixie about five years. Frankie had introduced them at a meeting.

She had been fresh from treatment and the beautiful "new girl" that at that time was wowing the rooms of AA.

She had already been through her mandatory detox/treatment center romance and was concentrating on getting sober. Chill had liked her right away she had shined like new money.

He had asked her out to dinner and quickly realized she was friend-zoning him. He had decided to stick around because she had seemed genuine. She wanted him as a friend not a resource. She had quickly became his confidant and he hers.

She was indeed beautiful but what stood out as her biggest character trait was she just seemed decent.

Much like his sponsor Frankie she had a kind heart and cared for people. Chill hadn't known how much he had needed someone like her in his life.

She had helped him through many rough nights. Most of those nights had been about Liza Beth and his relationship.

He knew that to Liza Beth he was mainly a convenience and a fall back plan.She trusted Chill and knew that he loved her.

He doubted she ever meant to cause him harm or heartache. She was like a wolf and he a sheep. The wolf did not pity the sheep. Predators devour prey . its prey's purpose.

She used Chill because he made himself available to be used.

If he stopped making himself available she would just use someone else. Chill knew there would be no shortage of people willing to take his spot.

He doubted he   could live with her moving out of his life. The thought that she could move on and not give it another thought tormented him.

He wanted to be important to her, he wanted to matter to her, to be more than an afterthought.

Pixie answered the phone and could tell something was wrong.

"What's going on, buddy? Don't say nothing. I can hear it in your voice. Is it Liza? What has she done?"

Chill chuckled miserably. Damn girl! You're good. But she ain't really done anything except damn near got herself killed.

Chill's accent got stronger in times of stress of anger. He was talking with a huge drawl and Pixie caught it.

Are you okay?

Chill replied softly. No I'm not. I'm not okay at all. I may never be okay again.

Where you at?

I'm at the hospital at the E.R. Liza Beth's in the exam room getting a rape kit done.

Oh Chill, baby, I'm so sorry!

Do you want me to come there?

Chill hesitated a second. He knew there was nothing she could do to help Liza Beth. He also knew that Liza Beth would probably want to keep the whole incident a secret. The girl thrived on her secrets. She liked to live several lives simultaneously.

Chill told Pixie, Yes, I do. I want you here, very much.

The pretty lady didn't hesitate.

I'm on my way. I will be there as soon as possible.

You hang in there, okay?

Chill replied through quiet sobs. Yeah, hurry. I'm about to lose it.

Chill kept replaying the girls story through his mind. He could see the fear and pain on Liza Beth's face. Rage mixed with powerlessness. He wanted to lash out at something. He couldn't comprehend how anyone could be so callous as to not see her value.

To Chill, there was nothing in the world more precious than Liza Beth. He knew all her lies, her secrets and knew her to be mean and selfish. He associated all these characteristics with her disease.

He didn't make excuses for her behavior. He was not oblivious or even misguided. He had seen her at her worst and been treated badly by her. He had stayed and was not a victim. His love for her transcended everything else. His heart and soul connected with something inside the girl that it didn't connect with any other person.

He realized that he loved someone that was probably incapable of loving him in return. He also knew it didn't matter. He loved her and for a guy like Chill that was everything.

Numerous times Chill had vowed to himself to stop having anything to do with Liza Beth. He would set out determined to be done with her. He would fill his life with work, art, and other women. For awhile he would have some success. He would think he was free of her hold over him.

She would call him, sometimes after weeks, and say casually; hey you want to hang out? His resolve would vanish and he would reply.

Sure. Where you at?

She would tell him and he would go get her.

On the way to get her, he would admit to himself that he hadn't really been trying to *forget* her. He had been killing time until she *remembered* him.

In a way, it was very sad and very tragic. He continued to give his love and his heart to someone indifferent to him. The truth was he was a coward in the ways of love.

Liza Beth's and his relationship would become the prototype for Chill's relationships with women.

These beauties would invariably be involved to some degree in other relationships.

Chill was commitment-phobic.

His childhood had undermined his sense of self-worth. He didn't feel worthy of any better treatment.His Grand Sponsor had explained to him once that we teach other's how to treat us.

Chill had taught Liza Beth that it was okay to treat him the way she did.

Chill was not a victim. He was just spiritually sick. Liza Beth was a great source of joy and torment for him.

He had been taught his entire life that love and pain were intertwined. He knew no other way. If loving someone didn't hurt, he wouldn't trust it. The irony of the deal was that Chill had learned more about recovery and trusting in God from loving Liza Beth than any other single thing.

He had learned the value of forgiveness. He had learned not to take another person's disease personally. He had learned not to retaliate when harmed. Love was not a contest. He had to treat other people decent even if they didn't treat him decent.

Liza Beth could lie and cheat and misuse him and   he still had to treat her decent.

In order to stay sober he could not give into anger.

The principles of recovery are easy to talk about. By keeping this girl in his life he had had to live by these principles. They were not theory. For him they had become fact. He often felt pity for the lovely Liza Beth.

Much like his brother Parker Dell, she could not see the blessings in her life. She could only see what was missing. She always felt incomplete.

Chill had learned the value of gratitude. He was not always grateful and he knew when he wasn't. His life became difficult when ungrateful.

He never regretted meeting Liza Beth.He treasured every moment with her.

He knew whatever happened that he owed her much more than she had ever taken. He had met her two weeks after her 18th birthday. He had been forty-one.

She had been at the height of her "girlhood" and knew not its value. He had been of an age and temperament to know its value as priceless. She had seen an opportunity to have some fun and a little adventure.

He had seen a treasure and had been determined to soak up as much as he could gather.

Here he sat desolate and heartbroken. Some heartless beast incapable of comprehending the depth and travesty of his actions had befouled his precious Liza Beth. A part of him knew that this experience was also necessary.

The man and the attack upon Liza Beth were consequences of her life choices. Liza Beth's higher power had seen fit for her to endure this experience.

We grow and learn through pain. This was a hard lesson.

Pixie arrived and gave Chill a huge hug.

Are you okay? Chill's friend inquired? Not really but you being here does help.

They sat in the waiting room for an hour maybe longer.

They talked about nothing and everything.

Pixie gradually got the gist of what Liza Beth had told Chill   They both knew there was more to the story and carefully avoided talking about it.

A nurse came out and with good intentions and   tried to bolster Chill's mood.

The nurse explained that the police had convinced Liza Beth to call her attacker and get him to admit the attack in front of the listening police officers. The nurse probably assumed   Chill a father figure for the young girl.

She probably thought him a kindly friend of the family here to lend support. It was obvious that she had not made the romantic connection between Liza Beth and the aging fat man.

The nurse continued, "Yeah, he was all apologies and 'you know I love you and would never do anything to harm you.'"

It was obvious the man and Liza Beth were involved in more than a casual encounter.

Chill sat stoically. He showed no emotion.

Pixie, bless her soul, did not push it.

She knew the big man's only concern at this time was the young girl's health and well-being. There would be plenty of time later to contemplate the depths of her treachery.

Pixie knew he would forgive her and find some way to continue to love her and keep her in his life.

It often amazed Pixie how this man; so seemingly intelligent and capable in so many areas of his life, could be so insane when it came to Liza Beth. Pixie was indeed a sweet and loving person but she did not like anyone misusing her friend.

Chill often reminded her that he was the one that chose to remain in the relationship.

Pixie had listened to the big man inventory his relationship with the girl on dozens of occasions. She had to admit that he owed a lot of his spiritual growth to his relationship with the girl. In a very unhealthy relationship he had constantly reviewed and revised his own behavior. He had struggled to not cause harm. He worked hard not to manipulate the girl with her disease.

He knew he enabled her at times and knew himself a coward. The thought of her not in his life overwhelmed him at times.

Pixie knew Chill tried his hardest to love Liza Beth in a way that was unselfish and would cause the least harm.

The hour continued to grow late and Chill realized that his friend Pixie had helped him through the hardest part.

He told his little hippie friend that it would be okay for her to leave.

She sensed that he was past the critical point and agreed to leave. She really didn't trust herself not to give the little bitch Liza Beth a piece of her mind. She very much wanted to tell the girl how selfish and cruel she was but knew that if she said anything it would also hurt Chill.

Pixie knew how to be a friend and so she agreed to leave. She made Chill promise to call her the next morning and give her an update.

At 5:30 the nurse came back out and told Chill he could go back to the exam room. The police officers were leaving and Liza Beth was sitting on the exam table.

She was wearing gray sweat pants and a paper smock. Her clothes were in a paper bag on the bed. The officers had taken her shirt and underclothes for evidence.

The girl looked a hundred percent better than she had upon arrival at the hospital. She was actually smiling and had a gleam in her eye. Liza Beth was a fighter and taking action against her assailant had done her good.

She hugged Chill tightly which surprised the big man. Seldom did Liza Eth show him affection in public.

When they had first met she loved to set in his lap and lean on his shoulder. She had shown him off to everyone.

Chill had felt like a king when she had done that. It was her pattern when she met someone to overwhelm them with her attention. She would call in the morning just to say she loved him. Again at night she would do the same. She would send texts throughout the day.

Chill had been hesitant to be sucked in by her a first. It just seemed too good to be true. It had continued until Chill had bought in completely. He returned the affection and the attention.

He made Liza Beth his world in return.

The funny thing was it seemed the moment that Chill returned the young girls attention Liza Beth began to lose interest. The more obsessed he became with her the less interested she became in him.

It seemed like her whole plan was to convince him he had to have her and could not live without her. Once he was convinced she had become bored. She only liked the infatuation stage of a relationship. Once beyond the honeymoon period intimacy and relationships became tiresome.

When you first meet people you share your hopes and dreams. You talk about your childhoods and everything is filled with mystery and delight.

After a period of time these conversations turn into stories about each other's day of what was on TV.

Liza Beth was seeking adventure and romance not drudgery and the mundane. Love is much more about commitment and sacrifice than it is adventure and romance.

Love became precious through dedication and loyalty. Liza Beth had no appreciation for traits such as these.

She was young and beautiful and finding people to love and appreciate her was as easy as breathing. She was the master of reading people and giving them the exact person they needed her to be.

The only problem was that once she tired of the thing she felt no compunction about going on to the next thing.

Chill had been seeing her for about three years at this point. It was probably the longest relationship she had ever maintained with anyone outside her family.

Chill figured the main reason that he was still in Liza Beth's life was because he had such low self-esteem.

Everyone else would cut their ties with the girl once her behavior got intolerable. Chill really didn't have anything else going on in his life. As fucked up as Liza Beth was she was the only person that consistently sought Chill's company.

If she was only there for convenience and refuge; so be it.

She brought chaos and heartbreak but she also brought the only thing resembling love into Chill's life. For some reason, Chill was not a man people sought out for long periods of time.

He had never been allowed to be comfortable as a child in the company of other people. Every time he had let his guard down it had been used against him by the people that were supposed to be friends and family.

Liza Beth may cause Chill harm but mainly through indifference. She had kept his confidences and never been malicious.

It probably wasn't from any noble character traits. More likely she had never retained any of Chill's deep heartfelt confessions of love and hope. As the young often do she had probably listened politely and waited patiently until her turn to speak.

Sometimes she would surprise him and recount some tidbit of information he had shared.

She was a very clever girl. In many ways much wiser than Chill.

She realized that the big man made a much deeper impression upon people then he realized. People didn't avoid him because he made them uncomfortable.They avoided him because he was overwhelming.

He was often too real in conversations. Chill didn't realize that 90% of all conversations were bullshit and filler. People talked about shit that didn't mean anything as a way of just getting through life.

If you asked Chill "how you doing today?"

He could respond in any manner of ways.

He might say, "I'm feeling really evil and hate most everybody right now."

Or he might say, "why do you want to know?"

Chill's mind was always racing. He loved knowledge and no subject was taboo. He did insist that a dialogue be interesting. Slow witted people irritated the hell out of Chill.

He had observed that a lot of people that were mean spirited often talked in clichés.

Liza Beth realized people respected and feared Chill and for the most part he was oblivious. A lot of people talk about not caring about other people's opinion of them.Chill really didn't.

Other people's opinions of him had little to no effect upon his decision making about his life.

If asked about this Chill would be surprised to know other people had an opinion about him.

Liza Beth knew Chill inspired people with his message of recovery.When he talked recovery he kept it simple and honest.

He was able to explain things in a direct, straightforward way. He was very effective because when he shared it was to convey insight and information more than to stroke his ego.

Chill took recovery seriously. He loved to joke and have a good time but even his jokes often made a valid point.

Chill loved to point out the absurdities in life .People that didn't know him often thought him irreverent and sometimes took offense.

Seldom did they speak of their discomfort to Chill directly. If they had they may have been surprised at Chill's reaction.

He would sit and listen and if their point was in any way valid he would take it into consideration.

If he agreed that his behavior or words had been harmful, disrespectful or disruption he would strive to do better and try to make amends if possible.

Of course if he reviewed their comments and decided they were full of shit. This verdict would be forthcoming and expressed with fervor.

"Go fuck yourself, nobody asked you," might be an appropriate response.

Chill and Liza Beth gathered her things and exited the E.R.

The morning air was crisp and it was still dark.

Chill knew Liza Beth was probably going to need to go get high. He wasn't sure what he would do.

The day before he hadn't been willing to take her and she had found a way.

If he didn't take her today would she leave and be gone for weeks, possibly forever. He pulled her close wrapping his arm around her. She sank into his warmth.

"Are you okay?" Chill inquired.

The girl responded yes, just really tired. I want to go home, get a shower and just sleep for about ten hours.

Chill's heart leaped.

Awesome we can definitely make that happen. Hell we might even get a little girl breakfast on the way home.

Oh baby, that would be great. Oh we need to stop and get cigarettes too. Please!

Okay, okay, you know I will.

After stopping at a Speedway and McDonald's Liza Beth was starting to nod off in the car.

Chill, baby!

Yeah, baby doll.

Will you take me to a meeting in the morning.

Sure! You know I will.

Chill held his hopes in check. He knew by the next morning the girl would be getting dope sick. She would not very likely be going anywhere but to get high.

Sometimes they fooled you. Liza slept the day away. She took a shower and put the grey sweatpants back on.

Somehow they had become something more to her. She was like that she would find security and comfort in something and keep it with her for days.

This would last awhile and then just as suddenly be replaced.

Somehow the grey sweatpants were a symbol for Liza Beth. They represented her trying to take back whatever had been taken from her.

It was a simplification but Chill knew truth when he saw it.

The girl may not consciously realize what she was doing but Chill lived and breathed this girl. She was coping sometimes little things were not so little.

Surprisingly at about four in the afternoon the girl had reached out to Chill she whispered hold me.

He had embraced her and she had offered herself to him. He had been hesitant because of her injuries from when the man had ripped her birth control from her body.

"The doctor said it would be okay just be gentle. I need you to love me Chill. I need you to clean me of his memory."

Chill made love to her and after she laid in his arms and cried. She told him about being scared and that she really loved him and that she was so grateful to him for letting her stay there.

He hadn't realized till that moment that she was moving back into his home.

Liza Beth had lived with Chill three or four times previous.

He wasn't sure if she ever moved out voluntarily.

Chill was not an easy man to live with and he refused to take too much shit under his own roof.

The rules were few and simple. He did not want anyone in his house that he hadn't approved. No guests while Chill was not home.

If you couldn't come home at night you didn't live there anymore.The last one could be adjusted. If Liza Beth made Chill aware of where she was and it seemed legit she could stay other places.

Chill knew she was incapable of following these rules.Her disease would not let her.

Addiction and alcoholism were about obsession and impulse. Liza Beth may have the best intentions in the world and still not be able to do right.

It was a primal thing that affected parts of the brain that functioned without conscious thought.

Chill knew these things from having lived with his own disease.He also knew recovery was possible.

He doubted Liza Beth was anywhere close to being ready to stop. He realized that the main reason she was here with him was she had ran out of options. He was her fallback plan and had been for years.

She kept him in her life for occasions of this nature.Hers was a love of convenience. Chill was like coming home for Liza Beth. It never occurred to her that she would not be welcomed into Chill's home.

The world might be a dangerous place full of uncertainty but Liza Beth had not doubt that Chill loved her.

She would ask herself why he loved her and could not come up with an adequate answer.She knew Chill had sex with other girls but she never saw them as a threat.

Chill was like an old hound dog loyal to the core.She never questioned his love she took it as her due.

Chill envied and admired her ability to take affection from other people for granted.Chill couldn't ever remember being able to do that.He often considered himself unlovable and had serious self-worth issues.

As a result of these feelings he had learned to live with himself. He valued his time alone and knew peace in his own company.He often thought of himself lonesome until the moment someone moved in with him.

Liza Beth was a slob but easy to live with.

She never cleaned but she   was funny and clever.She knew to give Chill pussy on a regular basis.

He was easy to live with as long as this particular need was addressed.Chill could become very unpleasant to the point of pure evil if not given regular sex. It wasn't an act. The man got mean if he didn't ejaculate on a regular basis.

Masturbation did not help it had to be through sex.

When Liza Beth lived with others   Chill got to fuck her every time he saw her.

That's why she came over it went without saying. When she walked in the door she started taking off her clothes.Chill had the same arrangement with about three other girls.

They didn't come around as much as Liza Beth but when they did it was for the same reasons.Chill knew they all were involved with other men and women.

Somehow he had become several pretty young girls dirty little secret.He wasn't sure why they came to him. He guessed because they didn't feel dirty or judged when they spent time with Chill.

He tried to instill in them the principles of recovery.Honesty is one of the major requirements of working any recovery program.

He tried to be honest as possible in all his affairs.He had went to his sponsor and asked if he owed the girls other lovers any kind of explanation of amends.

Together they had developed a checklist for Chill's behavior.

1. Was he lying or manipulating a   person to get his way?
2. Did he truly care for the girls that shared his bed?
3. Were they with other men (to his knowledge) when they started fucking Chill? If they were, don't expect them to   be faithful now.
4. Be careful to   not enable.

Chill struggled mightily with the fourth one.

A dope fiend is a focused entity. Every action an active addict is involved in is to further their Disease . This may not be a conscious fact but Chill had found it to be true.

In order to stay sober his own self   Chill had had to get honest.

He knew he was not a nice person.He knew his own fears and insecurities kept him in sick relationships!

He was not a victim.He loved the girls in his life. He loved Liza Beth with all his heart.

These relationships were not healthy relationships.

Chill also knew that he had grown spiritually by being in relationships with these girls.They may have started out as relationships of convenience but at some point all four girls had realized that Chill was the one person with whom they could be themselves.He loved them unconditionally. It hadn't happened overnight. There had been may many fights and hurt feelings.

Chill had contemplated murder and suicide with every girl he had ever loved .He was an all or nothing kind of guy.He loved with all his heart and he got hurt to the depths of his soul.

Every time he had kicked Liza Beth out of his life he had been determined never to see her again.

She would stay gone for two or three weeks and then she would call. His anger and resolve would vanish.

His friend Pixie told him that Liza Beth was his heroin. He was hooked.

He had laughed and asked, "Well, if she's heroin, what are the other girls?"

Pixie had laughed and said they are your methadone and suboxone. It had been funny but it had a lot of truth.

Liza Beth decided to move back into Chill's home. The two fell into a routine. Liza Beth had decided to get sober again. This was another reason she kept the big guy in her life.

He did the deal. He went to meetings and worked with other drunks no matter what else was going on in his life.

Chaos and gloom may take over everything else but he would continue to do the things that had worked when he had gotten sober.

Those things still worked.

His sponsor and a lot of old timers kept the solution simple. They had a saying. Trust God, clean house, and work with another alcoholic.

Chill knew Liza Beth was in his life for a reason beyond the obvious.

He trusted his higher power that if he was harming the girl she would be removed from his life. He was also assured himself that if she kept showing up some purpose must be being served.

He tried to examine his own behavior on a daily basis. He constantly scrutinized his motivations. He knew sometimes he was selfish and self-centered. Whenever he caught himself wrong he tried to make amends quickly unless to do   so would cause harm.

They would attend an AA meeting every morning at 8am. This would be after a forty-five minute drive each way to the methadone clinic in Indiana.

Liza Beth loved these mornings together. She considered it their time.

Chill didn't quite see it that way. He saw it as him spending his morning, time, gas, and money to get her methadone. It wasn't them spending time together it was her using him to get her dope. After they went to the clinic and to the morning AA meeting they would return home.

Chill would want to make love and often Liza Beth would not. She had already gotten what she need and didn't see why she should be bothered.

Chill would try to remain calm. He didn't make a lot of money and he was committing the majority of his resources to keeping Liza Beth happy. He thought it only fair she do the same.

If you ain't gonna come off no pussy you gonna have to go.

What? Are you fucking crazy?

Who the fuck talks like that? She would say.

Look here, girl! Chill often sounded like a hick when angry. The more hillbilly his accent the more pissed off.

Look here, girl! You know I do anything for you but you ain't   gonna play me for no punk.

I house you, I feed you, and I buy your darn methadone and then you think you too good to give me any pussy. You sleep till I gotta go to work and then you go hang out with your friends till late.

Oh my God! Listen to yourself! Do you know how fucking creepy you are when you get like this. I just gave you pussy like two days ago. You act like you're gonna die.

Well, let's see you go three days without what you need. See how fucking happy you get.

These fights were on the surface about sex but in truth they were about intimacy. Liza Beth had a pattern of establishing a home base from which to launch her operations.

She may be the most beautiful girl around but she was no prize to live with. Chill had found out through years of experience that it was a lot better to be the guy she was cheating with than the guy she was cheating on.

Being Liza Beth's boyfriend had its benefits. You got to parade her around and have everybody envy you.

Your appeal to other women was increased by association with a pretty girl.She was beautiful and awesome in bed.

When Liza Beth decided to take a new lover or "take a boyfriend" she became the women of that man's dreams.

She could read a man and she would be his every wish. She would be super attentive and in bed his every desire would be fulfilled.

She loved falling in love. The infatuation stage of a relationship was like a drug for Liza Beth.The problem with falling in love with Liza Beth was as soon as a man became seriously hooked, she got bored.

Once a man made her his world and was willing to die and forsake all others she would lose interest.

She liked the process of falling in love.The act of sustaining a long term relationship involved a lot of hard work and commitment. These actions were much much too mundane for the lovely young girl.

Chill envied Liza Beth her ability to attract people to her.

She was like a brilliant light and her suitors mindless moths willing to be devoured within her light.

Chill knew that Liza Beth was quick to start new relationships . She was also one to hang onto old relationships.

Just because she had moved on did not mean she was through with a man.

Chill knew from firs hand experience that as long as a man remained useful Liza would keep his number.

She was a great net worker and had a way of making each guy feel unique and special.

Chill had seen this ability in many women. . When he was younger his uncle had taken him to titty bars.

The ladies at the dance clubs would sit and mesmerize the guys for a couple of songs. As long as you were buying drinks and spending money they would sit and be your girl.

The trick was why they sat with you, you would be convinced they really liked you, when five minutes later you new "girlfriend" sat in someone else's lap and kissed him she was just doing her job.

His uncle had been a very wise man and had told Chill the biggest secret.Guys that went after girls like that were wanting to be misused. They want a bad girl so they can blame all their problems and failings on their bad woman.

The truth more often than not is these men are afraid to be in a committed relationship with a decent woman.It was too much responsibility and the pay-off too unsure.

Chill knew he loved Liza Beth but he also knew that every time she had lived with him he had been miserable.

He knew that when she was with him every time she left the house on her own he had to wonder about her actions.

He knew as an addict she had to get money every day. He knew that her beauty was the easiest way to get money.

He actually preferred when she lived with someone else.He just hated being lied to.After Liza Beth's attack and the long night at the hospital, there was a brief period of stability.

She quickly found a job at a fast food place, some roast beef joint.She had thoughtlessly told some old acquaintances about her good fortune.

Word of her new employment and sober lifestyle made the rounds and soon reached Liza Beth's attacker.

One afternoon after dropping the girl off at work. Chill had headed toward an AA meeting. Before he reached the meeting site his phone rang. It was Liza Beth, she was frantic and sobbing.

Through her distress and frenzied exclamations Chill was able to determine that her assailant had shown up at her workplace in a van that she didn't recognize.

He had offered her drugs and money to come with him. She had told him to leave that she was sober and didn't want anything to do with him.

She told him she was having her manager call the cops and that she had made a report of his attack upon her.

The man had tried to grab her arm but a friend from her work had held her. He had cursed her and told her it wasn't over and then drove away in his new van.

If Chill had waited ten minutes he would have been there to confront the men.

That night when the two were alone Chill confronted Liza Beth about the man.Girl, I know this man ain't some stranger or one night stand! I been around you long enough to know that this motherfucker is somebody you been fucking for awhile.

No! I promise he's not. He's nothing!

Bullshit! Just stop! It doesn't matter! What matters is I need to know everything you can tell me about this fucker so I can protect you from him! You're lying will only help him not us.

Can you not see by now you don't have to lie to me about this kind of shit!

Who is this motherfucker? And what does he mean to you?

She started to reply. He's nobody. I promise he means nothing. He's just some guy.

Chill laughed a crazy ironic cackle. Hah! We're all just some guy! Tell me the truth. Just say it! You know you want to. It ain't about to change anything between us. I love you even when you're not very lovable.

You're the one that always says you want it to be just you and me. Then you're the one that always cheats—first.

Chill was no saint he loved Liza Beth but he certainly didn't sit and wait on her.

The difference was when Chill fucked other women he did not start relationships with them. He kept things up front.He fucked them because she was not around. She was always number one for Chill.

He wished Liza Beth was capable of doing the same.

She just could not stand to be less than his everything.

She didn't share her toys.

Liza Beth finally conceded and told Chill some truth. He was very certain that her story was far from the entire truth but he could feel in the gaps.

Apparently while living with her boyfriend she had been working at some restaurant and had met "Mike" while at work.

She had been at the drive through and he had flirted with her.

He had asked her point blank if she got high and was interested in partying. It had been that easy.

Chill's blood turned to ice. He could not fathom how Liza Beth could just give away something he valued so much to a complete stranger.

The truth was it made it better for the pretty girl.   She got so tired of men treating her like gold.

So many girls bitched about where are all the nice guys? Liza Beth knew they were everywhere.

She made a specialty of finding guys that were obviously not up to her caliber.

They stepped all over themselves to please her. Whenever they caught her in a lie or cheating or whatever they told themselves what they needed to hear to keep her in their life.

A part of her loved giving herself to some nameless faceless stranger. She liked to fuck and it got her what she needed.

At heart, she was a very practical girl. She coaxed men to fall in love with her because that's what they wanted.

It also was the easiest way to get them to take care of her. It was a lot easier to have two or three "boyfriends" than to go out and hustle every day. She was young and beautiful and made sure they were taken care of, she owed them nothing. The truth was they were taking advantage of her as much as she was using them.

Chill agreed with the girl for the most part. The lying and deception tainted the arrangement.

Liza Beth in her youth and relative naivete did not realize that she could have maintained these same types of relationships with men and not lied. The payoffs may not have been as abundant and the girl did not like to share.

The man's name was Mike Cheri. She had met him at work .This had been the only time she had been to his house. Everything she had already told Chill about the attack was true.

The only thing she had left out was that she had already been involved with the man. Chill had already surmised that the man was no stranger.Liza Beth's story was convincing and consistent with what she had previously told him.

Chill needed to know the truth for his own sanity. He had a feeling this man was not just going to disappear. It seemed to Chill that Mr. Mike Cheri felt he was owed something. Chill felt he might be right.

Chill had sat and listened to Liza Beth's story. He had remained calm on the outside .Inside he was seething .He knew the girl had put herself in harm's way and that she had shown poor judgment. He also knew the man that had abused her had used her disease against her.

Whereas Chill loved and cherished the young girl this interloper saw her as an object to be used, abused and discarded if she became a liability. Liza Beth was lucky to be alive. Her own scheming and conniving had made her a perfect candidate to be murdered and thrown away like so much garbage.

Her entire relationship with this man had been a secret up to this point .He lived in a remote area about sixty miles from the city .No one knew she was with him or that he was linked in anyway with her.

That's if what she had told Chill was the truth. He really had no way of knowing. Her story indicated this was a recent relationship and that the man was some kind of abusive individual.

His showing up at her work indicated to Chill that the man was not finished with Liza Beth.It also made Chill inclined to believe the connection between the two was of a more intimate nature than Liza Beth had indicated. He knew Liza and knew how she operated. He knew that her talking about her family and especially her son usually happened when she was very comfortable and contented.

It was pillow talk the kind of conversation she indulged in when she had a good nod going and just after sex.

He could picture her lying in the crook of the man's arm her head tilted on his shoulder and chest. Her left hand would be holding a cigarette. The ash would be as long as the cigarette Her right hand would be cupping the ashtray lying on her stomach atop her nude body.

This scene pictured in Chill's mind hurt him deeply. She hadn't just given this stranger her body.

She hadn't traded some physical act for a night of drugs and money.She had shared "herself" she had given the essence of Liza Beth to this man.

It stripped away any pretense for Chill that somehow he was special to the girl. He meant no more to her than this man.

He was a resource, a backup plan.He had fallen for the hook just like the rube in the titty bar. He had told himself she loved him and was only with the other guys in order to feed her habit.

It hurt to realize these things but it really didn't change anything. Liza Beth's love for Chill may be a fiction but his love for her was real.

In the middle of her disease he knew she was probably incapable of loving anyone .He had known this when he met her .She had made no secret of being a heroin addict. He had been seven years sober and around drunks and fiends for most of his life.

He had seen she was up to no good and she had seen he was lonely and useful.

They had been perfect for each other.

Chill decided to suck it up. She might not love him but she was in his care. He loved her and there was someone out there who wished to harm her.

Chill at heart was a violent man. His every instinct told him to go and destroy this threat to the woman he loved.

The biggest problem was there now existed a link between Liza Beth and this Mike Cheri.She filed a report of the initial attack and then had filed an official report within the jurisdiction in which the attack had taken place.

Nothing had been done. The police were treating it as a domestic case.To them it was some dope fiend tramp had gotten upset with her sugar daddy.

If they went to the trouble of arresting the man more likely than not the girl would never testify against him.

Her being an addict made it even less a priority. Chill seemed to be the only person truly concerned. He was the person that still held Liza Beth in high esteem. No one else could see her value in the way he did.   For all intents and purposes the world considered her a throw away girl.She had no respect for herself or society. It was like to the world   she got what she deserved.

"What'd she expect?" was the unspoken statement.It was no accident that throughout history prostitutes and drug fiends had been targeted by rapists and killers.

Liza Beth the treasure of Chill's world was just another junkie to society.

Things between them had deteriorated. She had started lying and coming home later and later. He told her if she didn't come home at night she couldn't live with him.

The first night she didn't come home he put her stuff on the porch.

She called him and asked if he was serious. He had said yes.

Her   disrespect for him knew no boundaries. He had to be able to live with himself. He told her "if they can fuck you, they can feed you."

She had screamed back that he was just   like all the rest. He might say he loved her but when it came down to it he was just after the pussy like every other motherfucker.

She had concluded the exchange by telling him to take his AA and all his recovery bullshit and stick it up his ass.

She called later that day to tell him she had rented an apartment less than two blocks from his home.

He had asked why?

She had laughed and told him because I love you and I need you near.Chill's heart had raced but his good sense quickly told him that it was manipulation.

It was more likely that whoever she was fucking lived nearby and had encouraged her to rent the apartment.

A month went by and Liza Beth's behavior got worse and worse.She only stayed with Chill me or two nights a week.

She had started having very violent dreams and would wake up screaming.She had quit the fast food roast beef job. She had gotten her a job serving at some hillbilly joint.

Chill had worked for years as a bartender and knew most of the people that comprised her clientele.

She had tried to just drink but it hadn't lasted long. She was in full flight addiction and starting to be noticed by the police.

If Chill had ever doubted the disease concept of addiction he had doubts no longer.She was getting sicker right before his eyes. It broke his heart while at the same time it gave him hope. He had seen others do the same.

She was trying to "get done." She was turning herself over completely to her disease.She had stopped lying to Chill for the most part. He had caught her with other men and it had made no difference he still loved her.

One day she called hysterical. The Mike Cheri man had shown up at her job and was starting shit. She seemed more worried about losing her job than being harmed.Chill got her calmed down he picked her up from work and she spent the night in his arms.

The next day Chill started some deep soul searching. He was determined to protect Liza Beth.He had to inventory his mindset before going forward.

Did he truly believe Liza Beth to be in danger?

Was he seeking her approval or trying to carry favor? Was he wanting to get revenge?

In essence before he could take any action he had to determine that he was not acting out of his own self-interest.

At any other time faced with a decision of this magnitude Chill would consult Frank B or Pixie Skye.

Franky would make him break it down. Was he acting out of fear? What would his higher power do? Seek God in all your actions, etc.?

Pixie would be more practical. Is she lying? Are you certain this man is a threat? Can you live with your actions? Can you stay sober and live with your actions?

He asked himself all these questions. He prayed about it again and again. Several times he started to speak to his friends about what he was planning but could not. If he talked to them and then went through with his plan he would be making them complicit.

They would have to come forward or share in his guilt.

Chill knew facts were facts but that truth for an individual had more to do with belief. He not only asked himself if he could live and stay sober if he took action against Liza Beth's attacker.

He asked himself if he could live and stay sober if he did not take action.

He knew he could not protect her from herself but he was pretty certain that he could eliminate this one particular problem.

Once he had made a decision to take action he sought to do it in a way to cause the least harm!

Chill considered himself to be doing service work.

This man Mike Cheri had harmed someone Chill held dear. Liza Beth was probably not the first girl this man had harmed.

If he wasn't stopped, he would most likely harm other girls.

Chill was not scared to go to jail.

He knew if he did go to jail that people that loved and cared for him would be harmed and disappointed.

He did not want to harm these people so he would need to minimize his risk of being caught and prosecuted.

It had been about five weeks since Liza Beth had moved from Chill's home. Over three months had passed since the actual attack upon Liza Beth.

Mike Cheri continued to harass and pursue Liza Beth. He had called Chill's phone and left threatening messages. Chill had not responded in any manner. He had just pushed the button to disconnect.

He had been doing his research about Mr. Cheri. He knew he belonged to the Iron workers union and was a member in good standing. He knew the man's address from taking Liza Beth to file a restraining order against the man.

He had driven to the man's home on three separate occasions, always using a borrowed car. He had made sure not to stop at any local businesses near the man's residence and kept contact with people in the area to a minimum.

He had determined that Cheri was a small time dealer.   He sold a little pot but mainly pain pills and other prescription medication.

Liza had said that the man had told her he was connected with the local law enforcement. He had grown up with all the men   that were currently on stuff at the police department. The community was so small that Chill felt the man was probably telling the truth.

Apparently ; when high Cheri liked to brag. He had told Liza Beth a lot of interesting things. Chill had coaxed the information from her on various occasions. He had been careful to pose his queries into the man's affairs as needed information in order to be aware of any threat the man may pose.

When Liza Beth spoke of Mike Cheri, she always spoke with contempt and dislike in her voice. Chill did not think she was faking. He could sense she really disliked the man and feared him.

It seemed like some part of her felt that she deserved him in her life. It was as if he represented some dark penance for all the grief she had brought others.

The man had gotten into her head and fucked her up in a bad way.

He had told her she was a common whore and nothing but a junkie.

He was grooming her. He was using her own insecurities and drugs to undermine her self-worth and esteem. Removing her sense of self and replacing it with something weak and malleable.

The girl was young and short-sighted. Her only goals were to get high and stay high. The man was playing an entirely different game.

He was playing the long game. He was willing   to spend whatever money and time it took to own her.

His home was isolated most likely on purpose. If he could get her desperate enough to move into his home she would be totally dependent upon him.

Mike Cheri intended to make Liza Beth his very own sex slave. From what little contact and information Chill had with the man he had classified him as a paranoid redneck with abusive tendencies.

Whereas   Chill had taken great pains to not use Liza Beth's disease against her. Mike Cheri had no qualms about manipulating the girl with drugs and money.

Many people would say if she put herself out there like that she shouldn't be surprised when she gets paid back in kind.

To Chill the man was a predator and needed to be stopped. Liza Beth was no innocent. Chill knew she had gotten into a relationship with the man of her own free will.

Chill also knew that as young as she was there were a lot of things she didn't know or understand.

A girl of Liza Beth's beauty was a rare thing. Men like Chill and Mike Cheri might get a shot at a girl like that once or twice in a lifetime.

The youth and beauty; that Liza Beth took for granted and squandered so recklessly upon unworthy suitors, was a fleeting thing. She had no concept of her value to men such   as Chill and Cheri.

Chill knew in his own sick way that Mike Cheri was as obsessed with Liza Beth much like himself.

The difference was Chill had eleven years sober at this time and Cheri was still in active addiction. Chill could see the girl as a person. Her welfare and health were more important than his own selfish desires.

Cheri, in the midst of his own disease, could only see the girl as something to be conquered or destroyed. She was his bought and paid for. She had made promises in order to get what she wanted from him. It was time for her to pay what she owed.

Chill understood the mindset he had been around it his entire life. It seemed almost everyone had an agenda. If he got totally honest he guessed he also had one. As much as he loved Liza Beth, there was a part of him that resented her.

It irked him that she could place so little value upon his love. Her indifference and disrespect were like poison to his soul.

He knew in his heart that he had the option to walk away and if he chose to stay he could not blame her. Yes, there was a part of him that understood Mike Cheri very well.

A dark part of his own soul felt Liza Beth owed him something. It wanted her to feel the pain like she had made him feel the pain .But if he looked past the hurt there was a deeper truth.

He wanted her to love him to feel for him like she had said she did. He wanted the dream girl to be real. Mostly he wanted to be someone special to Liza Beth. He wanted to be as important to her as she was to him.

His friend Pixie had told him more than once that Liza Beth was his drug of choice.

She was his heroin. He wanted to be her drug of choice but knew it would never happen. Mike Cheri wanted to take a simpler tactic he would isolate and control the girl with drugs.

The big problem with Cheri's plan was Liza Beth's capacity for drugs far   surpassed his capacity to obtain drugs.

He wanted to manage the unmanageable.

On a cold Wednesday afternoon in February Chill decided to take action.

Liza Beth had called him frantic the previous Sunday. The Mike Cheri guy had shown up at her work.

He had threatened her in front of several of the bar's customers. A few Chill was sure she was fucking on a regular basis. He had been forced to leave but had not went quietly.

She was concerned that she might get fired if he kept showing up at her work. Chill thought she really underestimated the threat that the man represented.

As a result of Liza Beth telling Chill about the incident he hadn't been able to sleep.

What kind of man was he if he just sat around and waited for another man to abuse his woman? The fact was the motherfucker should already be dead for putting his hands on Chill's woman in the first place. Fuck the dumb shit! He needed to do something even if it was wrong.

If this fucker ended up hurting Liza Beth because he had been too chicken shit to do anything he would not be able to live with it.

He borrowed his brother's truck. Dell had been glad to loan it to him. He had tried to get him to sit and bullshit but he had told him he was pressed for time.

It was just after full dark when he arrived at a spot right above and behind Cheri's house. His house was situated at an angle on a small rise overlooking the highway. His nearest neighbor was about an eight of a mile down the road. Sound carried well in the country so Chill had decided not to use a gun unless it was a last resort.

There was a covered carport over a gravel driveway. The house was a rundown affair. It was a thrown together ranch made of brick and siding with a dog pen at the back.

There was no dog Chill had checked.

A neglected woodpile ran the length of the back of the house.

There was a building in the backyard that looked to be storage for some junk auto parts and old beer bottles. The place looked like it had been pleasant enough at one time but had fallen onto hard times.

Liza Beth had told Chill that Cheri had a brother but that they were mostly estranged.

There was an elderly lady that lived down the road that he got his pills from that was known to drop by on occasion.

For the most part the man was a loner. This was idea for what Chill had in mind.   The back door was a sliding glass type and pretty simple to circumvent. Chill had brought a tire iron to pop the door out of slot so he could gain entrance.

It hadn't been necessary The door hadn't even been locked.

This door opened onto a makeshift mudroom cluttered with work boots and various tools. The mudroom connected to the kitchen door which was locked.

Chill looked around the room for a minute and spied an old Folgers coffee can nestled neatly on a ledge.

The fact that the can was "placed" neatly among all the chaos made it peculiar.

On a hunch he picked it up. It was full of drywall screws but taped to the bottom was a set of three keys.

Chill noted that one looked like a house key, one a car key and one appeared to fit a padlock, probably to the outbuilding.

Chill tried the house key on the back door. It worked perfectly. He replaced the keys to the coffee can in case someone knew to look there later.

Chill wore a pair of old jersey work gloves. They were thin an available everywhere. He had considered wearing plastic gloves but when he used them at work they often tore.

He wondered how come on TV when people used   plastic gloves they never tore or shredded.

At this point, Chill was still undecided upon exactly what he was going to do to Mike Cheri. He was determined to render the man no longer a threat to Liza Beth. He had toyed with several ideas. He had considered castration but felt that it was likely to lead back to Liza Beth then to him. He knew a severe beating and a threat of more to come would not suffice.

He had dismissed the idea of crippling the man because it would cause hardship on whoever ended up   having to take care of him.

He was determined to cause a minimum of harm with this endeavor.

Chill had decided he had probably just better kill the man. It was the safest way to ensure   he would no longer be a threat.

It was also the least likely way to get caught.

He had struggled with the concern that Mike Cheri's death could cause hardship to others.

Were there people dependent upon him?

He had asked Liza Beth if he had any family. He did have a son that was grown. They hadn't spoken in years because of a fight over a wrecked car.

There was the brother but she had said they weren't close that Mike actually owed his brother money. She had said he had bragged about his home being paid for and that he didn't owe a dime on it.

A fire would endanger firefighters, so he had ruled that out.He had prayed for direction and the power to see God's will on the ride to Cheri's home.

He was confident a solution would reveal itself.

The house was warm on the inside. It was surprisingly neat.   Dishes   were washed and stacked neatly on a drain board. One coffee cup sat in the sink.

An automatic coffeemaker sat on the counter it looked as though it was programmed to make a pot of coffee at 9:30 pm.

It was almost 7:30 now. If Mike Cheri was a man of habit that gave Chill plenty of time to figure out the man's demise.

He looked into the refrigerator and noted a half-full fifth of Jack Daniels Old No. 7 and several long-necked Bud Lights.

Jack had been Chill's last drunk. Cheri had decent taste in liquor.

The woodpile not withstanding the house seemed to be heated with a combination of gas and electric. There was a woodstove in the front room but the room appeared to be rarely used. The furniture was old and worn. Some of the pieces looked older than the house.

There were very few pictures and the ones that were displayed were old. School pictures of children that were now in their forties.

An old black and white picture of a smiling couple hung over the covered fireplace.Chill touched his hand to the stove. It was cold.

Chill surmised that this room was seldom used. The inhabitant saw no reason to heat it.

Beyond the kitchen was a little room about eight foot by ten foot. It had probably been intended as a dining room.

The room contained a huge La-z-boy recliner, a small sofa and a large flat screen TV atop a five drawer chest of drawers.

A small end table sat beside the La-z-boy. It was cluttered with pill bottles and beer bottles. A small laptop computer resided upon a small coffee table in the center of the room. The room stank of cigarettes, whiskey and sweat.

This was ground zero. This was the room in which Mike Cheri spent his time.

Chill perused the pill bottles and started to get an idea. Beneath the La-z-boy, he found an old cigar box full of rolling papers and a quarter sack of weed. Several half-smoked joints were in the box along with about seven Lincoln logs Xanax bars.

The collection of pills on the end table had the labels mostly torn off but Chill was able to determine they were a mix of Percocet   fives, tens and a huge bottle of perc 30s that had to have at least a hundred pills.

Old Mike wasn't as small time as Chill had thought it seemed. On the coffee table beside the laptop were several huge scented candles and some incense. It was obvious to Chill these items had not been used recently.

The La-z-boy had a pocket on the side for books, magazines or whatever. Inside this pocket Chill found a wall maintained 38 Smith and Wesson. The gun was very old its handles worn smooth. It was fully-loaded, and the action of the trigger was smooth.

It was a nice weapon.

He knew Mike was a felon and briefly considered setting him up for a drug and gun charge. He discarded the idea because it depended upon too many factors and other people. If the man was arrested he had a home to put up for bond it would be months before any court date. He made good money and could probably buy his way out of any trouble.

Chill was determined to permanently neutralize this threat.

Underneath the TV in a drawer, Chill found a familiar item.

It was a small zippered bag. It had an Indian bead design on it and Chill would know it anywhere. He had given it to Liza Beth for her to put her makeup in. She had used it mostly to put her drug paraphernalia in.

He unzipped it and sure enough it contained all her "tools." There were five brand new hypodermic needles, the kind used by diabetics. Her contact case was in there. She used that to mix her dope in.

She would place a piece of heroin into the contact case squirt water onto it, break it up with the plunger side of the needles. She would then grab a   cigarette and rip a piece off the filter and use the cotton to strain the dope into the syringe.

A glass crack pipe was also in the case and at least three lighters. There also appeared to be two packages of dope.

One looked to be at least a gram. The other was probably a twenty.

Besides the two packets of heroin, there was a cigarette cellophane with a huge crack rock inside. It was well over a two-gram rock. There were some papers also folded up inside the beaded pouch.

Chill put everything back into the pouch and replaced it in the drawer.

It had been November when Liza Beth had been attacked by Mike Cheri. It was now the middle of February and Chill could recollect at least a dozen times that Liza Beth had had that beaded bag.

Something wasn't adding up and Chill was getting a very bad feeling about everything. It was possible that Mike Cheri had stolen Liza Beth's beaded bag without her knowing.

That was possible but there was no way   in hell that she lost her pouch with that much dope inside and didn't raise holy hell.

Chill had seen Liza hunt for thirty minutes for a lost piece of dope. She would dump everything out of her purse and search and search.

He had once had to drive her in the middle of the night to scour a parking lot for a lost packet of heroin. She had found it.

There was over three or four hundred dollars' worth of drugs in that pouch and no dirty needles. It was like it was waiting for her. Liza Beth had said that Cheri would smoke crack but that he didn't care for heroin. He would snort pain pills but he preferred to be wide awake.

She said he had a hard time coming on pain pills she could just imagine him trying to get off on heroin.

Something was very wrong here. Chill was almost at the point of leaving. He knew if he didn't follow through with his plan tonight he never would.

He sat on the edge of the couch and tried to think.His mind raced with different scenarios. None were good.

He stopped and took a deep breath and said a small prayer to himself. God show me something, anything, so I know what to do.

It was at this point the phone rang. It scared Chill at first because he wasn't expecting it.After a couple rings, the voicemail answered the call.

A female voice came on the phone and the rest of Chill's world crashed around him.

It was. Liza Beth's voice.

"Hey Daddy, can't wait to see you tonight. I'm not sure if I work the bar till close or not. Call me and let me know if you got everything on my 'list.' Ha ha," she laughed sweetly. "Love you, baby, it's been too long."

The wind left Chill's chest.

The treacherous whore was still fucking this motherfucker!

Here he was at the fuckheads   house about to murder the cocksucker because he was a threat to Chill's poor sweet Liza Beth.

Chill started to lose control but his years of recovery had taught him anger was for other men. He had been taught to "pause when agitated" to use reason when overwrought with emotion.

After about five minutes of just breathing and trying not to think Chill regained some 'semblance of composure.

He did a mental checklist of his situation.

He was here to stop Mike Cheri from causing Liza Beth more harm. Liza Beth had lied to him and mislead him about her relationship with Mike Cheri.

The man was using Liza Beth's disease against her in order to manipulate and use her sexually.

Chill had to reflect a hard moment at this point.

Didn't he himself do the same thing? He may love Liza Beth and want the best for her but would she be with him if she was clean and sober?

When he had met her she had been sober and had moved in with him. He had no delusions about her reasons for moving in with him at the time.

It was convenience pure and simple. It got her out of her parent's house and got everyone off her back.

Chill had been around long enough to know that the girl was most likely going to use again. She had reservations a plenty. Chill had evaluated her sincerity to himself. He had come to the conclusion that not only was she not done she really hadn't gotten started.

He looked at her youth and beauty and the ever-present challenge in her eyes.

She was not a timid   girl. He liked that.

She looked him in the eye when he asked her what was her drug of choice.

She had replied heroin as though now what.

Do you still want to play?

Chill was old school and knew not to underestimate anyone.

He had looked right back into those eyes and without saying a word they had come to an agreement.

Chill wanted her in his life he knew if he turned his back upon this opportunity he would regret it his entire life. A girl like her was an adventure whatever pain and heart-break that she may cause in his life would be a price he was willing to pay.

Chill had told himself he may not have her in his life long but he would make every moment count.

There was a difference between Chill and Cheri.

Chill loved Liza Beth with all her flaws.

His love was real and true and did not depend upon her behaving in any certain manner.

He realized due to the depths of her addiction that she was at this time incapable of loving anyone.

He just like Cheri was a resource. Someone to manipulate and facilitate her using.

That's a hard pill to swallow when you love someone.

It may be hard but it was true. Chill could not afford to let sentiment or emotion hold sway over his actions.

The girl was in danger from Mike Cheri.

The girl's biggest danger was herself. Chill could not protect her from herself but Mike Cheri was a problem he could eliminate.

He knew that at best it was a short-term solution. There would just be another guy like Cheri once Cheri was out of the picture.

Liza Beth liked to get men to make her their everything. She wanted them to worship her. She despised herself and sought self-worth through the eyes of others. She needed that validation.

Mike Cheri was obsessed with her to the point of distraction. This admiration fueled her ego and his money fueled her drug habit. She was incapable of seeing the inherent danger in the situation.

At some point, Cheri's money and resources would run out and Liza Beth would move on to the next man.

The problem that she was unaware of is that once you make yourself a man's everything, he's going to be a little pissed when you try to go away.She would be taking with her the only thing he valued.

Deep down Chill knew she didn't love him and was using him .His own self-hatred and loathing made him think   he probably deserved no better. He knew their relationship was based on lies and two people using each other.

Cheri saw Liza Beth as a lying, cheating, junkie, whore out to use him up and throw him away.

She was like a drug for him and no matter how much he hated and despised himself he wanted her.

Her false words and promises along with her delicate youthful beauty were as close as he would ever know of love.

Chill understood this man to the depths of his soul for he felt many of these same things.The key difference between the two men was Chill's long term practicing the principles of recovery.

He knew he was responsible for his own actions and emotions.Whether Liza Beth's love for him was real or not, Chill had to be honest.

When he told her he loved her, it was real.He could not afford to take her disease personally.

She did not lie and cheat and fuck other men to hurt Chill. She did these things because they helped her get drugs. She probably never even thought of Chill until she needed him.

When she had looked in his eyes and said, "I'm a heroin addict." She might as well have said that.

"I am a heroin addict and I will use you to further my addiction for that is what I do.

"Are you willing to accept the fact that I love nothing and my disease will take everything from me and those around me?"

Chill had understood that statement without it being said. He had never thought Liza Beth would have stayed in his life this long. He had thought her disease would have taken her far away from him.

One thing was still true Chill loved Liza Beth even the sick, twisted, deceitful whore she could become in the midst of her disease.

It didn't matter how she treated him he still loved her. At times he despised himself and wanted to die. He had often contemplated suicide but realized it was self-pity and would not change Liza Beth.

He wanted her to feel something for him. The reason he could ignore the cheating and lying was because he knew she didn't care for any of these men.

The fucked up thing   was a part of him felt she didn't care anymore for him than she did for them.

He had come to this house with the intent of killing Mike Cheri to protect Liza Beth from Mike Cheri.

Chill was no longer sure that that was the truth. Was he protecting Liza Beth or was he protecting his own self-interest.

For some reason, Liza Beth kept Chill in her life he was some type of anchor for her.

She would never let Chill know she needed him because that would give him power.

Outside the house Chill could hear a car pulling into the driveway. He glanced out the window and could see his target.

Mike Cheri was about Chill's age but looked older. His hair was uncombed, and he was unshaven.

He worked construction and his clothes were that of a working man. Jeans, T-shirt with company name on pocket, steel toed boots and a large battered plastic lunchbox in his left hand and a case of Miller Lite in his right.

That decided it for Chill. The prick drank Miller products. Chill decided the man had no redeeming qualities. None.

Chill hadn't drank in years but had never been able to stomach Miller products and had low opinion of those that did. He would rather drink falls city or strohs or even weidemenn.

Chill picked up a large scented candle from a lamp table beside the couch. It was encased in glass and covered with dust. Most likely a relic from Mother Cheri. Ol' Mike didn't seem like the type to frequent bed bath and beyond or peir one.

He knew Liza Beth would never spend money on candles when that same money could be applied to dope. She was a practical girl.

Cheri's arrival made Chill's indecisiveness vanish. He was committed to his course of action. If Cheri seen him and lived he would have no trouble identifying the intruder in his home. Chill's size alone would let Cheri know his identity.

Chill's plan had been to subdue the man and then make his death look like an accident. He decided this would work but Liza Beth's voice on Cheri's answering machine inspired him to slightly alter his original course of action.

Cheri stepped into the door he was whistling and had a joint hanging from his lip.

He placed the lunchbox on the kitchen counter by the sink coughed and spat into the sink opened the fridge placed the case of beer inside ripped into the box pulled out a can and opened it. He drank a good six swallows while holding the joint in his left hand. He pulled the beer from his mouth, let out a belch that lasted at least four seconds.

Chill almost laughed but contained himself.

Cheri tilted the can back to his mouth and finished it. He threw it into the sink and grabbed another he popped the top but did not drink. He placed the joint in his mouth and drew from his pocket a bic lighter he lit the joint took a big hit and chased it with another drink. He turned toward the living room and the hallway that let to the bedrooms and bathroom.

Chill was standing just beside the doorway in the hallway.

When Cheri stepped through the door, he was taking another long hit. His eyes were half-closed as he inhaled deeply.

Chill never hesitated an instant he was right-handed by nature but the way they were positioned forced him to swing the heavy glass candle with his left.

Cheri's eyes briefly flashed with recognition before the heavy glass cylinder connected with his forehead.

Chill put the whole force of his enormous frame behind the blow.

He had hit the unsuspecting Cheri between the eyes. The wall behind him and the doorway had caught him.

He hadn't fallen and this had confused Chill for a moment. Chill had been putting men to sleep with his bare hands since he was sixteen. It was highly unlikely Mike Cheri was still conscious.

The top part of the candle had exploded in a shower of glass and wax Chill held in his hand a good eight-inch piece that weighed a pound.

He swung this and hit the man again in approximately the same place. The man continued to stand.

His eyes had rolled back into his head but he was still standing. Chill looked closer and realized that the man's enormous chain keyring was wrapped around the door knob and that this was keeping him from falling. His body was slack and his pants were pulled way up to one side by the force of the pressure being applied just as he noticed the door latch gave way. It wasn't a knob but a lever type latch that went up and down. It sprang off the door hitting Chill in the arm and left a large red indentation.

When Chill looked down at his arm, he noticed his hand was bleeding. The candle had seemed like the perfect club. It had been over two-foot long and probably weighted six to eight pounds.

Chill hadn't considered that the impact would cause the candle to break and cut him.

As his adrenaline faded, he noticed his arms and face were peppered with minute cuts from the shrapnel produced by the impact.

The first blow had not caused much in the way of debris but the second had caused major havoc.

Fuck it! Chill thought it's too late to worry about it now.

He figured if   he ever got in this situation again he would bring his own weapon. Ha!

Cheri was lying half in the kitchen and half in the hallway. He was on his side and blood was pooling under his head. He was bleeding in torrents. Chill was no stranger to head wounds, having had at least seven concessions over the years,   he   knew the man was still alive. It took a beating heart to pump blood.

Head wounds bled a lot but were not usually serious.

Chill doubted the blows had caused any permanent harm. He almost left at this point but he knew that Cheri had seen him. It may have been the briefest of glances but Chill had seen the man's eyes focus with recognition right as he had swung the candle.

It was okay he had never intended to kill the man with the candle. He had always planned to make the man's death appear like overdose.

He would continue with this as his plotted course.He had decided to make some adjustments to his original plan.

Liza Beth's phone call to Mike Cheri had given Chill an idea.She wanted to spend time with Mr. Cheri well Chill was gonna help her with that.He had taken the beaded bag and Mike Cheri's phone. He quickly sent her two texts. She was working at the bar, but he knew she would leave early with the right motivation.

The first text was from Cheri's phone telling her he would be late picking her up probably around three and to not be mad because he had everything on her list.

The second text he sent from his phone telling her he wanted her to come over that he had a present for her.

She responded in about five minutes saying she was at work why didn't he just drop it off. He had anticipated this and replied with I just ran into an opportunity and made some money. I also found something of yours that I know you want very much.

It took about fifteen minutes but his text had done the trick his phone rang.

Hey, baby. I t was Liza Beth. I'd love to come over but I'm not feeling well. I need to get right.Chill was not opposed to giving Liza Beth money but he hated taking her to get dope and she knew this.

He told her don't worry I found something that will make you feel better. I got dog, hard and cash

Liza Beth's response was electric. Oh yea! Damn, baby, what'd you do? Rob a dope man?

Chill laughed and told her fucking A! and if you want in on it, you better get over here quick.

She hesitated briefly. Okay, I can be there in thirty, but I can't stay, I got a meet later it's real important.

Chill chuckled. Whatever you know me. It won't take me long to get what I need but once you get what I got I doubt you leave anytime in the near future.

Alright, I'll be right there. Love you, baby!

I know you do, girl! Right now you love the hell out of me.

Chill's plan was simple he would let Liza Beth get high and once she was properly incapacitated he would implement phase two of his diabolical plot.

Although greedy for drugs, Liza Beth was not without suspicion about Chill's readiness to supply her with drugs.

He had often given her money and even taken her to score upon occasion. Mostly to keep her with him. He did not like to do these things and often warned her how these actions could poison what was true and honest in their relationship.

He told her "if you ever get sober, I will probably be one of the people you have to cut out of your life."

She had laughed, "that's crazy you got nine years clean and you do this shit for real." She was talking about recovery.

He had said that doesn't matter to your disease if you keep using me as a way to get high and I keep enabling you because I'm scared to lose you it will just make it impossible for me to be part of your recovery because I'm too much a part of your disease.

She was like dope for him he had lost the power of choice and would accommodate her to make that day go well even if it meant jeopardizing any future together.

This would become a pattern.

When she had arrived at his house and seen what he had for her, she had voiced her concerns.

What's up? Why do you have this? Were did you get it? Why do you have it?

Chill responded, "What's the matter? You don't want it? I can take it back."

No! You know I want it but what about recovery and having a future together you always said that if you ever started using drugs to control me that it would ruin our chances of being together when I got sober.

Ah fuck! I don't know. I say a lot of shit and I believe most of it. I don't know what's going to happen more than anybody else. Shit I don't even know myself.

Hell I might be high tomorrow and I never expected you to stick around this long. Plus the way you get high you may not get sober.

Well, thanks! That's a fucked up thing to say.

Chill had tried to be light hearted but the nights events and the young beautiful girl's betrayal weighed heavy upon him.

Do you want this shit or not? You want to hang out with me or do you want to meet your friend?

Quit being a dick! I'm here, right?

Well you don't act like you much want to be I got everything you want right in front of you and instead of thank you Chill I love you Chill all I get is why.

Fuck, I don't know   why maybe cause I give up I don't know I'd like to hit that pussy it's been a while and you know I get a little mean when I ain't had none.

Liza Beth laughed, "Calm down, big boy. I got you. Don't worry about that! You kill me the way you fiend for pussy. Let me go in the bathroom for a minute and get right and I will be right back. I been needing some decent head and I know you can hook me up!"

Hell yea! Chill responded. Sucking Liza Beth's pussy was probably Chill's favorite thing in life. He loved fucking the beautiful girl but when he ate her out was when he felt most needed and alive.

The long-term heroin use often interfered with her having an orgasm but he could eat her for hours keeping her in a sexual coma. She told him that he ate pussy better than anyone.

He wondered if she lying but thought maybe on this point she was telling the truth.

Sex between the two had always been good they shared a common goal they both wanted her to be satisfied. Chill loved the girl to distraction and her body was to him a shrine a place of worship.

She was every centerfold of his youth come alive.

She grabbed the dope and her purse and belt and headed toward the bathroom. He hadn't given her a little piece of the crack but a large chunk of the heroin.

He knew the heroin was strong because he had given Mike Cheri a shot before he had left his house.

He had duct taped the man to a kitchen chair and noticed he was regaining consciousness.

The man was hurt bad probably had brain damage.

Chill had no idea how much to give the man and figured it didn't matter he wanted him dead; so now or later it didn't matter.

He had injected the man in the back of his hand because he hadn't wanted to fuck around with trying to find a vein in his arm.

Chill had been around enough to know a lot of fiends fired into their hands.

He wasn't sure if Cheri was left-or right-handed, but he had fired into his left.

Chill watched a lot of crime shows and was worried about leaving forensic evidence.

He thought about it a minute and laughed! Ain't nobody gonna give a fuck if this asshole shows up dead.

There won't be no investigation cause nobody will care.

Just another dead dope fiend good riddance.

From all the information Chill could gather on the man he had very little family, just a brother that he was semi-estranged from. Liza Beth had told him the man had dealings with the local law but that he wasn't real well liked.

Cheri made most of his friends with drugs and cash.

Chill figured Liza Beth was probably not the first girl Cheri had raped or abused but he was determined to make her the last.

He had injected the man once then waited and injected him twice more in the same hand. He wanted it to look like a drug binge.

He hadn't figured out how to make the bruised bloody face look like an accident but a plan was forming.

Once Liza Beth had returned from bathroom they had "made love" or had sex.

Once Chill had orgasmed, the girl had tried to make a call and had gotten no response. She had texted and again retired to the bathroom.

While she was in the bathroom, Chill checked Cheri's phone.

Sure enough, she had sent the man a message.

Hey, I might be a little late, is that cool?

Chill sent back "No problem, I had to work till   two I will pick you up in the morning and then we will have all day to play."

"Awesome. I can't wait. Did you get everything?"

Chill responded, "I got everything and more. Don't you worry."

"Great! I love you, Daddy!"

"I love you, baby girl!"

Chill burned at the nerve of the little tramp.His sperm still hot inside her she made plans to be with another man.He   again   realized he meant nothing to her and that his love meant nothing to her.

For the first time, he could remember he hated her.

He hated the part of her that could so casually dismiss his love, loyalty, and sacrifice as something inconsequential.

Logic left the man. The twelve steps and a spiritual answer were not available to him for the first time since he had gotten sober.Anger and self-pity had overcome love and devotion.

He became determined to make her see him as having value and worth. He wanted power over her like she possessed over him.

His plans for Mike Cheri started to take a new and more deliberate form.

Over the next three hours, he plied the young girl with sex and dope. Finally, she lost consciousness. He knew once she passed out she would be out for hours.

He knew she wouldn't remember the last two hours she was awake. Her drug use had a distinct pattern once she got to a certain level of intoxication she started talking about her childhood and how she had been cheated of being a child.

She had three stories she told over and over when really high. She never remembered telling them.

Chill never minded her at these times because she was always very accommodating to him sexually when in this state.

He knew he should feel bad for taking advantage of her at these times but he didn't.

He used her for his own gratification and often it was their best sex. She would become hornier and hornier right up until she faded out. Sometimes she would pass out before he finished and he would just hold himself inside her and study her beauty.

He would gaze upon her face and marvel at her beauty.

He realized of the two of them he was probably the far sicker person. Liza Beth had the excuse of being on drugs. Chill at this time was coming up on a decade sober.

He also knew addiction and alcoholism were progressive and although sober his disease was still present.

At forty-four years-old, he had had a lot longer to get this sick.

Once Liza Beth had lost consciousness Chill had dressed her in sweets and a cotton tee   shirt. He had carried her to this car. Driven to where he had parked the "loaner" car and driven back to Mike Cheri's house.

He had carried Liza Beth to Mike Cheri's bedroom taken off her clothes and put her into Cheri's bed naked he had gotten undressed and laid down beside her. He stroked her body seeking arousal. Liza Beth had responded and Chill had gotten inside her but was not able to complete the act. He had already shot twice that night and just didn't have a third.

Liza had seemed to float in and out of consciousness and Chill hadn't been concerned. It wouldn't be strange for her to remember him fucking her and he doubted she had any idea of her surroundings at present time.

When he went to check on Mike Cheri he   had been surprised to find the man still breathing. Although shallow the man did indeed still breathe.

He had fallen over and struggled one leg was free from the tape and he had apparently thrown up.

Chill removed the tape placing it in a garbage bag he also removed the clothes the man was wearing.

Chill retrieved the bottom portion of the candle and placed it in the bed with Liza Beth. He placed Mike Cheri beside her and fixed up another shot. This on he made very large obviously on overdose. He injected the man and waited. It didn't take long. The man convulsed once then again and went rigid then limp.

Chill waited fifteen minutes than checked for a pulse. There was none the man was at last dead.

Liza Beth was no longer in danger from this man.Chill had brought Liza Beth's purse and clothes all the items she had brought to his house with her.

He placed the beaded pouch with the remaining drugs on the night stand beside her.He took her hands and soaked them in Cheri's blood and smeared it upon her body.He placed Cheri halfway on the floor half on the bed as though he had convulsed out of bed.

He placed Cheri's phone on the night table after sending one more text to Liza's phone telling her he would be picking her up in ten minutes and her reply "k" Chill was not worried about any of these things being investigated everything would be taken at face value.

Chill retrieved Cheri's wallet, belt and keychain from his pants. He put the keychain and belt on another pair of pants that he retrieved from the dirty clothes basket at the end of the hallway. He threw the pants onto the floor but left another pair of boots inside them.

He placed the boots Cheri had been wearing into the garbage bag with the duct tape and work clothes covered in blood.

The wooden kitchen chair would also go with Chill it just could not be explained.

Chill took the money from Cheri's wallet and put it inside the beaded bag on the table beside Liza Beth's spoon and needle.

He quickly left the house because it was getting near daylight and he wanted to get away before anyone noticed the car he was driving. Cheri had lived in a small community and somebody just might take note.

He had been able to return the loaner car and retrieve his own and had returned home to wait for Liza Beth's call.

Chill's world changed drastically after the killing of Mike Cheri. Some of the changes he had expected; others he had not anticipated.

Chill knew that his relationship with Liza Beth would be altered by the events of that fateful night. His decision to go through with Cheri's murder had been about protecting her.

Once Chill had discovered Liza's treachery; of still seeing the man, Chill's resolve had strengthened but his original purpose had become divided.

His actions were no longer purely altruistic. Liza Beth's betrayal had hurt him. Hurt his heart, his pride, and his ego.

He had wanted to punish her to make her feel something for him. He wanted her to need him and to have power over her. He had figured that upon awakening Liza Beth would observe the carnage around her and surmise that she was in a world of shit.

Chill had reasoned that the girl would panic and call him to come get her and rescue her from her circumstances. He had waited all day and she never called. He began to worry. What if she had called 911 trying to save Cheri? Maybe she had been arrested?

Could she have overdosed herself and Chill not have noticed? Was he to blame for two deaths?

He tried calling her but her voicemail was full. It was always full. Dope fiends always screened calls.

The phone was their main tool for getting high. Since the advent of cellphones no one knew phone numbers except dope fiends. Chill knew at least five girls that could recite a half-dozen phone numbers after only hearing them a couple times.

Liza Beth could catch numbers with ease and keep them and discard them at will.

No she hadn't called that first day nor the next. On the third day, his phone rang and it was her.

Hey baby, I'm at the gas station down by your house, can I come hang out?

Chill was overwhelmed with relief and confused.

Liza, baby, where you been? Of course, come on over. Shit I been worried to death.

Oh, baby, it's cool. I'm fine I'll be there in a minute.

Chill's mind was racing.

What the fuck? The last time that Liza Beth was conscious she had been at Chill's house.

She should have questions on how she wound up at Mike Cheri's home. Chill decided he would just wait and see what the girl said and work from that.

The funny thing was Liza Beth acted exactly the same way she had always acted. She never made mention of the events that had occurred on the previous Saturday night.She seemed totally unaffected and nonplussed.

Chill wanted to shake her and ask her what had happened after she had awakened in that room of death.

How did she get away? Who had she called? Did she think she had killed Mike Cheri?Did she think his death an accident? Did she suspect Chill in any way?

He could not ask any of these questions.

To do so would be to admit guilt or at the very least involvement. As far as Liza Beth knew Chill had no idea that Mike Cheri was still a part of Liza Beth's world. For him to inquire about the man would be very suspect.

Chill tried to be as normal as Liza Beth appeared.

He asked her if she was hungry or tired and if she needed anything.

The girl responded.

"I could eat but baby what I really need is some money. Not a lot just like maybe forty dollars. Chill had started to protest but stopped he knew that if he refused she would leave and he wouldn't see her until she had gotten what she needed and maybe not even at that time.

Okay, sure, but what's in it for me? I haven't seen you in days and all you want is money if I give it to you are you coming back?

Yes! Shit, I will take care of you now   I will only be gone as long as it takes me to get right!

If you can do sixty, I will stay the night. Baby, I've missed you. I really have! It's been rough the last couple of days.

Chill said okay. Here's eighty; get what you need but I don't want you leaving again tonight.I love you, Baby! The beautiful girl leaped in to his arms.

If you give me a ride, it won't take near as long.

Chill drew the line. No! You know I hate that. I got to be able to live with myself.

Okay! Okay! Chill! Chill! Ha ha, that's funny, Chill. Please, Chill. No, baby, I'll be right back. She grabbed the money and started to head for the door.

Aren't you forgetting something?

What's that baby?

You said you would take care of me now and then come back for the night.

Oh? Yeah, no problem. Can you make it quick? Please? I'm starting to get a little sick.

Chill felt like a shit fucking her when she didn't feel well but he knew that there was always a chance she wasn't coming back that day.

She might have trouble scoring and be gone hours she might find a better offer and be gone for days.She might buy the wrong shit and die. Better get it while it could be got.

It was hard to love a dope fiend but Chill couldn't help himself. Despite all the lies, deceit and general bullshit he loved Liza Beth and he tried to make every moment count.

He knew each time he saw her could be his last so he tried to treasure their time together. She may be a junkie addict and a throw away girl to the rest of the world, but to Chill she was his everything.

He still saw her as the beautiful young girl that had so freely given of her heart and soul when they had first met.

She had read him her poetry and shown him her room.

She had shared her dreams and trusted him with her fears in that trusting unguarded way belonging only to the young.

She had been a temptress and a seductress while maintaining an innocence.

She thought herself so wise in the ways-of-the world and Chill had taken great care not to abuse or misuse her.

He had fallen hard for her and thought that she would only be in his life for a short time. She was too magnificent to stay his for long.

He had been determined to see her all he could and to love her the best he could.

He had devoured her body and her youth. Drinking them in like a starving man. Trying to store memories to last him a lifetime for when she was gone.

That had been seven years ago and those habits remained and he was glad. He realized that no matter what had happened in his life he had no regrets about loving this young girl.

To Chill his love for Liza Beth had been his most worthwhile pursuit. Truest to his heart and his nature.

He was not an easy man nor a very nice one. He possessed a strong sense of integrity and lived by a personal code.He knew that Liza Beth at this point in her life was incapable of loving anyone. She was sick physically and morally and spiritually bereft. He also believed that there existed a bond between the two of them that transcended all these things.

He was "all in" whether wrong or right. When if came to Liza Beth there would be no half-steping.

He had killed for her and now came the hard part. He would have to learn to live with that killing.

Chill knew if he was going to be of any use to Liza Beth he would have to find a way to stay sober as well as alive.

Liza Beth had taken care of Chill that day and she had quickly returned.They spent the day together and it had been good. Sometime in the night Chill had awaked to find the bed beside him warm but the girl missing.

He had gotten up to piss and seen a soft glow in the other bedroom. Liza Beth was sitting in the dark smoking a cigarette.

Chill approached her and spoke softly sensing the girl was in distress.

Baby girl, you alright?

Yeah, baby, I guess I'm okay, just sitting here thinking how bad I fucked my life up and how many good people I done shit on and wishing I could just die or get desperate enough to want to get better.

You know—the same ol' shit! Ha ha!

As she spoke the last words and gave a little lilting chuckle, her voice broke and Chill could hear her trying not to cry.

He knelt beside her and cradled her in his arms.

Liza, baby, he whispered in her ear. I love you with all my heart.

She had laughed a sad half sobbing laugh. "I know you do but why? I mean, how the fuck can you love me? I hurt everyone and everything I touch. I fuck people over to get dope every day then I hate myself and to keep from thinking about it I have to do more dope which means fucking over more people."

Chill smiled and held her close. Baby, you're almost there.

What?

You're almost there. You're at that point they talk about in the "Big Book" where they talk about "not being able to imagine a life with or without alcohol" but in your case drugs and alcohol.

"The jumping off point it's called."

So now what do I do?

Well, it's been my experience and the book talks about it. "You will either seek out and experience some sort of spiritual help or go on to the bitter end." Which the book says is jails, institutions, and finely death.

You just said dying would be better than to keep living the way you're living.

It seems to me you're not getting much relief from the dope anymore.

What do I do? Chill, I don't want to live like this. I really don't I hate myself so much sometimes and sometimes I hate you for loving me.

I know.

It'd be so much easier if you would just give up on me and not love me so much.

Chill didn't know what to say he had never considered his love for Liza Beth a burden for her but he was instantly able to grasp her meaning.It was like an unwanted responsibility she didn't want to disappoint him. She wanted to be worthy   of love.

Chill tried to explain his heart but lacked the words. He wasn't sure he understood himself.

His love for her had transcended pride and ego.

His love was not based upon merit or her actions.

He loved her simply for all that she was and all that she wasn't.

He took care not to let her disease control both their lives. He continued to take the actions that treated his own alcoholism and addiction.

He tried to hold himself accountable and was the most part successful.

He had given into resentment fear and rage during the Mike Cheri incident. These "character defects" had caused him to take an event that was entered upon with the intention of protecting Liza Beth; and instead using them to manipulate and control her.

He had wanted her to need him to shield her from a lie he created.

However sick and twisted she may have become, she had done nothing to him as low as this one act. He wanted to confess to her the events of that night but knew he could not.

It was not out of fear of consequences for he knew that learning to live with the lie he created was going to be a far more daunting task than facing the truth.No, he would not use that night's events as a way to control the love of his life.He would instead seek to use that tragic set of circumstances as a launching point for Liza Beth's redemption.

The solution remained the solution and there was no reason for it to fail them.

Baby, Chill whispered to the sad desperate beautifully young girl.

Pray, just pray. Open your heart and let whatever power that guides the universe enter your heart.

I try, baby, but I don't know what to say.

That's the easy part, baby. The best prayers don't have any words. Just open your heart to be filled.

Seek guidance only in the sense of doing the next right thing and serving the will of the divine spirit.

Chill, you told me you don't believe in God!

No, baby, I said I don't believe in the God that people have handed me all my life.

I believe there exists a commonality among everything. A thread that connects everything. I believe that science and religion are not at odds with each other.

There are patterns in nature that repeat themselves on all planes. The smallest atom follows the same principles as our galaxy.

With the sun being a nucleus and planets being protons and neutrons.

Out galaxy could be one speck on the fingernail of a being so large that it doesn't even acknowledge our existence.

But that being exists on anther galaxy on anther fingernail.

God is everything and everyone. Prayer works just like gravity. It is an action taken.

I believe that prayers are answered but that the universe is an expedient bitch and never wastes effort.

A person prays to want to get off drugs the universe hears that prayer.

Now for a person to want to stop doing something the pain of continuing has to be more than the relief of stopping.

Now addiction has the added measure of obsession so normal consequences may not apply. The universe nevertheless hears the yearning of the addict and bam!

Arrested

Jails detoxes   more people than anyone.

Chill, I don't want to go to Jail.

Baby, you keep going like you are there will come a time when jail seems like the only safe place.

THAT FUCKING SUCKS! I'm not praying for that.

Chill laughed. Chill, baby, I told you to pray with an open heart. Quit being the director. Just seek solace and spiritual succor.

Quit trying to use prayer as a leash to make God answer to your commands.

Work with the spirit of the universe seek harmony not discord.

Damn, Chill, where do you come up with all this shit?

I don't know.

When I first got sober I was told to seek a God of my understanding.

Well, I read a bunch of stuff and I noticed some things.

Most religions, prophets, whatever had simple guidelines for living most were similar in nature.

The formation of religion itself seemed to be for divisive purposes. A way of segregating people in order to justify abusing them.

How so? The girl inquired.

Well in all religions there seems to be an us and them component.

The chosen and the non-believers—now that seems more like a man-made concept.

If I am one of the chosen and you are not I can do whatever I want to you and God won't mind. Hell, if I do it in his name I can murder you and rape you and enslave you and it will be for his glory.

I know that's an over-simplification of the way religion works.

I know billions of people have lived and prospered by following the tenants of various religions.

The way I see it people want God handed to them. They want someone else to think about the nature of God to figure it out and then hand it to them.

For me a spiritual relationship with God of *my* understanding is the most vital and critical process I will undertake. I do not want someone else to establish that connection for me.

If I'm wrong, I take full responsibility for my beliefs and I try not to force them on anyone.

My higher power has no problem with others having their own concept of God.

People afraid to think and believe for themselves make easy targets for those that have no qualms about pursuing their own agendas in the name of salvation.

For me kind people seem to be happy people and most in tune with the nature of the universe.

Grateful people seem to be happy. If I want to be happy and free from jealousy and resentment, I seek to be like these people.

I don't know if works for me at least so far it does.

Liza Beth, the way I see it, it's simple. The big book says that all our problems come from self.

Alcoholics by nature are selfish and self-centered. We are never satisfied. No matter how many good things we have we always want more.In order to change that all we have to do is be unselfish and grateful.

Ha ha, fuck you! How the fuck am I supposed to be grateful when all I want to do is die.

You know that sucks for you that you can't find anything in your life worthy of gratitude.

The strange part is you are the person in my life that I consider my greatest blessing.

Bullshit! Chill, I know I've broken your heart a dozen times.

I've seen you cry over me.

I remember you telling me you wanted to die when you found out I was living with Bryan.

That's all true, Liza Beth. Every one of those things is true.

That's the paradox of love. You are the source of my greatest pain as well as God's greatest gift.

That pain and my living through that pain made me stronger.

All the spiritual growth involves pain, loss, redemption, forgiveness, and finally gratitude. At least it has in my life.

You are the biggest treasure in my life and as a result when you are not in my life it's like a part of me is missing.

I'm not trying to make you feel like you owe me anything when I say that.I love you and it's not something that's going to stop anytime soon.

I know more about you then anyone more than you know and I love you.

Chill, stop! Okay? I got it you love me and I guess I know that but it's hard for me to trust love. Love gets you hurt. Love makes people weak.

I know baby girl love is your biggest weapon. You make people love you at the drop of a hat.

You got the gift of beauty and charisma. You become their everything.

Once they love you though you lose interest. The game is making them fall in love but you walk away once they do.

You ever wonder why?

Why what, baby?

Why you walk away or lose interest once you get someone to fall in love with you.

Never much thought about it. I guess I just get bored.

Well, I've put some thought into it and I've got a theory.

Do you want to hear my theory?

Sure, I always love to hear you break shit down it makes me sleepy.

Oh! Ha ha ha, I put you to sleep. I think I'm offended.

No, you're not, and that's one reason I love you. You know I meant that you calm me enough that I can sleep. You're about the only person that can.

Funny you should say that because it plays along with my theory.

When you meet someone that ignites that spark of interest in you it's usually unexpected.

I've noticed you can read people very well and assess their vulnerable areas and their strength.

Within moments you have them at ease because you are beautiful yet you will suck them in with self-deprecating remarks that are totally honest.

Beauty and honesty are how you get people to fall in love with you.

You give so freely of yourself while you are getting them to reveal their souls.

The only problem is once you've told them about yourself and they've fallen deeply madly in love, they become boring.

Relationships become work and you are no longer the star. If you get with someone you have to share the spotlight.

You love people falling in love with you, not the responsibility of being in love.

The reason we get along so well is we both like having you as the center of attention. I fall in love with you again and again. Sure you get bored with me but not like everyone else. They fell in love with the presentation and then became disillusioned.

I fell in love with you. I saw through the presentation the first time we met. I knew you were dangerous and up to no good. I wanted you anyway.

You were like a dare. I couldn't wait to jump in. Fuck the risk!

Seven years later, I know so much more about you and my love has   only grown. You have lied and deceived me hundreds of times but one thing has never changed for me. I still know and hold onto that honesty and truth that you gave so feely when we first met.

That's why you love new relationships you get to be that young innocent girl presenting herself to her new lover.

New love let's you be honest and innocent even while you share the vilest acts. You text your new lover from your current lover's bed and tell him you wish you were with him. He doesn't think ahead to the future when he's no longer the new love.

When I met you, you were with someone and I didn't care. I knew if you would cheat with me, eventually you would cheat on me.

It would hypocritical for me to get mad. That's why I've always told you not to lie to me. The lies make us adversarial instead of confidants.

I can never be of use to you if you ever get sober if you have to lie to me about your past. I don't think you lie to me for the same reasons anymore. I think you don't want to disappoint me or hurt me more than as a way to manipulate me.

The reason I say that is because we've been through so much that you know I'm not going to push you   out of my life.

Of course, it maybe you lie to keep me from finding someone else to love. Nevertheless that essential truth; that you gave me in the beginning, I have hung onto and that's the Liza Beth I know and love.

Chill, Baby, I do love you but you know you're full of shit, right? I mean, you know that, okay? Let's get that clear.

Yeah, maybe! I think I'm just like everybody else at the end of the day.

How so, Big guy?

I tell myself whatever I need to hear so I can keep getting this good young pussy!

They both broke into chaotic laughter and it was good between them free and easy. If it could stay that way you could keep the world. At bay.

Addiction don't give two shits about love. Chill held the lovely young girl's nude body in his arms. She rested peacefully. He knew in the morning she would be gone.

She would need more dope and she would need to be away from him. Chill understood a little bit of him went a long way with most people. He had spent most of his life alone and appreciated his own company.

Other people were fine in small doses. He collected data like a sponge. Too much of other people and he had to decompress.

He knew this about himself and accepted it. As a child his biggest goal had been to go unnoticed around his family.

The company of others had always brought pain even when it brought joy.

He had learned to associate the two. His adult relationships had held to this model.

His relationship with Liza Beth was a prime example of how emotionally fucked up his childhood had left him.

His brother's constant bullying and abuse had conditioned him to choose mates that treated him with indifference or abuse mixed with love.

He knew these things and often despised himself for not being able to change. No matter what success he found in life; inside he remained that inept frightened child tortured and abused. His crime ; being himself.

The things he had said to Liza Beth he believed.

He was scared for her, her disease was taking over her life.

He was conflicted about his killing of Mike Cheri. Had his actions somehow caused Liza Beth to become more unhinged than before?

He did the only thing he knew to do; the thing that seven years of practicing the principles of recovery had taught him.

He put the situation and Liza Beth in the hands of God.

A   New Chapter

Liza Beth did leave early the next morning

It was almost two weeks before Chill saw or heard from her. It was a Wednesday afternoon and his phone rang.

She started talking as though they had just seen each other that morning. Hey, baby, it's me. Can I come over? Do you have any money?

Chill laughed. He was relieved to hear her voice. It did irk him a little that the first thing out of her mouth was to ask for money.

He didn't comment though because he kept reminding himself he wanted Liza Beth to be honest with him.

There wasn't anything more honest than a dope fiend asking for money.

Chill knew he would give her money and that she would probably stay a little while and be gone again.

He didn't care. He would take what he could get and be grateful. A dope sick Liza Beth trying to score money was still better than anyone else as far as Chill was concerned.

She may be just using him but like the old song says "Use me up" was Chill's response to Liza Beth.

It wasn't even a choice Liza Beth was Chill's heroin and he had no defense against her. He figured if God kept her in his life this long there had to be a reason.

Chill had been able to find out a few details about the demise of Mike Cheri.For all intents and purposes his death had been ruled an accident.

Chill had went to the library and discreetly looked through the local newspapers for Cheri's little hamlet.

It seems there had been a fire in the house and Cheri's body had been found inside. No mention of drugs in the article. Cheri's death had been ruled accidental due to smoke inhalation.

What the fuck? Was all Chill could think at this turn of events. Had Cheri somehow survived the night? No, he was dead.

Chill was positive of that. He had shot almost a whole gram into the man's arm.It had taken at least three hours to get Liza Beth from Chill's house to Cheri's.

The man's body had not moved in that time.

The blows to the head had probably killed him. The heroin had probably been overkill. Had Liza Beth set a fire to cover her tracks? If so, how had she gotten home without being noticed?

Chill had more questions than before and no way to answer them. It was in his best interest to let it lie.

As far as the world was concerned no crime had been committed. The man's death was ruled accidental. The house had caught fire due to an overturned kerosene heater.

If Liza Beth had indeed covered up Cheri's overdose and concussion with a fire from a kerosene heater she was fucking brilliant.

Chill had severely underestimated her and a shiver went up his spine. Could she as easily do something similar to him if she thought she had a reason?

He knew desperation made people do things beyond their normal abilities and inclinations.

She was an addict and desperation a common state. This line of reasoning gave Chill mixed emotions.

On one hand, he was apprehensive about what "his love" might be capable of in the future. On the other hand, he was exhilarated by her will and determination.

He liked to think of Liza Beth as a young girl, innocent and naïve in need of his protection. Liza Beth used that little girl thing to great effect on Chill and others. She had a couple other "personalities" for the younger men but the "daddy's little girl thing" got her far in life.

Deep down Chill knew of the two of them Liza Beth was far more capable of looking out for her own self-interest.

Chill knew that she was also her greatest danger to herself. She was far more aggressive and predatory than Chill.

Chill was under few delusions. He knew he was not a nice person and quite selfish in his own pursuits.

He was not Liza Beth's "victim" by any means.

She could blame her actions on active addiction; he however had years of recovery.

The weeks following Mike Cheri's death did show a change in Liza Beth. Her drug use escalated and her life got more and more chaotic.

Her visits to Chill became less frequent. When she did show up she was always stoned ; often to the point of being incoherent.

She seemed hunted and haunted by her own mind. Chill had always admired her quick mind and caustic wit. This new Liza Beth was a sad imitation of the girl he loved. She hardly even called him by his name anymore.

She would call him hon and baby and he realized it was because she didn't want to risk saying the wrong name. He was just a faceless, nameless man that she could use to help her stay high.

This was the cruelest joke the universe had ever played on Chill. He could not save her from herself and all he could do is watch her turn into a stranger.

Addiction was stealing the love of his life from him and he was powerless to stop it. She went at getting high like it was a mission.

One night while holding her close she confessed through crying eyes and muffled sobs, she was determined to either die or "get done" with dope. She would get on her knees and pray for the desire to want to stop.

She had met some guy at the bar where she worked that had a lot of money.His family owned some type of business and he had to travel a lot.

Liza Beth moved into the man's home and quit working. The new guy "Aarron" gave her money everyday and a car to drive.

He even let her have a credit card to use when he was out of town. She had found the perfect sugar daddy and was making the most of the situation.By this time, Liza Beth didn't bother to lie to Chill about other men.

She didn't tell him everything but she didn't try to convince him he was the only man in her life.She still showed up at Chill's house. He wasn't sure why.

She didn't need him anymore for money of dope.Chill may have represented some anchor or stability for Liza Beth. He often wondered exactly what the girl's true thoughts and feelings were toward him.

He doubted if she knew.He knew he loved her beyond the dictates of pride, ego or good sense.

He knew it wasn't just about sex for either of them although that's mostly what they did. They were both practical people and their relationship dealt in little bullshit.

Liza Beth knew he loved her and that he was someone that would not turn his back on her.

Chill in turn knew that somehow Liza Beth needed him and that was enough.During this time with Aarron, Liza Beth's behavior and drug use got so frantic that the inevitable happened.

She got arrested. Some bullshit traffic stop early in the morning. Chill never got all the details and figured he probably didn't want to know.

The police found a syringe in the car and she was charged with a paraphernalia charge. She passed the breathalyzer and only spent the night in jail. Liza Beth had been in trouble before but this arrest started a new trend for the girl.

Over the next two years, she would continue to go in and out of jail time and time again.Chill realized that God had heard her prayers. Her higher power was giving her the desperation to change that she had sought.

Her sugar daddy "Aarron" disappeared and was of little use to Liza Beth during her incarceration.

If he couldn't fuck her   well "fuck her" was his attitude. This was a hard time for Chill. He was still dealing with the death of Mike Cheri.

Chill believed strongly in Karma and knew actions had consequences .Chill also believed in a program of recovery and to seek God's will and work with others whenever things got confusing or overwhelming.

A lot of new guys started asking for rides to meetings and a couple of little tramps started coming around on a regular basis.

He stayed busy to the point of exhaustion; still sometimes his brain would not shut up.It wasn't guilt as much as an awareness of a debt owed.

He prayed for relief and God again answered. Chill's relief came in the form of a couple of misfit drunks.

Lonnie "L.A." Haze and Gerred "Gerry" Phelps had little in common except they were both addicts and alcoholics and felt a connection to "Big Chill."

Chill had been asked to give his "lead" or share his story at a meeting held in a local treatment center.

Lonnie and Gerry had both been in attendance at the meeting.

Lonnie had been at the meeting because he was a guest of the state while Gerry had come with a friend of his father's.

It was Gerry's third meeting and the first where another alcoholic shared his experience, strength and hope.

Some places call this type of meeting a "speaker" meeting in the Northern Kentucky/Ohio area they are referred to as "lead" meetings.

Chill had been apprehensive about giving this particular lead.

It had been a long time since he had shared his story and to be honest, he wasn't sure what to say.

When sharing their experience strength and hope in this manner, alcoholics are told to tell "in a general way" "What it was like" "What happened" and "What it's like today."

They tell what their life was like when drinking the event or situation   that led   them to stop drinking and to seek a life in recovery.

Finally, they share what their life is like living in recovery. Chill had no concerns about telling how it was or what happened.

The how it is today part made him more than a little apprehensive.

Chill's story was not typical. He strived to apply the principles of recovery in his daily life to the best of his ability bur he knew his being sober was a minor miracle. His association with active addicts and their disease affected his life.

He knew he was spiritually sick and wasn't sure he had anything to offer the new comers at this meeting.

It didn't matter what he believed. He had been asked to share his story and so he would share his story.

Chill had been taught early on not to turn his back on AA.

You never knew where or when a solution was going to be placed in your life.

Chill spoke from his heart and tried to be as honest as his ego would allow.

Early in his recovery he had interjected humor into his story but the longer he stayed sober the less he felt the need.

He spoke of his childhood and how the family dynamic was instrumental in his own feelings of inadequacy and lack of trust.

He told how alcohol and later drugs and alcohol formed a bridge between him and his family. That bridge extended to allow Chill to interact with the world.

He had always known alcohol and drugs were a big lie. He knew at an early age to avoid his brothers while they were intoxicated.

Their faces may have smiles and their voices sweet and soothing but if you got too close those smiles would change to snarls and voices held threats and savage insults.

He had held off drinking until eleven years old and then everything changed. Chill often stated he knew he was alcoholic before he ever took a drink.

He had known that once he drank he would change. Drink was like all other lies in his life; they all came with guilt and shame.

No matter how much fun he had or how much affection and attention showered upon him during his sprees, he always awoke feeling like he played himself.

His family and his life had went to great lengths to teach him humility. Drugs and alcohol made him a braggart and a blowhard.

He became obnoxious, grandiose, vulgar when intoxicated. This type behavior embarrassed him to no end. He hated it in others and could not stand it in himself.

He was the exact kind of drunk that he would not endure today. A lot of the "character defects" that became overwhelming and obvious during active alcoholism and addiction continue to manifest in recovery. Chill noted to the crowd that the people he hated to hear share in meetings were the ones that were most like himself when he drank.

He shared that often he endured these people for the very reason that they irritated him to the extreme. It was not some backhanded form of penance. It was an honest attempt to learn through listening and observation.

Often it is easy to see in others what we are blind to in ourselves.

He had come to a realization that the biggest benefit his sponsor and sobriety network had been to him was to point out to him those things his disease or ego would not let him see within himself. His best friend "Pixie" often sat and listened to him "inventory" his current life situation. Her mentoring technique was simples she let him keep talking until he dug out the truth.

He could rationalize and justify almost any behavior. He would just look at it until he could find some way that God benefitted from his actions.

Chill's argument was all actions served the will of the universe. God was in everything. Sometimes situations were so severe or shitty that "God's" will was giving the person the "gift" of enduring pain and spiritual growth through that trial.

Pixie would point out Chill's self-will and how his actions could possibly cause harm to others.

Chill liked to joke that he didn't owe amends when his actions annoyed or harmed other people. He felt he should just tell them "you're welcome" for the opportunity that he bestowed upon them to practice love and tolerance.

The big book states that " Love and tolerance is our code." At these times, Pixie tells him that his thinking may be logical but also full of hypocrisy.

His seeking God in all actions was just a little too convenient for his own benefit. During the telling of Chill's lead, Lonnie Hayes's brain started clicking into unfamiliar territory.

The big guy started talking and it was like he was telling Lonnie's story. Everything the man described rang true in Lonnie's ears.

When he talked about his brothers being his heroes and his biggest source of self-loathing, Goosebumps   had run   up Lonnie's back and arms.

No one had ever spoke the feelings and emotions that Lonnie had experienced in a way so exact.

Lonnie himself had never been able to express the insight that Chill had upon Lonnie's life.

Gerry Phelps had sat restless at the beginning of the meeting and Chill's story had little effect upon him. Then Chill began speaking about the day of his brother's death and the following events. The big man spoke about learning to live with the guilt and shame of his own actions.

Gerry became entranced perhaps there was some light at the end of his own tunnel.

Chill spoke of willingness and how even if a person was not able to make an amends. The person had to remain willing to make that amends. God would find a way for some relief to enter into that person's life. Gerry wasn't sure he believed the giant but he believed the giant believed.

He knew he needed to talk to the big man after the meeting. This was no small thing for Gerry. He was a man given to introspection and not prone to sharing his thoughts and feelings with other people.

He had only gotten close to a handful of people in his life .Only two people   had he trusted enough to open up his soul and dreams. Both were dead. His heart was so full of pain that his own death would be welcome.

Chill talked about living with that kind of hurt and this gave Gerry hope. He approached the big man in the main meeting room. The room had cleared out and only a couple of die hard treatment stooges remained.

They were quickly wiping down tables and emptying garbage cans making sure everyone could see that they were good little AA members.

Gerry approached Chill tentatively. He held out his hand.

Chill shook the young man's hand he looked him in the eye and said, "What's wrong?"

Gerry stammered out, "I liked your story. I mean, I under stood what you were saying."

Chill just looked at Gerry and said, "Okay, now tell me what's on your mind?"

Gerry was taken aback. He wasn't sure how to proceed.

He had a lot of shit he needed to unload but didn't know how or with whom to unload it.

Chill's "lead" had touched him. He had identified with the feelings and emotions that the big man had shared.

He just wasn't sure he had the words or the courage to ever speak a loud his own pain and heartbreak.

Chill could see the scrawny young cat had something on his mind.He wasn't sure if it was about recovery or if this kid was someone from his past.

Someone he may have wronged or someone he owed amends. Chill didn't enjoy making amends, but he didn't shy away from making them. He believed strongly in paying what was owed.

His biggest problem at present was wondering if there was any way he could pay the karmic debt owed for the death of Mike Cheri.

He hadn't lost sleep over Cheri's death. Liza Beth was alive and somewhat her old self.Her using had progressed and Chill hadn't seen or heard from her in over a week. He wasn't worried. She would show up when she needed him.

One thing he was pretty confident about was that Liza Beth would be back. Wherever she was at or whoever she was with would not maintain her interest for too long.

People tended to become boring for the young beauty. Once they had heard her story, fallen madly in love with her and spent all their resources on here, they became dull.

She wasn't mean about it and there wasn't any planning to her actions.It's just that other people' stories didn't interest her much and broke people tended to be pitiful.

Chill understood this about the girl and accepted it as a part of her. He never regretted his time, money or whatever resources that Liza took from him.

For Chill there existed nothing as precious as Liza Beth. Her presence and beauty in his life; however brief was worth whatever he had to pay. Chill's only regret was he didn't have more to give her.

His little hippy friend Pixie would ask him how come he never got mad when Liza Beth would leave him and be gone for days and weeks.

Didn't it bother him to know that she was with other men and sometimes women?

Chill said yeah it sucked to know she was with other people.

He didn't tell Pixie that whenever Liza was gone, he didn't blame Liza.She was just being true to her nature.

He blamed himself. If he had more   resources or was more interesting, or handsome, or rich or whatever she would stay with him.

He knew with the disease of addiction that there was never enough. He was the perfect mate for a narcissist. He refused to be mad at Liza Beth. He wanted her in his life in whatever capacity she wished to be in his life.

It is easy to love people when they act right. It's a lot harder to love an addict in the midst of their disease.

Liza Beth may wake up with every intention of being the most well behaved loving young lady in the world. Two hours later she may be lying in some dope boy's arms telling him whatever he needs to hear to get what she needs.

The power of choice had been taken from her. As bad as it is for the people that love an addict they still have some choice. The addict does not.

Of course it still hurt to be lied to and used. Sometimes Chill wondered if Liza Beth even cared for him.

All that passed through Chill's mind in an instant while he looked at Gerry. Chill again wondered what Gerry was and why he was here at this moment in his life.

Chill had been around recovery long enough to know that blessings often came in disguise.

His   own recovery had started after being arrested. The police and jail often became the frontline in the war on addiction.

More people detoxed successfully in jail than treatment centers. For a lot of people e any way less severe did not work.

For some, nothing worked. The drink and the drugs took them.

"What's your name, buddy?" chill asked the young man.

Gerrard   Phelps was about five nine in stature and weighed about a hundred and sixty-five pounds. He wasn't small but he wasn't large. He was lean and fit. His body was nothing but bone, sinew and nervous energy.

Next to Chill the man seemed tiny. Chill stood about six three in height but weighed around three hundred and eighty pounds.

Most people would be surprised to know he was that heavy for he didn't move like a large man.He had always been large as a kid but he was now immense.

Unlike a lot of big men, Chill was not awkward in his size and he didn't apologize or joke about his size.

He had been teased and bullied as a child due to his size and would not brook any crap about it as an adult.

If someone made a comment about his size he would very curtly tell them "if you ain't fucking me or feeding me, it ain't none of your fucking business."

That seemed to stop any further comments. He definitely did not go for the "jolly fat man" role in life.

Once in a bar, a young man had patted Chill's immense beer gut.Chill had grabbed the man and yelled "What the fuck, buddy? I ain't your fucking Buddha."

The man's brother had been standing close and told his sibling to "cut the fat, fucker!"

Chill's friend Elzie Wester had smacked the man in the mouth for his comment. Elzie had started calling Chill Buddha afterwards. Paradoxically, Chill had let him because he knew Elzie loved him and had his back. Elzie wasn't making fun of Chill.

Liza Beth had never said anything about Chill's size and he knew she never picked a man because of his looks. She didn't like pretty men. She wasn't sharing the spotlight with anyone.

Gerry began to speak.

My name is Gerrard   Phelps. People call me Gerry.

"How long you been sober, Gerry?" Chill inquired.

I got 97 days today, but I only   been coming to meetings for a couple of weeks.

Well, shit, 97 days is 97 days Chill replied.

"Do you want to sit down a minute, Gerry?" Chill asked the young   man while pulling out a chair.

Chill had learned a few tricks since coming into the rooms.Always stand between the new guy and the door was one.Get 'em seated and get 'em talking was another one.

Gerry said, "Uh, okay, I guess."

"Now, Gerry, what do you know about this recovery shit everybody keeps   talking   about? Huh?"

"You think there's anything to it? You think this getting sober shit is a good deal or what?"

Chill liked to ask odd seemingly off the wall questions to newcomers. It did two things : :First, it calmed them down and got them focused toward the topic of recovery. Second, it evened the field.

The situation was no longer the earnest newcomer and the wise old sage of an old timer.

It became two guys talking. Two guys   with a common goal and an interest in the other's point of view.

Too often a new comer thinks he hasn't anything to offer when he first gets to the rooms of recovery. Old-timers and people that have been around a while will tell you that the new person coming into the room is vital to the program.

No matter how long an addict or alcoholic is clean and sober, they are never but one drink or drug away from that next debacle.

To work with other alcoholics and addicts is an opportunity to practice gratitude and to treat one's own disease.

A man twenty years sober still has the disease of alcoholism. The difference in his life is that for twenty years he has been able to successfully treat his disease. The disease is progressive so therefore treating it has to be ongoing.

After sitting down with Gerald Phelps and listening to him begin to tell his story; Chill realized he was relaxing for the first time in weeks.

The simple act of hearing another man's raw pain and emotional torment soothed the big man's own gnawing spiritual ache.

Chill was not some spiritual vampire; parasitically feeding upon another's despair. Gerry's tale of woe evoked in him empathy.

They shared a common bond. Gerry's story was similar to Chills in some aspects.

His family had been a big influence upon him. His people had also been hardworking and intense. The emotion of rage seemed to be suitable for all occasions. Their families were people who cared too much and were unequipped to provide a home fostering emotional stability.

Chill's father had seldom drank at least not a home in front of his family.

Gerald's father had been a daily drinker and a petty thug.

Both families were from the south. Chill's father had been raised in rural Tennessee hill country at the foot of the Appalachians.

Gerald's family had originated in Alabama down near the Tennessee state line.

Their fathers had worked hard all their lives with little to show for their efforts.

This lack of success in life had made them bitter and resentful.

Chill's father lived a dual existence. To the outside world, he presented a happy go-lucky Mountain man quick with a joke and a smile. He exuded charm and made friends easily. He worked for the National Park Association in the Big South Fork region and often encountered tourists and people on vacation.

Many of these people would return to their homes with fond memories of the "nice mountain man" that had been so entertaining on their trip.

At home Chill's father was cold and distant. The family sat in silence in the evenings when his car pulled into the drive. They waited to see what kind of mood he was in before speaking.

If he was in a good mood they could be in a good mood but always on guard to not upset the father. Gerrys' dad had bee a light-hearted man in his youth.

He had gotten his high school sweetheart pregnant and married her. In truth his wife had never made it to high school. Meg Evans, later Phelps, had met Gerrard "Big Gerry" Phelps the summer of her fourteenth year. He had been nineteen and about to go to Vietnam.

She had just graduated middle school and was due to start high school in the fall. They had met at a dance held in town every week at the local skating rink. The skating rink was where the younger kids and kids without their own cars spent Saturday night.

The more well-to-do kinds spent the nights driving the loop endlessly around town. Smoking dope and drinking beer.

Gerrys' dad had driven his Daddy's flatbed ford to town to pick-up his little cousin Darnell who was sixteen.

Meg had been Darnell's date and Gerrard Senior had offered to give them a ride home.

After a couple of joints and half a fifth of Heaven Hill vodka Darnell had passed out.

Gerrard never one to pass up a good opportunity quickly "seduced" the young Meg. Unfortunately for our Romeo, Meg had been a good girl and Jerome had been her first lover.

Five weeks later, Meg's uncle and Daddy broke the news to the young lothario about his upcoming nuptials.

He could marry the now pregnant teenager or he could face charges of statutory rape and most likely be shot.

Gerrard married Meg in August. She was three months gone at the time.

He shipped out to basic training in October and was home by February.

Baby Gerrard arrived the same week as his father.

Gerrard Senior had gotten kicked out of the Army before finishing AIT. The real story never came out but it was something to do with liquor and an non-commissioned officer's wife.

He switched from happy-go-lucky to miserable bastard. He often bemoaned how his wife had tricked him into marrying her and that he felt trapped. He continued to work and to drink and as he aged he got sullen and morose.

Chill told Gerrard some of his history and Gerrard shared some of his own.

Their dysfunctional past helped to form a bridge.

Gerry said he didn't know much about AA and that the whole twelve stop thing seemed kind of stupid.

Chill responded that he understood Gerry's point of view.

He then asked Gerry was he willing to do some things just based on faith.

Gerry wasn't sure he figured he needed to know what sort of "things" before he could answer.

Chill told Gerry a little more of his own story.

Gerry had heard his lead and how Chill had gotten sober. He now told Gerry about those first weeks of treatment.

He spoke of how he had woke up in jail covered in blood and felt relieved. He had been relieved because he was alive.

He had been relieved because that nameless dread that had been in his life was over. For years, he had known the way he was living was wrong and that it couldn't last.

Someone or something sooner or later was going to happen. This feeling had hung on him for at least three years.

The "Big Book" of Alcoholics Anonymous mentions a feeling of this type and talks about loneliness   and despair.

Gerry listened to Chill speak and started to relax.

He started telling more of his own story and as he spoke he seemed to gain confidence.

After about thirty minutes of the two men conversing back and forth, a lull developed in the conversation.

The mood seemed to   change and   become somewhat solemn. It was at this point that Gerry decided to take a chance on the whole recovery deal.

"Chill, do you think this shit can work for me?"

Chill didn't hesitate. "Yes! Yes, I do. I don't see any reason it wouldn't work for you."

Gerry began, "I understand that part of the steps is making amends for shit you done wrong."

Yep, Chill said, the ninth step is when we make the actual amends but the fourth, fifth, and eight all play a part in dealing with that part of recovery.

We call it dealing with the "wreckage of the past."

Yeah, well, what if a man has done something so bad that there ain't no way to make amends for it?

Chill felt his blood turn to ice. He knew immediately that Gerry Phelps coming up to talk to him was no accident.

Chill's higher power was sending him relief from his own personal hell. Chill avoided the term "God." He preferred thinking of his higher power as a force behind the universe linking every person, animal and action.

To call such an entity God was to place human-like characteristics upon it. He didn't want to limit his higher power by labeling it for the sake of convenience.

This time he couldn't help himself "God" was sending him help for his problem.He was doing so in the way that Chill trusted and understood. His salvation and solution was presented to him in the form of a fellow suffering alcoholic.

Chill knew before Gerry ever spoke that whatever happened next would involve he "Chill" telling Gerrard   Phelps what he "Chill" needed to hear.

The man's moral dilemma would be such that its solution would mirror the solution of Chill's own situation. Chill did not possess the ability to see a way out of his own darkness. He was mired in his own ego and fears. His own self-absorption blocked him from believing he could be helped.

Paradoxically, Chill had been around recovery long enough to believe whole-heartedly that everyone could be helped.

Miracles happened everyday and Chill knew that Gerry   Phelps was a miracle sent by his higher power.

The funny thing about miracles and rescues and rewards in recovery; they often come disguised. They arrive in the form of apparent adversity or even outright calamity.

Chill's brother's death and his own subsequent arrest had been Chill's biggest and most tragic miracle in his life to date.

It had been the darkest time in his life also the hardest but he had survived. Upon awakening in jail, he had been covered in blood, some his own, some other people's.

He had felt relieved. He had gotten stopped and at last the power of choice had been restored.

This had been the beginning of his journey in recovery.

He had witnessed many such "miracles." Mother's losing their kids to social services, husbands losing their wives' to divorce, people losing their jobs.

Great upheavals in a person's life hold enough impact to get that person to pause and become willing to do something different. A person's life is worthless until the person puts value on something or someone.

Chill never realized he had anything worth losing until it was taken from him. Today his life held value and he treasured everything and everyone in his life. He knew this to be true because anytime he got ungrateful and didn't do the spiritual maintenance on the people and things in his life, he lost them.

Chill had a worthwhile life full of people that he treasured. They sometimes did not treasure themselves or could not see Chill as having value. That did not matter. He was not responsible for their behaviors or attitudes.

He knew that a person's life was a rich as he let it be. The secret was not in having a lot but finding gratitude for what life gives you.

Chill knew that true gratitude involved work.If you were grateful for people in your life, you let them know. It was called maintenance. In order for anything to remain in good working condition it had to be maintained. This included relationships with people.

There remained people in Chill's life that some would deem "toxic" or at the very least "unhealthy."

Chill's relationship with Liza Beth at first glance would seem extremely unhealthy. It was co-dependent in that both people used the other person.

Chill believed that keeping Liza Beth in his life and learning to love her in spite of and beyond her disease had been the single greatest contributor to his own spiritual growth. Gerry 's story was pretty dark. He had enlisted in the army on the delayed-entry program with his best friend, Randy Marcus.

They had been best friends since second grade. They had lived within a quarter mile of each other their entire lives.

Randy's mother was Gerrards' mother's ex's baby mama but Gerrard had a different father.

The two ladies had become friends when they realized they both had an ex in common.

Both ladies were raising children by themselves. Gerrys' father was still alive he was just gone a lot. He was either away at jail or living with various other women.

When he did show up he was often drunk and mean.

Gerry and Randy had enlisted in the army at the end of their junior year.

They had attended ten weeks of basic training during their summer break before their senior year.

They figured that they would be in great physical shape for their last year of school.

Their plan had been that all the girls at their school would just melt and throw themselves at the two patriots. This plan had met with limited success.

They came from a rural area and a lot of people were very patriotic and supported the troops even if they no longer believed in the war.

There also existed a fairly large contingent of the population that did not support the war or anyone involved. This contingent was comprised largely of the younger people in their town.

It seemed to Gerry that half the school considered them heroes and the other half thought of them as sell-outs.

Gerrard   and Randy didn't know exactly what they felt about the war. Enlisting had seemed like a way out for them. Neither boy had been particularly motivated toward athletics or scholarly pursuits.

Their families certainly did not possess the where withal to send them to college or sat them up in business.

Neither had political aspirations or knowledge.

A recruiter had visited their school and he had been a very convincing man. He had asked them where they saw themselves in five years, or ten years.What did Florence Alabama have for them in the future?

Well, the boys bought the man's spiel hook line and sinker.

Neither could see himself prospering in North Alabama.

Florence was a big town almost 40,000 but held little opportunity for the two young men.

They had seen the pretty young girls in their school run off to the University of North Alabama .They wanted part of that   action.

The recruiter sensed their interest in money for school and quickly sold them on the army's new G.I. bill.

He may have oversold it a little but he really hadn't needed to. The boys were ripe for an adventure and the split training enlistment seemed ideally suited for their needs.

They envisioned their senior year as something Grand. They would be in the best physical shape of their life and have pockets full of spending money.

They had enlisted as combat engineers and as such they did their basic training and AIT (advanced individual training) at Ft. Leonard Wood Missouri.

Chill had done his own basic at Leonard Wood and wondered how the boys had liked the mountains Being from Kentucky, Chill had grown up in mountains but he had a feeling the boys from North Alabama may have been a little out of their element.

Gerry and Randy had done well in basic. Their final year of high school went pretty much as they had planned.

They returned to Leonard Wood AIT and things changed.

The boys learned that the army, once you're in it, can be a very different place than the organization represented on the T.V. and them smooth talking recruiters were not beyond lying.

Their AIT was being extended by three weeks for additional training in IED (Improvised Explosive Device) detection and removal.

Combat engineers were encountering a lot of booby traps in the performance of their duties.

Gerry and Randy were to be deployed to Afghanistan, knowing this fact gave them incentive to appreciate extra training. Randy had a knack for bomb removal during training. Of course all the devices used in training had the explosives removed.

To make for more effective training the actual explosives would be replaced with live fuses. The fuses did hold some explosive and were very effective training devices.

As a result of Randy's performance during training he was offered further instruction in IED detection and removal. He was sent to "Bomb School."

Gerry was deployed with the rest of his unit.They had a good laugh the night before Gerry shipped out.

They toasted their recruiter and the army's "Buddy Enlistment Program."

The nature of military service is such that Gerry had already formed close attachments with other soldiers in his unit.

Randy would be missed but Gerry had been okay with the split.

Basic training and AIT   had helped him gain confidence within himself.

He was anxious to test himself. Thus far   army life had been good to him.

He was judged solely on his own performance and action.

His worth was determined by personal performance not by who he was kin to or how much money his family had in the bank.

In Florence Alabama, his options had been limited by family and station.

Gerrys'   view was perhaps a little naïve.

His youth and experience kept him from seeing the larger picture. For him, the army had elevated him to a status that equaled his peers. He was treated as well as all those around him .What he wasn't able to consider was that those around him were already much like him. They, for the most part, had joined the military for the same reasons that he had joined.

They had felt limited or trapped within situations that held little promise of a better future. Promises of training, education travel and better living standards were the carrots dangled before eager young eyes.

Many young men and women that entered into military service had vague ideas of patriotism.

They were committed to the "idea" of America.

The America they envisioned and had been promised had not been the America they had experienced.

Often hailed as the "Land of Opportunity," many of America's youth found themselves facing very limited opportunities.To pursue the illusion   of the American Dream.

Gerry and Randy were reunited once Randy had completed his extra training.

During this IED detection training, Randy had made the acquaintance of another soldier named Manuel Freeks. Everyone called him "Manny" or "Man Freek."

Manny was 27 years old and on his second enlistment.He had already served two deployments in Iraq and none in Afghanistan. He had achieved the rank of E-6 a staff sergeant but had been busted down to E-1 and worked his any back up to E-4.

It was a miracle that he had been retained within the military.He liked to boast that he had more article-15s than any other active-duty soldier.

Gerry had no way of determining the veracity of this claim. Everyone knew Manny was two things. .

He was a fuck-up and a fighter. He was the guy you wanted with you when the shit hit the fan.

Manny had started his military career as Eleven Bravo, Infantry.He had seen a lot of action and had quickly rose in rank. He was a good soldier but he had one flaw. He was an alcoholic, and, since joining the military, a heroin addict.

All his problems in the army had been direct results of incidents that occurred while he was intoxicated.

He had several arrests for fighting and two on post-DUIs. He had started using other drugs as a substitute for alcohol. Manny's reasoning was drugs did not make him as out-of-control as whiskey.

His drug use was a way to manage his alcoholism. He had stuck to cocaine and meth at first.He had been hesitant to try opiates because he did not want to lose his edge while in the field.

A lot of his fellow soldiers and superiors had over looked his use of stimulants.Some even secretly approved. The thought of a hyper vigilant person on their team seemed somehow comforting.

One day a convoy that Manny's team had been assigned to escort had come under fire. Manny received a fairly serious gunshot wound to his upper thigh. He lay in the hospital for a week in intensive care and suffered through six months of physical therapy.

During his convalescence, Man Freek got introduced to painkillers. He had been given IV drips at first filled with what he assumed was morphine.

His doctor had ascribed to the old adage of "keep the patient comfortable" and had freely prescribed painkillers to Manny upon request. He had experimented with fentanyl patches and oxycontin but found he had a preference for Percocet tens and thirties.

Oxycodone seemed to agree with his constitution.

Upon returning to active duty, he had assumed that he would be able to return to his normal routine.

Once declared fit for duty, the attending physician decided that Manny no longer needed the "comfort" of prescribed narcotics.

Manny was prone to substance abuse and susceptible to chemical solutions in life. It didn't take long to find a suitable replacement for his no longer prescribed painkillers. Ninety percent of the heroin produced in the world was manufactured   within the regions that he was now deployed. He had changed his MOS and volunteered for Afghanistan just so he could facilitate his heroin habit.

Randy and Gerry had some experience with drugs. They had partied in high school; but they had stuck to smoking pot and drinking until they had enlisted in the delayed entry program.

The looming specter of random drug testing had made them change their drug choices. They quit smoking dope because it stayed in your system too long.

Many benzodiazepine   drugs were also eliminated   for the same reasons. They had experimented with acid, molly, shrooms, cocaine and meth. Being true southerners and rednecks at heart they found beer and whiskey their go to choice   on most occasions.

Man Freek had introduced Randy   to the "delights" of heroin use. Within a very short time, Randy had developed a habit. He was able to hide the extent of his using   and his dependence for several weeks.

Gerry   had noticed the change in his friend but attributed it to their new environment and being homesick.

One night while drinking beer, Randy went to the bathroom and did not return for a very long time. Gerry went to see what was up with his friend. When he entered the bathroom, he found Randy slumped over and barely conscious.

Gerry was not stupid he knew instantly what was wrong with his friend. The fucker was on dope!

How the fuck could he be so stupid? They were in a fucking war zone! Everyone knew you couldn't depend on a fucking doper! Guys were fragging dope head retards on a daily just to make sure they didn't get people killed.

Gerry started smacking Randy's face trying to revive him."Wake up! You stupid fuck! Wake the fuck up!"

After a couple of good healthy smacks Randy responded.

"What the fuck? Dude! Chill the fuck out! Why you hitting me?"

Gerry was irate.

How the fuck can you be on that shit! We used to make fun of fucktards on fucking dope!

What the fuck?!? Man?

You trying to get killed?!

You trying to get me killed ?!

Randy had never seen his friend so mad.

Chill, dude. Just fucking chill!

The commotion alerted other troops in the vicinity. Several seen fit to investigate the disturbance. One of the attending parting was a recovering heroin addict named K.C. Jackson. K.C. was a twenty-four-year-old African American from Chicago by way of South Carolina. He had lived with his Grandmother in South Carolina until she had passed when he was thirteen.

He had then been sent to live with his Mother's oldest sister in Chicago. His mother had died of cirrhosis and no one was sure of what happened to his father. K.C. had started selling drugs at thirteen. He had started using at fifteen. He had OD'd at seventeen and enlisted at eighteen after completing a nine-month drug rehab.

He had six years clean and sober and was platoon sergeant for Gerry and Randy. He also had no time and little patience for dope fiends in the field. He had both men detained and sent to the command truck.

He then requested the CQ (Charge of Quarters) to alert the company "Top" sergeant that he needed to see him.

He wanted the company commanding NCO to see firsthand the state of the two men.

The first sergeant was a lifer a twenty-five-year man and he too had little patience. He asked the nature of the emergency and was told that two soldiers were suspected of drug use in base camp. He inquired if either had been on duty while intoxicated.

When told no he told the man standing in his doorway.

"Then it can wait 'til morning."

Randy and Gerry   were sent to their quarters and told to report to the first sergeant in the morning. No MPs were called no arrests were made. No formal charges at   that time.

Sergeant K.C. Jackson took it upon himself to be present the next morning. First Sergeant Thomalson noted this fact with mixed emotions. On the on hand, he appreciated the man's attention to detail. On the other, he wondered if the man had some personal agenda against the two men serving under him. Was he using some pretext of drug use to have these men singled out and punished for some other reason.

Both soldiers had exemplary records up to this point. Private Smith (Randy) had even received specialized training outside his MOS on the request of AIT drill instructors.

First Sergeant Thomalson had Sgt. Jackson's written report as well as statements of three other soldiers. He had not requested the Sergeant's presence at this informal proceeding. In fact, he wasn't sure that any   of this ordeal was necessary or a good use of time.

Sgt. Jackson, you sent a CQ runner to my quarters at 2:30 am about this matter. I'm assuming you deem this a critical issue.

Yes, First Sergeant! The young NCO replied.

Okay, I'm listening. Give me your version of what transpired.

In a clipped, crisp, precise tone the young soldier elaborated the incidents of the previous night. His accounting of events was accurate and fair. Jackson strove to not let his own bias color his narrative.

Upon retiring to his trailer the night before he had reviewed the incident in his head. He wanted the two young men out of his platoon because he saw them   as a threat to his other men. After this initial threat to unit safety is addressed   he realized he wanted them to get help.

Drug use within the military was fairly common. Whenever possible the army tried to retain trained and experienced soldiers. The army had its own process for treating substance abuse issues.

Much like the private sector the military supported self-referral for treatment programs. If a soldier facing criminal or disciplinary action for substance abuse asked for treatment they usually received it. The criminal actions and disciplinary actions may still proceed but the   Army   would still pay for and support treatment.

First Sgt. Thomalson knew about the Army's policy on substance abuse and treatment as a preferred alternative. He thought the policy lenient and easily abused. He did however ascribe to being a "by the book" soldier and would follow regulations wherever they seemed reasonable.

After reviewing all accounts he decided to issue the two soldiers summary Article   !5s and dock them one day pay each.

As a precautionary measure and to cover his own ass in case of some future incident he had them referred to medical for evaluation. A captain Marcie Denvers conducted their intake evaluation and recommended both men be enrolled into the Army's track one outpatient program.

The track one program focused on information and educating the service personnel on substance use and abuse. It involved meeting with a group and a counselor once a week for four weeks. Watching some films and four ninety-minute classes on various topics. It was designed for early intervention and to avoid serious consequences. Randy and Gerry thought it a joke and did not take it serious. It did slow down their drug use because they were subject to weekly drug screens.

The track one program was not designed as treatment so much as a slap on the wrist. It met a requirement but was more of a nudge, nudge, wink, wink deal.

In a lot of ways the military still payed homage to the hard fighting, hard playing, hard drinking macho image. Getting a little drunk and in a little trouble was a rite of passage.

Sgt. Jackson knew better. He knew that heroin use was not dabbling. He believed Gerald was only drinking but he had seen Pvt. Smith totally senseless. He did not take alcohol lightly but he had intimate knowledge of a junkie's mind.

His own drug use and subsequent dedication to a program of personal recovery gave him plenty of insight. Jackson approached his First Sgt. in private with his misgivings.

First Sgt. Thomalson was known for being a fair Top Sergeant. He seldom got angry and he trusted his staff. Staff Sergeant Jackson had always been an excellent soldier and Thomalson valued the man's opinion.

It did seem to Thomalson that in this particular instance that Jackson had some personal agenda with these soldiers. Jackson had avoided telling Thomalson of his own drug history. He had been afraid that it would affect their working relationship. In truth, it was no one's business but his own.

On the other hand, if Jackson had disclosed his own experience to Thomalson the more senior NCO may have treated his misgivings with more consideration.

Thomalson spoke directly to Jackson. Sergeant, you are a good NCO. These two young men were definitely out of line but this is the first time either soldier has been a problem? Is that correct?

Yes, First Sergeant, both men have good work histories.

The incident in question was mainly one man's actions in the wrong. Pvt. Marcus showed up very intoxicated on drugs and Pvt. Phelps tried to cover for him.

Well, that's understandable on Phelps' part.

This Marcus, is he a bad egg? Speak freely, Sgt. What is your opinion of those two? I also want you to tell me why you feel this incident warrants my involvement. Couldn't this have been contained within your platoon or at least within a company level?

Sgt. Jackson was no fool. He could sense the senior mans' reluctance to pursue the matter.

He decided to cut his losses and decided to try a different tactic.

Both privates have been good workers. Up to this point I have had no complaints about their performance. Having said that I would like to request their removal from my platoon. I just don't feel comfortable taking these men into the field.

Bullshit! Thomalson lost his cool. You don't trust them so you want to unload them on someone else. That's not how it's done, soldier.

Yes, First Sergeant.

Your concerns are duly noted Staff Sergeant and will be included within these men's records.

Is that satisfactory?

Yes, First Sergeant.

Dismissed.

Randy and Gerry were returned to normal duty and after their four weeks of Track One assessment and "treatment" things returned to normal.

Gerry returned to drinking daily and Randy returned to using heroin. He did stop shooting it and confined his use to snorting and smoking it. The heroin available in this region was of such purity that it made little difference in how you introduced it into your system.

Sgt. Jackson continued to monitor his two wayward soldiers.

At about this time, Manuel Freek "Man Freek" had come to a crossroads in his life. His enlistment was almost up and it was time to decide whether to reenlist or to leave the army. If he reenlisted, it would be a minimum six years. He just didn't want to stay in that long. If he went home, he faced the daunting prospect of not having access to mass quantities of easily available, cheap heroin.

He was committed to some type of compromise. He had made some contacts locally and had gained access to a supplier that could get him all the heroin he wanted. He just needed to find a way to get it shipped stateside. He was not a short-sighted man and realized once home at some point he would need more.

.

Man Freek decided to enlist private Randy Marcus into his plan. Marcus was not the criminal type by nature but by this time he had developed a pretty good habit.

Heroin may have been plentiful and dirt cheap but addiction is addiction. Marcus could always use more . More money and more dope ; It was the nature of the beast . A man could never get enough .

Manfreak had served in the 82nd Airborne division and had attended jump school at Fort Lee Virginia . Fort Lee was also where supply soldiers were trained .

Manny had made some valuable contacts while stationed there and had kept in touch with these people.

He was able to make an arrangement with a First Sergeant named Lee Myers . Myers had become stationed at Fort Knox Kentucky. Manny and Myers arranged a deal in which 20 kilos of pure Afghan Heroin would be shipped home every month in Equipment boxes and returning soldiers personal effects .

Manny would obtain the uncut heroin from a local contact for the princely sum of 200.00 dollars a kilo or 4000.00 dollars American. For the twenty. This 20 kilo package would then be given to a friend in the supply room . This " friend " would pack it into the personal effects of a soldier returning stateside .

The soldier would have no idea that the heroin was in his property because it would be removed once the plane landed stateside.. One of First Sergeant Myers' personal agents would see that it was received and placed into the pipeline .

The system was simple and very efficient . Flights were scheduled 2 times a week and did not have to come from any certain port . All was required was for man freak to obtain the heroin and give it to his man on the Afghan side .

The man would pick a returning soldiers' personal effects ; stash the drugs inside then supply Manny with the name . The freaky one would in turn supply that name to the people on the American side.

The beautiful part was : If for some reason the package got intercepted ; the soldier whose belongings concealed the package would be blamed . The Army would rather prosecute one soldier one time ; rather than admit to having a international drug pipeline operating under their noses . Unless of course it was an officially sanctioned pipeline .

The risk was minimum and the pay off huge.

Manuel Freek was of Latin American heritage, he had contacts within the expanding Mexican population within the southern region of the U.S. .These contacts were ready and quite capable of distributing his product once stateside .Their $ 4000. Investment would net them 80,000.. This was still a bargain . The street value would be more than 10 times that once it was finally delivered to the consumer .

Manny and his crew were not greedy Manny took half for himself gave Myers the other half . Myers kept half and split the rest between the guys that handled the actual package on each end.

Mannys' guy on the Afghanistan side was being shipped stateside and he needed a replacement . He also needed someone to deal with the local contact in Afghanistan once he himself rotated home .

He had no problem finding a guy to cover packaging the product and placing it on the plane .He was having trouble getting someone he could depend on for dealing with the locals in Afghanistan . It was no small thing to ask an American to essentially place cash money directly in the hands of the enemy . It was very close to outright treason . Never mind the damage that the shit was gonna inflict once in the community. Manny needed a true capitalist motivated purely by greed . The problem with an individual of this type ; the person once established would not hesitate to cut Man freak out of the loop .

Manny decided if he could not trust men motivated by greed he would use one motivated by need. He would recruit an addict .

Manny approached Randy Marcus and explained the deal .. He outlined the low risk and the potential pay off.

Marcus would receive $ 5000.00 every other week and all the dope he needed.

The package would be increased to 30 kilos ; around 70 pounds; a still manageable Quantity .

The funny thing is it had never occurred to Manny that the drugs he was buying were probably helping to finance the war on his brothers in arms.

The war itself was almost an afterthought to Manny . His long term drug use and subsequent descent into dealing had placed him in the mind set where " it was just business ."

He had always been a good man in a fire fight and dependable in combat but he had lost his way.

Once Marcus was on board with the little smuggling plan; the only thing left to do was to make the introduction with Mannys' heroin contact in Afghanistan . Manny had been dealing with a family for about 2 years.

He had met a youngish man on the street and had scored personal dope from the boy on numerous occasions . One time when he had no cash he had traded a pistol for an ounce of really good dope. This had led to him buying larger and larger quantities .

The young supplier was about 17 years old and often visible around post he was affiliated with the local powers that be and no doubt he played both sides of the fence in the conflict.

The young entrepreneur called himself Artan and he was a very precise and intense individual Although lacking in years in many ways Artan was more mature than his American associates .

The man was always on time, cordial and efficient in all matters. He dressed non descript and went to great lengths to blend into the crowd.

Randy Marcus upon meeting the man had remarked ; " don't I know you? " Artan had replied 'No. I do not think so; you are mistaken." The statement delivered in a quiet clear voice , without accent or inflection and in perfect English.

Artan had spent 4 years stateside .During that time he had attended private school . He was not a native to Afghanistan ; his father hailed from Istanbul and his Mother had ties to Iran .

Artans' people had sold and traded heroin for generations .He had kinfolk in the mountains and his only political commitment was to his family. Governments came and went in his part of the world but certain things remained.

There was always a demand for oil, guns,, and dope

.His mothers' people had ties to oil , his fathers' to heroin.

Everyone traded guns.

Artan hated the Americans and their ways but he also hated the Taliban and it's oppressive nature. He traded drugs' information and guns with all sides in the conflict. His personal hatred aside he planned on eventually living within the United States. His mother and younger sister were already situated stateside . They lived in a small two story home in Evansville Indiana . This had been where Artan had attended school.

Man freak had just assumed Artan had lived his entire life in Afghanistan or some other nearby shithole. It would not have changed anything for the man he could not have cared less about the mans' politics, heritage or agenda. The man was good if his dope was good. . Mannys' bottom line was the business at hand.

Randy Marcus was not quite as jaded as many. He was inquisitive by nature and took an interest in people. Randy was certain he had seen Artan before but did not have a clue as to where or when. Randys' frontal lobe was not as impaired as Man freaks due to not having used as long. He may have hesitated to work with the young smuggler if he knew all of the mans' pedigree.

Once introductions had been made and everyone understood their role ; operations recommenced .

Manny continued to accompany Randy to meet Artan his final week in country. He was confident Randy could handle everything on his end and many was looking forward to his "retirement."

At first everything ran smoothly. Randy was cautious and made sure to stick to the routine already in place. It was all good for about 6 weeks.

The money became a problem. Randy had never considered what he would do with 10, 0000 dollars a week. His one major expense (heroin) was now free.

He could not deposit it in a bank or send it home without arousing suspicion. His actual consumption of heroin had decreased. His tolerance had increased but he had become very disciplined in his use..

He would shoot up one time in the mornings and snort or smoke throughout the day. This made him a little irritable. Just ask any IV drug user ; using any other way is just not as effective . The old saying among fiends is why take a bus when you can fly ? Shooting dope is like a plane, The dope Randy had access to made it like taking the shuttle. Of course he would finish the day with a big shot to fade him for the night.

Randy avoided most other soldiers except at work. Staff Sergeant Johnson had restricted Phelps and Marcus to on post duties. He did not trust either man in the field and did not consider them competent for patrol.

Phelps still occasionally got sent out to run some heavy equipment but no one wanted Randy Marcus trying to disarm any I.E.D.s.

Gerry Phelps noticed the change in his friend Marcus. He wanted to intervene but did not know how to proceed. Their relationship deteriorated and Gerry started hanging with other people.

A day came that Marcus sought Gerrys' company. He approached his friend and asked him to accompany him on a walk.

Gerry had been surprised but recovered quickly and agreed to walk with his friend.

" Whats' up ?" Gerry askrd . Marcus replied " Dude I need to tell you something . "

" I don' t want you to get mad at me but I got nowhere to turn; I ned your help."

Gerry Phelps got a sinking feeling within his gut .

Fucking doper bullshit ! was his first thought.

"This asshole done fucked up again He probably needs money for fucking dope."

He voiced his misgivings ." what is it ? You need money to pay off some fucking dope dealer ?'

Marcus laughed . " Aw shit man that is definitely not it ; a lack of money is not my issue.'

"what is so funny ? I don' t see anything to laugh about ." You can' t tell me your not getting high !. You' ve lost thirty pounds and you look like shit.'

Gerry continued ; " It' s only a matter of time before you get caught or worse . That shit is gonna be the death of you."

Marcus retorted ; " Whatever fucker!' " "I don' t need a fucking lecture , I know I am A fuckup.

I need your help." " If you don' t want to help me I understand it' s fine I will figure something out."

Gerry conceded the fight .

"What?"

"What do you need/'

It took about 15 minutes for Marcus to explain to his friend all the particulars of his situation .

Once fully informed ; Gerald Phelps looked at his friend and said " ARE YOU FUCKING STUPID ?" " This is the stupidest shit I have ever heard."

Marcus responded.

"Dude I' m making thousands every fucking week. Thousands.'

So? You can't spend it and it's fucking treason. " Gerry informed his friend.

This was a new consideration for Marcus .

"What do you mean treason /"

Gerry Phelps was incredulous .

" Dude your running fucking dope for the fucking Taliban ." "They use that money and buy fucking guns and bullets and kill American Soldiers ."

"This is the sickest most foul shit you could ever be fucking doing man."

"Plus all that fucking dope you are sending home is killing more Americans. 'Your working for the enemy."

Fuck you Gerry!" I ain't no fucking Taliban."

I'm just trying to get paid."

"Help me figure out how to get this money home and I will give you half."

Gerry was quite clear in his response.

" FUCK YOU ! FUCK THAT MONEY !"

There ain't enough money in the world to get me to push dope for the fucking Taliban."

Marcus shot back,

" Oh yeah? I got $ 60,000 in my duffel bag . Thirty is yours if you can figure out how we can get it home." " Plus I will give you another $5000 every week;"

" I need you man ; I need your help ."

For all his bluster and conviction Gerald was tempted .He hesitated and like any good dope fiend Marcus seized opportunity.

" Don' t decide anything right now."

"Take this; no strings attached 'and think about it. "

He handed Gerald $5000 in new $100 bills.

Gerald wondered briefly where the fuck do these hillbillies get all these new bills ?"

Neither Marcus nor Man Freak had ever considered it odd that the currency the Afghans always used was American.. They insisted they be paid in only US currency.

Where was Artan spending his share? Who traded in US currency in this region ? The obvious answer would be Americans . In this case other soldiers . The things soldiers have to sale are weapons of war .

These thoughts just never entered their minds.

Marcus handed Gerald the money then turned quickly and strode away in the opposite direction . He did not give him time to refuse or return the money.

Chill had sat quietly and listened to the young mans' tale .

He thought he knew where it was headed but hoped he was wrong..

Chill had served in the Army but not in time of war.. To place lives of other soldiers in such peril would be a deed beyond despicable . Chill did not know what to do or say ; so he held his tongue and let the man resume his tale.

" Okay buddy this is where it gets fucked up. " Gerald began.

Gerald had decided not to take Marcus up on his offer.. He had been raised right and knew right from wrong. He also knew that Karma was real.

Actions have consequences. It might take a while but this situation was bound to turn to shit. It would probably turn to shit sooner rather than later.

Gerald approached his friend and handed him an ammo pouch. Within the pouch was the $5000.

"Here dude I don't want anything to do with this."

"What do you mean?" It was not conceivable in Randy's dope ravaged brain that someone could turn their back on "free money." In Randy's mind Gerry Phelps' risk would be even less than his own.. All Gerry would need to do is mail that cash home to his Uncle.. They could divide it up later when they got home.

Randy trusted Gerald so implicitly that he never once considered the possibility that his friend could just send the money home and keep it all.

It also never occurred to Randy that Gerald would say no. Gerald had had his back since seventh grade. He had never let him down. Randy felt betrayed and lost.

Gerald handed his friend the money and told him he would not be helping him and for Randy everything changed.. The world as he knew it no longer existed .

Gerald continued talking; " Furthermore dude; as long as you're fucking with that shit I don't want anything to do with you' "

"What? I don't understand.' Randy just stood and stared at his friend his mouth agape. He had sought the help and comfort of his oldest and dearest and had found that avenue of succor closed, shutdown completely. He was devastated.

Gerald did not relent. " Dude what you are doing is wrong! It is just fucking wrong!" "It's fucking murder and ain't no way to justify it."

"As long as you keep fucking with that shit just stay the fuck away from me."

Randy started to recover and the cunning primordial part of his brain began to work. His survival instinct kicked in and he wailed at his companion," You ain't gonna say anything are you?' ' You ain;t gonna rat me out?"

'You do fucker and I will fucking KILL YOU!"

" I tried to do right by you and give you a chance to make enough money that you would never have to work again; now you coming at me like some little bitch." ' This ain't no afterschool special dickhead! " You better watch your fucking back! "

"You threatening me?" Gerald asked his friend. "After everything we have been through; you're gonna fucking threaten me?" ' It's not bad enough you're smuggling heroin for the fucking Taliban; you gonna threaten me.

"FUCK YOU PHELPS!" ' Watch your fucking back!

Gerald hit his once friend in the mouth three hard straight right hands. Marcus went down and Gerald followed. He hit him three more times then stood up. "NO MOTHERFUCKER! You watch your back! ' In case you forgot this is a fucking warzone.

People die here !'

Randy spit blood and rolled to his knees. "FUCK YOU Gerry! This ain;t over. He was right it wasn't over. Three days after their fight Gerald was sent to operate a bulldozer in A nearby village. . he was ordered to clear debris from an Artisan well. This was his third time clearing this very same well. The men of the community kept blocking it because the women liked to congregate there It had little to do with the war it was more about how the community operated.

Upon returning to post Gerald found the entrance to his barracks had been taped off and he was refused entrance.

An E6 flashed a Badge at Gerry. "My name is Larson I am with C.I.D..

C.I.D. was the Army's version of detectives. The acronym stood for Criminal Investigative Division, Gerald felt a sinking feeling in his stomach . He knew this was connected To Randy.

The E6 began a barrage of Questions.

" Are you Specialist Gerald Phelps?" " Yes . I am"

"What's going on ? What's all this."

"That's what we want to know . The big sergeant continued ; "Do you know of anyone that would have a reason to target you ?"

Gerald sputtered his reply." What? Target me? What are you talking about?"

Again the big Army detective responded. "Specialist Phelps today at approximately 1400 hours A K_9 Unit was doing a routine walk through of these Barracks. Upon entering your area of operations the K_9 unit posted. This is an alert position for this animal This particular unit is a bomb disposal animal. Upon further investigation by a bomb disposal team an Improvised Explosive Device was recovered from the inside of your wall locker. "

"The device was a shaped charge containing military grade C 4 attached to the electronic igniter from a disposable lighter. If you had opened your wall locker the igniter switch would have sent a jolt and blown you to bits.'

"Again I ask you; ' Is there anyone for any reason that would pick you as a target for termination?"

Geralds' blood turned to ice. His best friend of ten years had placed a bomb in his wall locker.

If he had not done it himself he had had it done either way there was no doubt in Gerrys' mind; Randy was responsible.

He considered telling the investigator about his friend Randy Marcus but vetoed the idea.

Gerald was not a rat and besides the Sergeant would want to know why Gerald had not reported the smuggling operation before the attempt on his life.

In the eyes of the Army to know about the treason and to not report it made Gerald a co conspirator. To know about his friends actions and not reporting it made Gerald as guilty as Marcus. He had chosen loyalty to his friend over loyalty to his country.

His friend had tried to murder him for his trouble.

Gerald decided to handle the situation himself.

Gerald Phelps was detained and Questioned for two days and told he would be shipped to a new unit for his own protection. The big C.I.D Sergeant was convinced Gerald knew who had planted the I.E.D in his locker and he wanted to detain the man until he told what he knew. Fortunately for Gerald A brand new 2nd lieutenant from the Judge Advocate Generals' Office intervened on his behalf and had him released. If the "Butterbar" 2nd louie had been in country a little longer he would not have bothered. The continued goodwill of an E 6 investigator was much more valuable than the gratitude of a lowly E 4 on his way out.

Randy Marcus had been questioned about the incident and somehow been cleared. Gerald knew he had to do something. It was not about revenge as much as the realization that his not doing anything was condoning what Randy and Man freak were doing. He was guilty of treason by not stopping his friends from committing treason.

He was jeopardizing the lives of fellow soldiers by letting the flow of illegal money and drugs continue to be traded by his companions.

Randy Marcus had laid out the entire operation to Gerald when he was trying to entice his friend into the "sweet deal" he had found.

Gerald knew his simplest option would be to contact the C.I.D investigator and spill his guts. The problem with this was he was convinced he too would get in trouble. The penalty for treason in wartime is death . Gerald did not wish to die or be responsible for Randys' death.

Instead of reporting his friends little operation he decided to sabotage the system . Killing Randy would just stop Randy. Manny and Artan would just find another " soldier ' to ship their poison . Gerald knew at $ 10,000 a week there would be no shortage of willing people.

He contemplated killing Artan and Randy while they made their next exchange. The problem with this course of action was ; outside of basic training Gerald had not had to fire a weapon. He had never killed anyone and was not certain he was capable of killing anyone. He was pretty certain Artan was capable and his old pal Randy seemed up to the task.

After some consideration Gerald decided to drop an anonymous tip to the C.I.D. investigator . He would drop a dime on his buddy Marcus. Gerald was sure once arrested and in withdrawal Randy Marcus would roll on the entire operation. Gerald was not sure it would work but he had to do something.

Gerald sent an E mail from the PX cafeteria . In the lobby of the building the Army had placed a group of about 10 computers . They were at the disposal of everyone and were for soldiers to make contact with home.

A man could be blown up in an armored personnel carrier at noon and arguing with his wife 2 hours later via internet.

Gerald also sent an E mail to his Company Commander . It was marked URGENT ! . He hoped by marking it it would not be ignored. The E mail outlined the operation and named people involved. He knew the E mail was not evidence but hoped it was enough to warrant the start of an investigation.

Gerrys' E mail worked very well and set into motion a chain of events that would forever change his life. Unknown to Gerald ; Marcus was already under investigation . Staff Sergeant Jackson had noticed Randy's spending habits and had made a report of his own . Jacksons' report had led to an investigation.

Not much had been confirmed; by this time, Randy Had become more discrete. They knew a lot about his operation but not the key elements ; where the money went and where the dope originated . Geralds' E mail provided these missing pieces . Manuel Freek provided the cash and Artan supplied the heroin.

Artan ; as it turns out' is already known to everyone . He is an informant for the local police and the U.S. Army. His only true alliance was to profit .

Randy Marcus and Artan were picked up and detained . When they were arrested Marcus was in possession of 30 kilos of heroin and Artan was holding several thousand in U.S. dollars . The heroin was enough to get Randy life in federal Prison. Artan would face the inconvenience of building a new network .

Both were quick to tell their stories in hope of making some kind of deal. Artan was recruited into the C.I.A and released to resume business albeit on a much larger scale and with less personal risk. Things did not go so smoothly for Randy or Gerald .

The E mail was traced back to Gerald , he was detained , questioned, threatened and asked to resign from the Army .Gerald was never formally charged with any crime . He was asked to give a lengthy and detailed deposition which was used to develop a case against Randy Marcus.

Randy was charged; with smuggling and a list of other crimes. The word Treason was avoided in order to protect the Army more than Randy. It would not play well on the evening news.

The investigation became tricky once stateside. Manny had become very rich and cautious.. He had insulated himself from direct contact with money or merchandise. He was no longer subject to the Uniform Code Of Military Justice. Civilian agencies work differently from the military. Their court system depends more on evidence and procedure. Civilian drug task forces like to build cases over time and learn every aspect of an operation.. Civilians like to catalogue assets and seize them. It could take two years to build a case in a civilian drug investigation.

Manuel Freek had "friends" pay visits to Randy's family in Florence Alabama. Randy's Uncle was murdered and his mother raped. Randy was found soon after dead in protective custody. His death was ruled a suicide.

Gerald's family did not escape unscathed. His uncle was shot coming out the front door of Gerald's parents home. He had been able to provide a description of his assailant. " Mexican " was his total statement.

Gerald and his family decided to relocate even though the family had lived and prospered for generations in Alabama. The move was prudent and serendipitous. Gerald's uncle Vincent was offered the opportunity to run a heavy equipment maintenance company. It was a union shop and his job was to inspect heavy equipment at all the mines within the state and surrounding states. It was a lot more money and Gerry was able to get a job running a backhoe as part of the deal. It was not witness protection because technically Gerald had never testified or been a witness. He had never dealt with Man Freak and as such posed no threat. Once Randy Marcus had committed "suicide" the threat to Gerald's family was considered minimal.

Gerald relayed this story to Chill and tears were running down his cheeks once he had completed the tale. The guilt he felt from his actions was eating him alive.

Chill let loose a long low whistle when the man finished. They had been at it for over an hour. Chill understood the man's perspective on the events and could empathies with the man's guilt and remorse.

Unlike Chill, Gerald had not directly killed anyone. His actions or lack of actions early on had resulted in at least 3 people being dead .That count does not include dead soldiers shot by bullets bought with drug money or dead addicts from overdosing on smuggled heroin.

If Gerald had reported Randy's operation when he first knew of it, could lives have been saved? There is no way of knowing but once a thought like that starts eating at a man's soul, It just keeps gnawing.

Yes ; God had sent this man to Chill to help him with his own shit. Chill reckoned he better listen close to whatever he was about to tell the younger man that sat before him. He was certain he himself needed to hear it as much; if not more, as Gerald Phelps. The big man began to speak.

" Alright buddy , that is a hell of a tale and I see some of your concerns. " " What exactly do you think you did ?"

' What do you mean? I just told you what I did. " was Gerald's response.

" Well' It's a fucked up deal any way you look at it but for right now we are concentrating on you trying to stay sober. . Right?"

"Right! I want to stay sober. I know if I drink I just aint worth a shit to nobody."

"Anybody Chill corrected. "Huh?' Gerald grunted.

" You said if you drink you aint worth a shit to nobody you meant anybody.'

WHAT THE FUCK EVER DUDE! You know what I Meant."

" Yes I do but it makes a world of difference in the meaning of the statement." " Details are important. Alcoholism is "cunning, baffling and powerful." Says so right in the "Big Book" of Alcoholics Anonymous.' It is also patient.

OK Gearald;

Let's break it down. What exactly did you do? What were your actions, what are the effects of your actions upon other people and what was the reasoning used when undertaking those actions?

Gerald interrupted. " What do you mean" Reasoning" ?"

Good question! When we review our actions we look for motives and patterns in our behavior,

'Alcoholics Anonymous ' talks about finding ' Causes and conditions" it's why we do a personal inventory.

Gerald interjected 'Your talking about doing a fourth step."

In a way; I am talking about the practice of using a personal inventory to better define what is going on in any situation. Here is the situation as I see it.

You are having trouble in your life due to your drinking and drug use. Right?

Well, yeah Gerald retorted. That is why I am here. '

OK! Good. Is this something new or something that has always been a problem but just recently gotten worse " Gerald thought about it for a minute then replied. I guess I always drank in an extreme manner. I just didn't drink that often.'

When I was in Afghanistan I was scared to drink too much so I avoided drinking for the most part.

Chill then queried. Would you say you drink for effect, or for taste?

Gerry shot back; Effect! for sure."

Aright! That is important. Chill continued; 'What effect does drinking have upon you? Gerald laughed. It gets me drunk.'

Chill also laughed. Of course it gets you drunk. The "big Book" talks about the "ease and comfort of that first drink.' Does that sound about right to you? Gerald nodded. Well; yes and no.

When I drink I relax. It's like something is lifted off my shoulders. At least that is how it used to be; now it's like I don't get any relief. It just makes me more anxious and full of self pity.

Sometimes I just get angry.

Chill spoke. The simple thing to say would be drinking doesn't do for you what it use to do. It no longer does for you what you want or need it to do.

" I guess that would be right. Gerald answered. Chill continued: I know sometimes it seems like we talk in circles when talking about recovery. The reason is we need to define exactly what we are trying to accomplish Gerald .

Gerald was tentative in his reply." I guess; I mean I am not really sure what you mean. When I drink I am useless. I can't do anything else once I start and my entire life turns to shit."

Ok! We are making progress Gerald my young friend. The "Big Book " of Alcoholics' anonymous talks about alcohol being " but a symptom" Our true problem lies within our thinking." It sounds like alcohol use to help you with your thinking problem but no longer works.

Gerald agreed. Well yeah ;I guess it did ok.

Chill continued. Have you given any thought about what can be used to replace alcohol as a solution to your thinking problem. Now understand that is not an exact statement . Alcohol provided some relief but it was not a solution. Good news is the 12 steps as outlined in "Alcoholics' Anonymous " ,claim to be a pathway to a true solution.

I have founf this to be a true statement from my own experience. The 12th step talks about " having had a spiritual awakening as a result of these 12 steps ." That spiritual awakening is the solution .

Chill further expanded : Personally I always knew alcohol was a lie. Before I ever took my first drink I had seen its' effect on other people.

My brother and my Uncles would all change once they started drinking .They would seem all happy and carefree but at the same time sinister and false. I knew not to get too close to them because at any moment they could turn into vicious snarling beasts. Once my own drinking escalated ; I noticed these same characteristics within myself.

I did not like myself sober so I drank . The time came that I hated myself drunk. When the lie of alcohol quit working I felt lost

When it got intolerable I reached out and asked for help. To put it simply I found relief in working the 12 steps.

I was not certain this would work and I had no reason to trust anyone in the rooms of recovery. I just hoped if this was a lie; that it would be a lie that I could swallow and that it would provide me with relief.

" What are you saying? " Gerald interrupted . Are you saying recovery is a lie?"

Chill laughed . NO! not really that is not what I am saying.. When I got here the whole thing just seemed too good to be true. The whole Higher power trip and all that shit, I just did not want to hear it. Just more do gooders trying to feed me their bullshit; so they could feel good about themselves.

"Well, Why did you stay?' Gerald asked.

Chill replied. Because I was desperate and scared. I was out of answers. I didn't care what happened next I just didn't want anymore of what had been my life.

I asked people to give me simple instructions like what to do that day .

I did not want to cause more harm. I doubted I could change anything ; I just did not want things to get worse.

Chill faced the other man. Gerald, you said you believe your life is unmanageable and you want to stop drinking. Do you believe alcohol is the reason your life is unmanageable ?

At the moment; Yes! Gerald shot back

Good answer. Consuming alcohol is causing the immediate conditions in which your life is out of control. Do you believe if you quit drinking that everything will be OK? Chills' question made Gerald pause and reflect a moment. His answer was short but honest . I' m not sure . I hope it does .

Chill was elated when he responded. Awesome shit ; hope. Hope gets us started , Resolve keeps us going. You felt hopeless and now you are seeking hope. Hope! It' s A big word.

Some people seek recovery for relief from circumstances . Once they get that relief they stop doing the actions that provided their relief and soon they again become miserable. Other people want relief from themselves..

I could not stand being the person I had become for even one more day. I absolutely did not care what I had to do to become someone different; I was willing to do it.

Resolve is maintaining that focus after relief has been obtained. That is a little in the future. For now lets' try to determine your causes and conditions. Gerald you are the best person to provide information about this subject.

Why do you think you drank? " I don' t know ." the boy responded. Well Shit! I guess we are fucked ! No help to be had today> Chill replied.

What?" Gerald asked confused.

Stop bullshitting boy! Chill took the gloves off. " Why you been Drinking/'

Because I hate feeling like a piece of shit.' ' Gerald shot back with fervor.

' Why you feeling like a piece of shit ? "

Gerald shouted back on the verge of tears. " Because I ratted out my friend and got people killed."

Chill now excited exclaimed. OK! Now we are talkin. Is that the truth? Is that what really happened?..

Geralds' reply was confused. " What do you mean ? I just told you my story." Chill clarified . I heard your story but that was not what I heard.

I heard your friend ; Randy Marcus, started smuggling drugs . He offered to cot you in. You told him no but not right away which tells me you considered it. You stated you believe in Karma and that it would come to a bad ending.

Your" friend " got scared that you would turn him in so he tried to kill you. You plotted killing him but decided to turn him in as a better option . It would be less dangerous for you and you would be safe.

You ratted him out in a way that was least likely to get you in trouble. You were determined to minimize your risk.

Once arrested your friend had no compunction about ratting. He told everything he knew about everyone involved. The other people involved took steps to ensure their own safety. They did this through intimidation and murder.

You feel conflicted because you think your actions ; your betrayal ' caused the death of your friend and the death of the innocents that were slaughtered. Chill paused. Does that cover everything?

Pretty much; Gerald replied . It's a little more complicated but yeah for the most part that sums up what happened.

Chill spoke. On the back of the coins we give out in meetings to commemorate anniversaries there is written on the back " To Thine Ownself Be True." What does that mean to you Gerald ?

I guess it means to not lie to yourself.

OK I like that response . So again Gerald do you think you have been lying to yourself ?

No. not really ; I know what I did and it sucks..

This is why we work with other people. I see inconsistencies in your story .The younger man looked at chill confused.

Really ; just what is it you think Inconsistent in my story ?

You claim to have a problem being a "Rat ". Is that some moral code ?

Yea; Of course everybody hates a rat.

OK but eventually you did "Rat" . Right ? Chill's look was confrontational. The smaller man held the gaze and replied.

Well Yea I did. I had no choice. This was said with conviction.. Chill continued.

Is that true ? You said you contemplated murdering your friend. That is not "Ratting" .

Sure that was an option. But I could have gotten killed or caught; all kinds of shit could have gone wrong.

Gerald I am going to share a little insight here. You have patterns of behavior ;everyone does. I am going to show you one of your patterns.

Ok , Show me . Please ! Show me.. Gerald s' voice began to rise he was becoming agitated.

Chill replied in a calm soothing tone. Don't get angry. Anger feeds the disease not the solution.

What I have noticed is your moral code is purely of convenience.

Gerald sputtered. What?

You got no conviction ! The big man spat these words and followed them with ; if you want the truth you are pretty much a chickenshit !

Gerald's face turned red. He was furious and full of anger and shame. FUCK YOU ! You fat tub of shit. !

Who the fuck you think you are ?

You Don't fucking know me..

Chill shot back . Wrong ! Yoyu just told me who you are . I know you because I know myself ! I am that same chickenshit motherfucker. I know the right thing to do but I hesitate.

I don't want to cause waves or have people mad at me ; so I don't stand up for what I believe to be the truth

You say you hate rats aint nothing lower than a rat. But, once you were scared enough you ratted.

You ratted and the people you ratted on reacted and people died.

Now you want to wallow in self pity and drink yourself to death. Well. You have that right.. the " Big Book" talks about accepting spiritual help or going on to the bitter end.

You have a choice . You let fear keep you from turning your " Friend" in when you discovered he was smuggling heroin.

You knew the money was probably supporting the Taliban. You chose loyalty to your friend over loyalty to your Brothers in arms.

That choice made you vulnerable to being held accountable. There is only one real hard question as I see it .

Did you choose not to report Randy because he was your friend, or because you were tempted to become his accomplice ? Did you decide not to be his accomplice out of a sense of duty or because you were scared?

Remember; There are no right or wrong answers at this point. Honest answers to yourself are the only useful answers.

Remove judgment from the equation. Observe only the truth within yourself. We have established you act out of fear but where did the fear rest?

If you had " ratted" on randy when you first discovered this mess the outcome may still have been the same. All the same people may have died or been harmed.

Would anything have been changed about YOU ?Would you feel different about yourself ? I can't answer these questions for you.

Here is the most Fucked up part ; The answers you get today may change over time.

If you stay sober and apply the principles of recovery in your life consistently you will become a different person.

That person you become may be able to look back on the person you are now and forgive him.

Your friend put you in a shitty situation .

Your friend was sick with the disease of addiction and alcoholism.

His thinking and actions were compromised by his disease and the chemicals.

Your own thinking and actions have also been compromised by your disease and drinking.

There is nothing to be gained by being resentful toward your friend nor indulging in your guilt.

Guilt is a luxury it has no place in recovery. Remorse followed by action is how we deal with shit . We cannot change the events of the past.. We can change how it effects our lives. We can use it as a learning tool for ourselves and others or we can wallow in it and drink and die.

We use the past by looking at it honestly, we determine what actions were appropriate and which inappropriate. We can resolve to conduct ourselves in a better manner moving forward.

If we owe amends we can seek to make things right to the best of our abilities. You must realize we are never going to be perfect at this process but we can remain determined to make continued progress.

This is how the process of recovery works.

I also have the choice to remain a whiny little bitch drowning in self centered fear and alcohol. Either way I am choosing not to drink today. How about you?

Gerald felt stunned. The big man had just ripped him apart and put him back together in a handful of sentences.

Somehow he did not feel lessened or compromised by big chills' analysis of him or his circumstances.

It wasn't about what had happened but what happens next.

Okay big boy; I hear you. Now after all that; how do I make it right?

Chill knew this part was what he himself needed to hear as much as Gerald.

You don't. Some things you just learn to live with. Your a guy; who in a moment of weakness or bad judgment did a shitty thing. As a result of your actions people suffered. The thing is: Do you want to keep doing shitty things and to keep causing harm?

No; of course not. Gerald replied.

Well then own that shit! Use it. The next time you are in a situation where you have to make a hard choice' choose out of principle not out of fear.. Remember if you are walking in faith you got company.

Lonnie

Chill had little time to reflect about his and Geralds' little talk .His other troubled child ; Lonnie " L. A." Haze grabbed him up when he exited the building.

Hey big guy I need to talk to you man.!

Can this Wait? Chill really wanted to go somewhere and process everything that had just transpired.

No man it can't . I need some relief from this.

Chill hesitated but he saw the determination on Lonnies' face. Alright can you sign out to take a ride with me.?

Lonnie replied ' Yeah ; no problem, I am signed out for the day.

OK , let's take a ride and you tell me this urgent piece of business.

The duo got in Chills' little car and drove aimlessly for a brief period. For all his bluster and determination ; Lonnie was having trouble getting started .

Chill in an attempt to ease the tension asked Lonnie if he would be interested in a Cheeseburger . Lonnie accepted the offer. Chill went through a drive through and got 2 value meals. He drove to the end of the parking lot away from other cars and parked . Chill handed Lonnie his food ' looked the man in the eye and spoke.

Just say it dude. Stop thinking and just start talking.

Lonnie began to speak and the man called Chill soon had chills running up his spine. Chills' higher power was working overtime today. He had sent him Gerald and talking with Gerald was going to help him live with the murder of Mike Cheri.

This talk with Lonnie would further help with the Mike Cheri ordeal; More importantly it would help Chill reconcile his ambivalent feelings toward Liza Beth.

Lonnie Haze possessed a certain elegance when he spoke. He was A natural storyteller and a hustler at heart. . Despite all his glibness he found himself struggling for a way to tell Chill His story.

Chill sensing the younger mans' discomfort, gave him some encouragement.

I find when I got something hard to say it's easier to keep it very simple and just say it.

Lonnie spoke. I think I owe an amends.

Either you do or you don't. Which is it? Chill responded.

For real; Chill, I am not sure if I should say anything.

Once again chill sent encouragement. I can see you are serious so ; Let's break it down. You're bothered by this . Right?

Yeah! I am bothered. I am very much bothered.

Chill continued; you think you may have harmed someone ?

I'm not sure. I mean I think I need to tell somebody this shit ; but, I don't see how it can help anything.

Chill was losing patience. Fuck it ! what's the story?

OK here goes nothing. You know before I got here and met you; I was out there pretty hard. I was hanging with some shady people and involved in some sketchy shit.

Now here is the deal : You and me , we think a lot alike.

You told me before that God uses everything and everyone. No action goes wasted , even bad things teach us lessons or give us experience. That experience we share and help others.

Chill interjected . That is correct . Sometimes our difficulties are sent to us so we can use them to help another drunk at a later time. They are not about us.

Lonnie squared his shoulders and spoke. I think I owe this girl an amends but I am not even sure she knows me.

Chill chuckled. That is pretty vague but I get it.

No! no! no. Listen; This girl was at a house when something really heavy went down. A really nasty fucker did some nasty shit to another nasty fucker and she was there.

The deal is though the chick was really out of it; I mean bad. She may not even remember anything from that night.

My bringing it to her may just cause her harm .

Alright , STOP! We know an amends is about making things right for the person we harmed. It is not about giving ourselves relief, especially if that relief is at the expense of another person.

I understand that Chill. I do understand but I got to get some relief.

Can I trust you Big Boy? I mean I understand that part of this whole deal is to share with my God and another human being everything.

I also know that there aint no legal protection here. If I tell you about some foul shit and you get all ate up about it ; aint nothing to keep you from turning me in.

Chill again   interjected.. Stop. If you are scared about telling me something ; don't. Tell it . Go to a priest or a counselor . Hell get a lawyer.

One thing you need to remember, we do not shy away from an amends just because it may mean we suffer consequences . This is life and death and we approach it that way.. Which thing you more scared of; getting in trouble, or getting drunk ?

Lonnie   shot back. I'm   scared of getting dead motherfucker !

If I drink or get high ; I truly believe I will die. I just don't think I got enough heart left to try and get clean another time. The   thought of it just makes me cringe.

On the other hand; If the shit I'm about to tell you gets out they's a motherfucker out there just might kill me point blank.

We   don't live in fear . Chill   replied.

Lonnie   laughed. Bullshit! Motherfucker! You might be big and bad , full of god and recovery but don't you sit there and tell me you don't' get scared. Shit!

Fuck! Big   man I've heard your lead. It's   why I picked you.

Chill   grunted and growled a response .Your right. Fear is a big part of my inventory. Anger   and fear ; which are the same. Anger   comes from fear. But; we don't live in fear. Today we have a higher power and part of this process is walking through the difficult shit no matter how scary it is.

When I wanted to get clean I was facing attempted murder charges. I was scared to death and just aching to do something.

I wanted to leave treatment and hustle money and get a lawyer. I spoke to some people about my fears. I was told I would never get a better chance to see if this shit was real.

a man told me to do what was put in front of me on a daily basis and let my God handle the rest..

The Commonwealth offered me eight years on paper and do 17 months in prison.

The state prosecutor told me if she had to take it to trial ' she would make sure that I would do eight years before I would even be considered for parole. She said I would probably do 12 of the 17.

I was scared but I was Naïve. I turned down the deal and decided to take it to trial.

That was in June and trial was scheduled for October. I stayed in treatment , graduated, and got a little temp job.

Now' you would think that I would have been worried with all that time hanging over my head. I was not worried . For some reason that was one of the most serene periods of my whole recovery.

I prayed about it' put it in God' s hands and quit dwelling on it.

If I went to jail' I would be going sober. Eventually they would let me out. I was guilty and if my higher power needed me in jail I was OK with it.

The day before my trial; that same prosecutor took me back in her office and offered me a new deal.

She told me that the more she had learned about the circumstances of my case' and about the people involved' the less she wanted to send me to jail.

She said to me: Mr. Frieze my best recommendation for you is to get away from these people and stay away.

Something had changed her heart. For some reason she had looked at my case and decided that I was not the piece of shit that she had originally thought.

I mean look at my case. I was a 350 pound man and went into a house full of people; most women and children. Once inside I near beat A woman to death with my bare hands.

These are facts! I did those things! I got to live with that. No matter what else that had happened on that day . I did those things.

I assaulted a woman in front of her children and Grandchildren. Yet; here this lady was looking at me and telling me to stay away from them. Not for their safety was she saying this. She was worried for me.

There is no black and white in life: it's all shades of grey. Recovery is the process of finding out exactly who you are' figuring out what you don't like about yourself and working toward being someone you can tolerate.

I know I'm a motherfucker ; that under the right circumstances, will beat a woman in the head with a twelve pack and then try and choke the life from her body. That's me ! I am capable of that type shit.

I also know that's not a person that I like or a person that society will tolerate. I also know ; from experience, that if I don't take a drink or drug , and apply the principles of recovery in my life, I don't beat and choke women in front of their Grandbabies.

I also know that that motherfucker is still there waiting. He's just as crazy and just as angry. If I don't treat my disease he fucking wins. Well; FUCK THAT MOTHERFUCKER !

That prosecutor took that 17 years and turned it into 5 years suspended with 90 days work release. I was shocked out after 51 days

I did do 5 years on paper and found out what its like to live as a convicted Felon. I had a college degree and worked in factories and warehouses for next 12 years and grateful for the opportunity.. I worked as a temp that entire time and that was because I worked for the temp agency before I went to court.

The hardest part about recovery is staying grateful. It is also A key element in staying happy in life. .

I'm lucky; in that, I have no trouble remembering how I felt before I got stopped. My life has never gotten so good that I take it for granted .I keep enough of a struggle present to keep a need for recovery vital and ever present.

Lonnie had heard much of Chill's story on another occasion. The big man's experience hit close to home on this night.

OK big dog ' here's what happened.

Lonnies' Dilemma / Chills' Grace

About three weeks after I got through Detox the house started taking us to meetings on the outside. Well' I kept seeing this really hot blonde chick at these meetings. You know her. I've seen you talking to her.

She is a tall pretty bitch goes by Liza. I heard someone call her Liza Beth.

A shot of adrenaline ran through Chill. Shivers went up his spine. He wanted to stop the younger man but knew he needed to hear this story.

Chill did caution the man. That girl is very important to me. She is one of the people I love most in this world. If you got something bad to say about her; you best say it careful because I will beat a Mudhole in your ass if you badmouth my friend.

Hold up buddy! It aint even like that but I do hope you know that little princess aint no angel'

Chill laughed. I am well aware of all her faults and can honestly say I love her with all my heart: warts and all. I would take a bullet for that girl.

Lonnie continued his story. There was something familiar about her and finally I heard her share at a meeting. It came to me from where I knew her.

It was about a month or two before I got stopped. It had to be November or December.

Me and this ol' evil fucker named Ronnie Byrd was hitting licks robbing houses over in Ohio.

Once we got in the country Ronnie starts telling me about his piece of shit step brother that deals meth.

He say that "Mike" his brother lived real close and that we could probably get some speed fronted. At that point' I had been up about three days. The last thing I wanted was more speed. What I wanted , was A big hit of dawg ., Heroin , Hairon you know what I am saying.

Ol' Ronnie says shit dude we can always sell the shit.

He also says his brother kept a good supply of prescription pills around to feed little whores. . He said his step brother had a taste for young girls. He said he liked them pretty and strung out. He also liked to comment. " the best thing about heroin was it brought down the price of pussy."

Chill cringed he had made the same statement to Liza Beth Hearing his own words three or four times removed put them in context. It was a pretty shitty statement ; it held a lot of truth.

The disease of addiction placed these women into a place where they were vulnerable to people like Mike Cheri . If he got real honest it made them more available to guys like Chill.

Chill was beginning to realize that Mike Cheri and himself were not so different. If Chill took a drug or a drink ; he had potential to be worse than Cheri. This did not make Chill feel good about himself.

He had often wondered if his presence in Liza's life was A good or bad thing. He had spent many sleepless nights soul searching over this very thing.

He loved the girl but had enabled her. Chill realized Liza was very much like a drug for Chill. His love for her had evolved from what it was when they first met.

Lonnie continued his story. We pull up at this cat Mikes' house. Ronnie turns the car off and tells me to sit still . He says his brother is A weird cat and not very trusting of strangers.. Ronnie says he will go inside and see if everything is cool. He said his brother might not be home. If he is not home we can rob his house.

I'm like " Dude, you gonna rob your own brother ?'

Ronnie just grinned. Fuck that Motherfucker! I'd like to cut his heart out., You know how family can be hah hah.

I am sitting in the car for like 15 minutes. Ronnie comes out of the house all crouched down with a big ass gallon jar in his arm like a Big baby . Under his other arm he had A couple of old shotguns. He throws the shit in the back . He yells come on! And grabs my arm.

We get to the back porch and Ronnie has A couple milk crates full of crap we can pawn. One box is full of knives and pistols. He was cleaning old boy out. I'm like " Damn! Any dope?

Oh Yea！ Ronnie   holds up a cigar box . He flips the lid and it is just full of shit. Pills,   crack,   heroin, and   a   big   piece   or   pure   ice. Ronnie   smiling exalts. " Jackpot! We   are   set.

We   load   everything   in   the car and   I   start   to   get   into   the   car.. Ronnie   says "Shit!' I'm   like   "What?" Ronnie   replies OK man we   got   to   go   back.   Thers' one   more   thing   we   got   to   grab. Im like   " What?"

Ronnie   is   like   "dude ; It's   kinda   fucked   up in   there.   Just   remember if   I go   down   ; you   go   down.

I'm   like   " Whatever dude. Let's   just   get   this   shit and   get   out of   here. "

Inside ; the   house was   a mess.. Furniture   was   turned   over   and   it   looked   like somebody   had   ransacked   the   place.. Damn Ronnie ! you tore   this   place   up."

Ronnie   laughed. Weren't   me place   was   fucked   when   I   came   in   the   door. He   stopped   me   and   said   "   look   in   there." He   was   pointing   toward   the   living room right   off   the   kitchen.

I   looked   and sitting   in   the   easy chair   half   on   the   floor   was   a   body.

I'm   like   Ronnie   What   the   fuck!?

He laughed. I   didn't do   it   but   that's   my   dumbass   stepbrother. He's dead   . Looks   like   he   got   his   ass beat   then   Overdosed. Rough   night.

I   stammered back: ' We   got   to get   out   of   here   Ronnie;   they   gonna   charge us   with   this. '

" We   going. We   going   but   we   got   to   get something. Come   on ！ It's back   here.

I followed Ronnie to a bedroom. It was dark inside and he flipped the light switch. On the bed; dressed in bra and panties was that Liza Beth girl.

At first I thought she was also dead. I saw spit bubbles at the side of her mouth and realized she was passed out.

" Damn aint she a pretty one?" Ronnie stood over her looking down like he was about to take A bite out of her.

I told him " Dude ! We got to go whatever you are thinking just don' t. We got to get out of here. I aint going down for no manslaughter and rape bullshit.

Ronnie looked at me like I had two heads. We leaving; that' s for sure but we taking her with us.

Why? I ain' t down with no kidnapping. Ronnie had laughed. Kidnapping?

We aint kidnapping. We is rescuing. We can' t leave her cause this place ain' t gonna be here in about twenty minutes.

Huh?

Ronnie went on My brother is dead. Looks like somebody beat him in the head. He probably deserved it. We just took everything valuable in the house. This place is insured and I am next of kin. This place is about to burn. Grab sleeping beauty there and lets' get out of here. I should leave her and let her burn too but she is a pretty bitch . I hate to waste snatch that fine.

We took the girl and carried her to the car , We shoved her in the back next to the stolen shit. Ronnie threw a blanket over her and remarked:

" You know that bitch aint got no clothes here cept for what she wearing . That and a   Tee shirt.

I' m Like   whatever dude; lets' go.

We got in the car   but Ronnie went back into the house then came running to the car.

`Just a minute'   Ronnie ran back into the house. He returned smelling like kerosene.

I asked " what' s up/'   Ronnie replied   "don,t worry I took care of everything.

What did you do /

I dragged Mikey over by the couch and wrapped one end of the curtain around his foot. The other end I wrapped around the kerosene heater I put the curtains on the kerosene heater .

It will look like he got high and fell over the heater and died. The fire will cover up all the stolen shit. No   house; no crime.

" Dude I am   fucking brilliant."

" As long as sleeping beauty don' t say anything; Lonnie reminded his shady   compatriot.

Ronnie laughed . " About what?"   'Shit she probably killed him ."

Chill interjected . " What did you do with her ?" He knew he sounded A little hysterical but hoped Lonnie wouldnot notice.

" funniest thing we rode back to Cinci and scored some more dog and sold some of the meth to a guy Ronnie knew.

She woke up a couple times and just asked for a cigarette and went back to sleep .Once she rolled the window down and puked down the side of the car. It was all water.

\She rolled window back up took a drink of bottled water wrapped herself in a blanket and went back to sleep. She never mentioned Mike or even asked us who we were.. Ronnie said she was a cold ass bitch but he meant it as a compliment.. The chick was unfazed like just another day for her .

She finally asked if we had any dope . Ronnie gave her enough to fix and she did a big hit like an old pro, lit a cigarette and nodded out.

She never seemed scared or even curious about where she was at, who we were or where we were headed. We stopped over in Hebron or Florence somewhere and Ronnie arranged to sell the guns we stole off Mike. She asked if she could clean up while we was at this guys house.

The guys Ol' lady was about her size and he gave her some clothes to wear..

Before we left A car pulled up with two young girls and an old guy about 50 . Dude looked like an old sugar daddy.

One of the girls knew this Liza girl. They bought a couple grams of meth and most of the dog we had left.

Liza said she would leave with them and thanked us for the ride and " poof " she was gone.

Lonnie stopped talking . He lit a cigarette , inhaled deeply looked at Chill and said. " Well?"

Chill reflected a moment and carefully chose his words

That is a wild ass story but I don't see where you owe an amends.

Lonnie thought a minute He replied to the big man's statement..

" That's fucked up. "

" What " Chill asked.

Man I was dying to get that shit out . I mean I been obsessed for like three days about telling you about this shit. The whole time thinking I needed to clear my side of the street.

Maybe you just needed to know she was ok. Did you ever worry that she might turn you guys in to the police ?

Not really Ronnie kinda covered that . He was like: " Who the fuck she gonna tell? What the fuck she gonna tell? Aint nobody gonna cry over that Motherfucker. " I remember asking Ronnie ; " Who you think hit him ?'

Ronnie had smirked . " I wish I had . Fuck that motherfuckerr I just hope his insurance was paid . I'm next of kin."

" Fuck if I knew who did him. I'd love to shake the fuckers' hand . Mike was a bastard I hated that Motherfucker. Give the fucker A medal.

"You know I guess I should feel guilty about robbing that guy but I really Don't . Is that wrong ?'

Chill looked at Lonnie and said. " I'm not sure." Right and wrong are just words man. We take actions in life according to circumstances and frame of mind.

The person you were that day did those things. The person you are today doesn't feel any guilt about those actions. The person you become may be bothered by those actions.

The great thing about it is you know what to do. Inventory that shit again and make amends if you feel one is needed.

Right now do you feel ok with this shit?

Lonnie reflected for a moment and replied. " I do I really do for some reason I'm ok with it. I told you and now I'm good.

I don't even feel a need to talk to that girl. It's the wildest thing. Two hours ago this shit was all I could think about and now it's just fading away.

Chill understood Lonnies' confusion and could tell him why he no longer felt the intense obsession to unload his story and make an amends.

Lonnie had been sent; on this day, to help Chill. This " confession" had been a gift to Chill's recovery not Lonnies' .

Chill marveled at the spirit of the universe correcting and connecting everything and wondered why he had been granted such a grand reprieve.

He had murdered Mike Cheri; a man no better but no worse than himself if he got completely honest.

He could tell himself that Cheri's death had been to protect Liza Beth . . He may have started out with noble intentions but once he had heard Liza Beths' voice on Cheri's recorder; his noble plan had become self serving.

He had killed a man and had plotted to use that mans' death as leverage to control Liza Beth. Her higher power had intervened and sent a couple of junkies to rescue her. And him from his crap.

He could sugarcoat it a hundred ways but the truth was he had killed out of self serving, ego driven pride.

Mike Cheri used money and dope to manipulate and hold power over women. He did these things because he was sick. He was spiritually sick and like all humans seeking love.

Was Cheri's love for Liza Beth somehow worse than Chills'?"

Who was Chill to make this decision?

The fact was Chill was spiritually sick himself. The only difference was he had been given the 12 steps as a solution and his life had become livable as a result.

He could never repay or make amends to Mike Cheri. He also knew that guilt and remorse were useless emotions to him. They were self indulgent and destructive,,

He had told Gerald Phelps these things and believed them to be true. Some things you just had to live with they could not be taken back or made right.

Chill had to live with the fact that at fifteen years sober he was capable of killing another human being. He was also capable of using that killing to hold power over another person that he claimed he loved. The most odd part for Chill was he could do these things and somehow stay sober.

Was he a sociopath? Had years of drugs and alcohol impaired him to the point of being a borderline personality?

He had no doubt he possessed narcissistic personality traits but unlike a true narcissist; he did feel empathy and other people did have value for him as people and not just resources.

Chill understood that bad acts and twisted sick shit also served the spirit of the universe.

Good and bad were human concepts. Nature was much more about balance. Humans thought in terms of predators and victims. Nature dealt with predators and "prey."

Liza Beth was a protected soul. She had been protected from Cheri and Chill. The universe had used people that were as sick as she and her oppressors to rescue her.

The greatest gift to Chill was he had never gotten a chance to " blackmail" her into some form of forced " recovery."

He realized if that had been allowed to happen it would have changed everything. He would not have been allowed to stay in her life and he probably would not have stayed sober. Honesty is A key element of recovery and a lie of this magnitude would have poisoned the big man.

His higher power had shown mercy. Chill knew gifts took maintenance and one this large could never be paid off or ignored. Lifes' burdens are often its' treasures. Attitude of the individual made the difference.

At the end Of Lonnies' story Chill was quiet but chuckling to himself. Once again his higher power had outdone himself. In one afternoon he had been sent mercy and grace twice.

Sitting and listening to Gerald Phelps had helped him come to terms with his murdering of Mike Cheri. Sometimes you just had to live with shit you had done and the best you could do was try not to cause harm.

Geralds' story showed Chill nothing was to be gained by taking a drink or a drug. He wasn't scared of jail and had been considering turning himself in for the murder.. He had held back thinking he needed to be free in order to watch out for Liza Berth. This was funny because he had convinced himself that murdering Mike Cheri was him protecting her..

Lonnies' story had shown him that Liza Beth had a higher power protecting her. It had protected her against Mike Cheri and from Chill.

She was not a sociopath. Liza Beth was unaware that Mike Cheri was dead or that Chill had been prepared to extort her to treatment with that death. Chill realized just how sick he was after being clean for over 15 years he was capable of murder and blackmail of the person he loved most.. He also realized that his God still found him useful and had granted him grace and forgiveness.

He did not need to worry about Mike Cheris' murder. No one was looking for anyone . His death had been ruled an accident . No murder meant no murderer. Chill knew the truth and had to live with it . He also had to find away to stay sober and help another suffering addict or drunk.

Chill Addressed Lonnie:

Not everything that happens to us is about us. You were sent to that house that day to save that girl. Her higher power used you and your unsavory friend to protect that girl.

Lonnie replied. "

"Why do I feel like I owe her an Amends?'

Do you still feel that way after telling me that story. You may just have needed to tell the tale.

Lonnie contemplated that thought.

" I'm not sure. I don't feel anxious anymore." Chill began speaking

. Lonnie I believe My higher power sent you to me to give me relief. That girl is very important to me and I have been in a lot of turmoil over her.. Your story has given me a great deal of relief from my personal burdens. I can't tell you the story without causing harm but I want you to know you have helped me today.

Lonnie did not know what to say. He looked at his watch and told Chill it was time for him to return to the treatment center. Chill drove the young man home in silence.

Both men were overwhelmed by the day. Lonnie was content his mind at ease. He was a little confused but happy..

Chill was not confused. he had witnessed two miracles in one afternoon. Some people would scoff at that thought. Chill knew the relief and healing he felt was miraculous. He had sat and listened to two fellow addicts and drunks share their burden and his had been lessened.

Nothing was different but his perspective. He was still a murderer and he had tried to blackmail the woman he loved into recovery. He knew these things about himself and knew he could live with that knowledge on this day.

In the morning he would try to do better.

He would start by going to a meeting.

Made in the USA
Monee, IL
22 March 2021

62702534R00184